EVERY MOTHER'S SON

A DCI ROBERT KETT NOVEL

ALEX SMITH

RELENTLESS
MEDIA

EVERY MOTHER'S SON
Published Worldwide by Relentless Media.
This edition published in 2021.

ISBN: 978-1-913877-06-4

Edited by Hanna Elizabeth

www.alexsmithbooks.com
relentless.media

ALSO BY ALEX SMITH

The DCI Robert Kett Thrillers

Paper Girls

Bad Dog

Three Little Pigs

Whip Crack

Run Rabbit Run

Stone Cold Dead

Every Mother's Son

Cry Baby: A Novella

The Softley Softley Thrillers

The Harder They Fall

Hard Luck House (Coming Soon)

Other Books

Six Days, Six Hours, Six Minutes

For Jamie

PROLOGUE

Friday

CAITLYN BROWN HAD ALWAYS THOUGHT THAT BEING A mother would be the most natural thing in the world.

But nothing in her life—literally *nothing*—had been harder.

The noise was the worst. The endless fucking noise. It was like living with your head inside a turbine. No, inside a *blender*, because it made her feel like she had knives in her skull, whirring through the tender flesh of her brain, turning it into jelly.

Dawn was almost here and Adam was screaming in his crib on the other side of the room the way he had been all night, the way he had been since she'd brought him back from hospital two weeks ago. It was the worst sound she had ever heard because it just wouldn't stop, it never stopped, not when she picked him up and cuddled him, not when she swaddled him in the cot, not when she offered him milk or kind words or kisses. He just screamed, loud enough to shake the world to pieces, loud enough to unravel the very fabric of existence, loud enough to drive her insane, to drive her to...

"No," she said. "Stop."

She rolled over in bed, her hands pressed against her ears so hard they ached. She had to sleep, she had to sleep but she couldn't because he wouldn't let her and now the sun would be crawling up over the horizon again bringing the heat, the humidity, the flies. And more crying, always crying. It was only May but it was unbearably hot, even here in the old Manor house.

Liam lay next to her on his back, out cold, his big, stupid mouth hanging open and his snores like buzz saws. How could he sleep through the screams? It was like he could make himself deaf by sheer force of will. Even in those moments where Caitlyn felt like she was losing her mind, when she pounded on his chest and pulled his hair and shrieked at him to pick the baby up, he barely even stirred. The whole thing had been his idea and now he wasn't even interested. Oh, sure, he'd play with the baby, he'd cuddle him, but the second Adam started crying he'd hand him back with an apologetic smile.

He wants his mum, he would say. *Every mother's son wants his mother.*

And Adam never stopped crying. He never fucking stopped.

She hated her husband. She fucking hated him.

As impossible as it seemed, the baby's screams grew higher in pitch. High enough, surely, to shatter the windows. To shatter her *skull.*

"What?" she snapped, rolling over to face the crib. "What do you want?"

He answered her with wet, choking shrieks, so many that surely he couldn't get a breath in. He was bright red and sweating, his chubby hands groping for the ceiling. He was so pathetic. So loud and so pathetic and...

So small. He was so small.

Caitlyn climbed out of bed, hating herself for her thoughts, hating herself for hating Adam and for hating Liam and for hating this whole fucking mess. It wasn't the baby's fault, was it? He was so little, so young. It wasn't his fault.

"Hey," she said. "Hey, Adam, it's okay. It's me, mummy."

She scooped him out of his crib—the hot, squirming, too-heavy mess of him—his blankets tangling, anchoring him in place so suddenly that she almost dropped him. He fought her, his screams like a fist smashing her in the face again and again and again. She couldn't even take him out of his crib without fucking it up. She couldn't even do that much.

"Stop," she said, her heart so high up in her throat that it was choking her, the rest of her body a hurricane of panic because the screaming just wouldn't stop. "Please, Adam."

She hugged him tight, *too* tight, swaying her whole body from side to side, bouncing up and down on legs that felt paper-thin.

"Oh God, please stop. I don't know what's wrong."

She was wrong. She was a fraud. She couldn't be his mother, she couldn't do it, she wasn't good enough.

A sob tore its way from her, something almost animal, primal. And just like that the cries caught in the baby's throat, the sudden silence leaving her reeling. He looked at her with eyes that hadn't even started to settle on a colour yet, his little wrinkled face trying to work out what to do with itself. He sniffled, whimpered, reaching for her, and her tears dropped onto him—huge and fat and hot. She heaved in a shuddering breath, every bone in her body shaking, her teeth chattering.

"Hello," she said. "Hello, Adam. You're okay, you're okay. I'm here. Mummy's here."

His face creased, his body twisted itself in her grip like some alien thing, and the scream peeled its way free.

"No," Caitlyn said. "No no no, please."

The noise he was making was enough to shred her into pieces, into bloody ribbons, and the strength of her anger terrified her. She dropped Adam back into his crib, clamping her hands to her ears again, throwing herself into the bed.

"No no no no," she said over and over, her voice swallowed whole by the noise of the child. "Please stop it, stop it, *stop it!*"

This was supposed to be a place of miracles, a place where wishes were granted, and Adam was her gift from God. How had it gone so wrong? He was broken. He was broken and she couldn't take him back, she couldn't do anything about it other than lie here and weep.

"Take him away," she said. "Oh God, please take him away. I can't do it. I can't do it."

A place of miracles.

"Please take him away. Please take him. Take him and end this."

A place where wishes were granted.

"Just take him."

Why was she so surprised, then, to open her eyes and see an angel in the open door—the vision blurred by her tears, smudged and shaken by the endless, awful screams.

Caitlyn looked at the crib once more and her son looked

back. His little hands reached for her and the swell of love she felt for him was huge and golden and wonderful.

"Wait," she said, trying to get out of bed, trying not to look at the angel that was drifting into the room. Her feet were wrapped in a fist of blankets and her top half slid onto the floor. "Wait, I take it back, I take it—"

But it was too late. The angel reached out with its too-long arm and the world went black.

And the last thing Caitlyn Brown heard, even as she knew she was dying, was her son falling silent.

CHAPTER ONE

Friday

Robbie Kett sat in the interrogation room on the world's most uncomfortable chair. It was far too small for him, meaning that his legs were bent uncomfortably and his back was arched in a way that made it difficult to draw breath. The bullet wound in his chest didn't help, of course, the pain needling its way between his ribs into the tender flesh of his lungs, echoing with every beat of his heart. It had been months since he'd been shot, enough time for the nightmares to pass, for the flashbacks to be mere memories themselves. But that little fragment of Keefe's bullet was still there, a reminder that life was fragile, and that time was short.

He stretched his back, the pain migrating from his chest into his spine. His head was aching too, the single light in the small room fitted with what had to have been a billion-watt bulb. Somebody had covered the walls in crude drawings, distorted figures who gazed down at him with twisted smiles and bulging, inhuman eyes—a serial killer's chamber if there had ever been one. His lower back started to cramp and he pushed himself up, only for a voice to spill through the open door from the stark corridor beyond.

"Please stay seated, Mr Kett. This won't take long."

Kett sat back down, the chair designed to make every part of him ache. He checked his watch and went to pull his phone out of his pocket, stopping when he heard footsteps. He gritted his teeth, steeling himself, well aware of how bad this was going to be.

You've been here before. You're strong enough to get through it.

"Just in here please," said another voice.

The door opened a little further and Kett was ready to say Alice's name. But it was *Evie* who stood there with a face like a slapped arse. She was wearing one of Alice's old green dresses, a hole in the knee of her grey tights. She didn't need to wear a uniform in nursery but for the last couple of weeks she'd wanted to and nobody seemed to mind. Her hair had shucked itself free of the bun Billie had carefully arranged that morning, and her cheeks were positively glowing. The four-year-old looked at Kett with a mixture of defiance and panic, the same expression she wore at home when she was guilty.

Behind her stood Mr Clapham, the principal. He was a short man whose immaculately styled hair seemed permanently at odds with his badly arranged face—a nose that was a little too small, and a forehead that seemed big enough for another set of watery brown eyes. Kett had never liked him, and from the expression the man was wearing, he didn't figure that was about to change.

"Evie?" Kett said, clearing his throat. "I'm surprised. I

honestly thought that I was going to see Alice walk through the door."

Because it *was* Alice who walked through that door, at least once a week, accompanied by her teacher or the principal or the school's eternally patient SEN lead. He'd heard it said that this windowless, cupboard-sized space was known as the Kett Room, and his oldest daughter had kicked off in here so many times he was amazed they hadn't padded the walls instead of decorating them with children's drawings.

"Robert," said Mr Clapham, using two fingers to pinch a nose that was permanently runny. He put the same hand on Evie's shoulder and Kett had to resist the urge to rip off her cardigan and set fire to it right here. "Thank you for coming in."

The principal spoke the words through his teeth, and then he ran a tongue over them as if to wash the residue away. He guided Evie to the little plastic chair that sat opposite Kett's, the glare of the bare bulb exploding in the vast expanse of his forehead. Evie slumped there and Kett took her little hand in both of his, holding it tight.

"What's up?" he asked her, but it was Mr Clapham who answered.

"Evie is here because of some things she said in nursery. Her teachers felt they were extremely inappropriate."

"Evie?" Kett said, not taking his eyes from his daughter, not letting go of her hand. "Is this true?"

"I'm not in the habit of telling a lie, Robert," said Mr Clapham. The principal was standing over Evie like an ogre and Kett glared up at him. The chair was making him feel like he was four years old as well and he tried to stand up only to feel his back cramp. He grunted, sitting as straight as he could until the pain pulsed away.

"It must have been something very serious to call me down here at..." He checked his watch. "Ten minutes to three. It must have been something that couldn't wait until pick-up."

"Yes."

"Do I need to call my lawyer?" Kett said. He tried to smile at Evie but she wasn't looking at him. Her hand flexed compulsively inside his own.

"No, that's not necessary," Mr Clapham replied, deadly serious. He put his wet fingertips on Evie's shoulder again and a flash of anger detonated in Kett.

"I don't think she's going anywhere, *Phil*," he said, and there was no mistaking the tone of his voice.

Mr Clapham pulled his hand away, sliding both thumbs into his pockets and rocking his hips back and forth like a cowboy from the movies.

"Look, can we hurry this up?" Kett said, the room growing smaller with every breath, the bulb brighter. The drawings on the wall seemed to be laughing at him. "What did she say that was so bad?"

"Evie, do you want to tell your father?" said Mr Clapham.

Evie shook her head, her mouth a grim line. There wasn't a chance in hell of getting her to talk when she clamped up like that.

"Why don't *you* tell me, Phil?" Kett said, the impatience gnawing at him.

Mr Clapham took a big breath, his immense brow furrowing like a wrinkled bedsheet.

"Evie called her teacher, Mr Trowbridge, a *farty butt cheese*."

Kett felt the smile pushing the corners of his mouth and he bit his tongue to stop it. He cleared his throat again, waiting for the rush of laughter to ebb away before speaking.

"Is this true, Evie?"

"I told you, I'm not in the habit of lying," answered the other man.

"I'm asking *her* if it's true," said Kett, squeezing Evie's hand gently. "Is Mr Trowbridge a farty butt cheese?"

Evie frowned at him.

"He won't let me sit next to Sophie," she said quietly.

"I rather think you've missed the point," Mr Clapham said. "Your daughter shouldn't be using language like that in school, especially directed at a teacher."

"I'm aware you've lived a sheltered life, Phil," Kett said. "But there are a lot worse words out there than farty butt cheese."

"Can you please stop saying it?" he replied.

"Will you stop saying farty butt cheese, Evie?" Kett said. "Mr Clapham doesn't like it when people say farty butt cheese so I'd be grateful if you could stop saying farty butt cheese."

"I'll stop saying farty butt cheese," she said, smiling.

"There's no need for the words farty butt cheese to come out of your mouth anymore, okay?"

"Mr Kett, I don't feel like—"

"Farty butt cheese," Kett said, meeting the principal's eyes. Mr Clapham gasped. "Are words that shall never again come out of Evie Kett's mouth."

"I will never say farty butt cheese again," Evie said, giggling.

"May I speak with you alone?" Mr Clapham said, fuming.

Kett pushed himself up from the chair, growling as the pain sloshed back into his chest. His face carried the scars of countless fights, a tapestry of violence, and Mr Clapham took a step back. Kett held out his arms and Evie scrambled into them. He lifted her to his chest, breathless with the agony of it.

"No, Phil, you can't," he said hoarsely. "You wouldn't want to be alone with me right now, I can promise you that. I'm getting a bit sick of this, to be honest."

"Robert—"

"I get that Alice gives you trouble. I get that you probably don't like me. But Evie's a good kid, she loves nursery, and she doesn't deserve to be hauled in here for daring to say a handful of words that wouldn't even make Elmer the Elephant blush."

"I'm not—"

"Listening," Kett interrupted. "I know, which is why I'm trying to help you out here. Have you looked outside recently, Phil? Have you seen what's going on out there? Do you know how bad it is? *This* is not a crime. *This* is not a bad thing. I can promise you my daughter won't call Mr Trowbridge anything else, will you?"

Evie shook her head.

"And she'll say sorry to him, won't you?"

She was a little more reluctant this time, but after a second or two she nodded.

"But Phil, if you call me in here again and put her in front of me then she'd better be guilty of something a hell of a lot more serious than this. Okay?"

Mr Clapham gulped like he'd swallowed a live frog.

"We done here?" Kett said.

"We're, uh, done," the other man said, standing to one side and flapping his hands at the door like it was on fire. "Just be sure to sign out. And perhaps next time we should call Evie's mother."

Kett actually laughed.

"Be thankful you didn't," he said. "Have a good day, Phil."

He walked out of the room, taking such a deep breath that the corridor seemed to break loose and dance around him. Evie clung on, heavier than she had any right to be, but there was no way he was putting her down. He pushed through the door into reception, making sure he was out of earshot before smiling at her.

"That man is a massive farty butt cheese," he said, and Evie broke into a laugh that was like birdsong.

Kett nodded at the receptionist and hit the button for the automatic door. The warmth of the day drew him out onto the playground, the air full of blossom and sunshine— enough to make the pain in his chest sing a little more quietly. Summer had landed early this year, and it had brought its A-game. He lowered Evie to the ground and knelt beside her, brushing loose strands of hair from her sweaty face. She seemed to have even more freckles now than when he'd dropped her off that morning. Her blue eyes seemed sky-big and he took a second to marvel at her.

"Please don't call your teachers names," he said. "I have enough trouble with your sister. I need you to be the good one, okay?"

"Sorry," she said, a genuine apology.

"It's alright," he said. "You're awesome, and don't let anyone tell you otherwise."

He stood up slowly, like a broken marionette.

"Let's go get the others. I feel like pizza."

"Me too!" Evie said, taking his hand and practically dragging him towards the Year 3 classes. Kids were escaping into the playground, making so much noise that it took him a moment to recognise the sound of the *Mexican Hat Dance* screeching from his trouser pocket. He pulled out his phone to see a number he didn't recognise.

"See if she's coming," he told Evie, watching her scamper over to the window of Alice's classroom. He answered the phone and put it to his ear. "This is Kett."

A breath, deep and broken.

"Hello?" Kett said, twisting his head away from the crowd to hear better.

Another breath, on the verge of being a sob. Behind it he could hear music, something choral.

And he knew. Somehow, even after all this time, he knew who it was.

"Mum?"

A third breath. Kett's skin buckled into goosebumps, his scalp swimming-cap tight.

"Robert," said Mary Kett, her voice making the day at once too bright and too dark, like something in the sky had broken. "It's me. I... I need your help."

CHAPTER TWO

"AND BE NICE TO EACH OTHER!"

Kett yelled the words through the back door, knowing all too well that they would be in vain. Alice was sprinting to the back of the garden, clutching her bowl to her chest like Gollum with the One Ring. Evie made it two steps before managing to drop hers, Smarties hitting the dirt. Moira was on them in a heartbeat, spilling her own in the process, both girls screaming.

"Be nice!" he yelled again.

He closed the door and let them sort it out for themselves. The house held him in its silence and its stillness, almost maternal. Fridays were Billie's busy day because she had her group in the morning—painting, on the surface, but all of the women who took part had suffered terrible traumas—and she volunteered at the food bank in the afternoon. She'd started talking about going back to work, which was just as well because Kett was still out of a job.

He peeked through the window to make sure the girls weren't killing each other. They were, but he was too tired to bother with it. He retreated to the table instead. His phone sat there, waiting for him, but even after he'd struggled into a chair he couldn't bring himself to lift it. He couldn't bring himself to call her back.

It had been such a shock to hear her voice. It had stunned him so much he'd made up an excuse, hanging up without so much as a goodbye.

Mary Kett.

For the first twenty years of his life, she'd been his mother, and for the next twenty, she'd been a ghost. She'd vanished off the face of the earth, nothing except for the occasional card and phone call and then, after a while, not even that. He knew she was alive because every now and again he'd checked the system for her name, but he hadn't spoken to her in nearly two decades.

And now she needed his help.

He picked up the phone and swiped it open, looking at the list of calls. She'd rung him from a landline and he recognised the area code. Thetford. Just forty minutes away. He knew she'd never left Norfolk but something about the fact she was so close made him angry. All this time, after everything they'd been through as a family, she hadn't once shown her face.

He closed his eyes, suddenly smelling vanilla—the soap she'd always used. Hairspray too, the house had been full of it when he'd been a kid. The scent was so strong, so real, that he snapped his eyes open again, expecting to find her standing right next to him. But there was just the house, steeped in sunshine, shoals of shimmering dust motes swimming in front of the window. Kett's heart was rocking in his chest and he put a hand to it, gently pressing.

Because in thinking about his mum he couldn't help but think about his dad, too.

About the day he'd found him.

And the day they'd buried him.

He pushed his thumb on the number and waited, his breath locked in his lungs as he counted the rings. Two, three, four.

The phone clicked but it wasn't his mum's voice that answered. It was a man, his greeting more like a dog's bark.

"Yes?"

"Uh," Kett spluttered out the breath he'd been holding. "I'm looking for Mary Kett. She just called me."

"You are?" the man said, and Kett wasn't sure if he was asking him to confirm his request or to identify himself. He did neither. The man on the line huffed quietly and his voice came again, muffled and ancient. "Mary, it's for you."

He said something else, too, that Kett couldn't catch. There was the scuffle of a phone being passed between hands.

"Robert?"

It was anger he'd felt, right up until he heard his name. Then something else rushed into him, something loud and dark and overpowering. He blinked, feeling the tears gathering, feeling the suffocating weight of all those years.

"Mum," he croaked. He cleared his throat, no idea what to say.

"I know this is... I know..."

The line crackled, the sound like firecrackers being let off. Kett's heart had climbed right back to the top of his throat and it sat there like a brick. He opened his mouth but he couldn't get any words out.

"Are you there?" Mary asked.

"I'm here," Kett said.

The man's voice, inaudible but urgent.

"We need your help," she said, her words fast, clipped, like they'd always been. He saw her in his head the way he'd imagined her for the last twenty years: small, slight, her hair cut short and neat and basket-tight with spray. She'd always worn glasses with transparent frames, religiously cleaning them with the hem of her long dresses every time she stopped for breath.

"I'm *fine*," Kett said with a little more sarcasm than he intended. "Thanks for asking."

Mary swallowed, sniffing. Kett heard the man's voice again, like he was yelling orders at her from the other side of the room.

"I'm *doing* it," she hissed, and Kett sensed the reluctance there, the shame. She hadn't wanted to speak with him, he realised. Somebody else had asked her to call.

A seed of panic bloomed inside his stomach. He remembered Keefe, his rifle raised.

They won't stop coming. They'll never let you go.

Hollenbeck. Was this them? Had they got to his mother?

"What's going on?" he said.

"Are you still a policeman, Robert?"

"No," he said, and he thought his mum might have sobbed. "Why?"

"I'm... glad," said Mary, hysterical. "Something's happened. Something... I can't say right now. Will you come?"

"To see you?" Kett said.

"Yes. Now. Please."

Even though it hurt to do it, Kett pushed himself out of his chair.

"Mum, I haven't heard from you in nearly twenty years and you call me out of the blue demanding to see me. What do you want me to say to you?"

"I..."

Nothing, just a dry swallow. Kett forced himself to take a couple of deep breaths. Outside, the girls had finished their Smarties and were leaning over something in the weed-strewn flowerbed.

"Tell me what's going on," he said.

"I can't. I can't tell you over the phone. But I'd like to see you. I need to see you. Can you come up? Today?"

"Down," Kett said. "I'm back in Norwich."

He heard her gasp like he'd shared impossible news.

"You're close. You could be here this afternoon."

"I could," he said. "But I'm not going to be. I have a life, Mum, I can't just drop everything because…"

He stopped, because it was the exact same thing he'd said to her the last time he'd seen her, standing beneath the great arch of the cathedral gates. It had been spring then too, fresh into the new Millennium. She'd asked to speak with him and he'd met her there, right after her choir practice, and she'd told him not to join the police.

I have a life, Mum, I can't just drop everything because you ask me to. It's my choice.

He felt reality lurch, as if time had snapped its jaws around him. He could have been right back there, a young man, the pigeons cooing overhead, the car bonnets shimmering, kids laughing to each other as they came out of the school and his mother's face creased with anger.

Then go do it. Go do it for your stupid father. But don't come crying to me when it all goes wrong.

He hadn't gone crying to her. He hadn't spoken to her again at all, not even when it had gone so terribly, terribly wrong.

Laughter outside. Whatever the girls had been looking at was now on the end of Alice's finger, all three of them crowding around it. Kett hoped it was a ladybird or an ant and not pigeon shit.

"There's something I need to talk to you about, Robert," Mary said. "Something urgent. It can't wait."

Kett thought he heard the man's voice again, he couldn't be sure.

"Has somebody asked you to call me? Somebody you don't know?"

"Somebody I don't know? Of course not, Robert. *I'm* asking you."

His mum was many things, but he didn't think she was a liar.

"It's urgent," she said again. "It can't wait."

He almost said no, and he almost hung up. But something stopped him. He caught the scent of vanilla again, the soapy smell that had filled the house every afternoon when he'd come home from school. She'd always greeted him with a terse smile and a brief, bony cuddle. Never full of love, Mary Kett. Always tight, always rigid, always reserved.

And always there for him. Through the bad days. Through his father's decline and death. Always there.

Right up until the day she hadn't been.

The girls were racing down the garden, screaming with delight. They'd never known their grandmother, although they often asked. Maybe this was a chance to fix that. Mary Kett was many things, he thought again, but she was blood.

"I'll come," he said. "Give me the address, I'll be there in the morning."

"Could you come tonight?" she said.

"No. The morning."

There was a muffled reply from the man, and his mother sniffed.

"It's a community called Whytetail," she said. "You'll

find us there."

"What street?" Kett asked.

"There's only one. I... You'll find me in the church."

Of course.

She swallowed again, and Kett waited.

"Goodbye, Robert."

And she was gone.

Kett dropped the phone onto the table just as the back door opened and the girls stampeded into the room, Alice barging past Moira and sending her flying. Kett helped his youngest up, all of them clamouring for his attention.

"It's amazing!" Alice said. "Look, Dad."

"It's prickly," Evie added, trying to grab something out of her older sister's hand. "I want to show him."

"I found it," Alice cried back, thrusting her hand into Kett's face. He reeled back at the sight of what sat there.

A stag beetle, its carapace as black as pitch, twisted and broken and very dead.

"It wasn't moving," Alice said.

"It's asleep," Evie said.

"Aleep," added Moira, poking it with her finger. "Ake up."

"I think you should put it back outside," Kett said.

"No, I'm going to make a house for it," Evie shot back. "Out of Lego."

"Let's do it!" Alice screeched, running from the kitchen. Evie was hot on her heels and Moira squirmed in Kett's arms until he released her. He watched her go, thinking of his mum, thinking of the beetle lying fat and black in his daughter's hand.

It's urgent. It can't wait.

He didn't believe in omens, of course.

But this seemed like a bad one.

CHAPTER THREE

Saturday

"ARE YOU SURE YOU WANT TO DO THIS, ROBBIE?"

Billie asked the question as she climbed into the passenger seat of the Volvo, slamming the door behind her. She turned to check on the kids, who were bickering in the back, then buckled herself in. When Kett didn't answer, she put a hand on his arm.

She'd let her honey-coloured hair grow out this year—just a couple of inches, but it made her look so different. It was the same length now that it had been when they'd met, as if she was healing herself by moving backwards. She was wearing her blue dress, too, the same one she wore on the screen of his phone, when things had been so different. The shitstorm of last year was never gone completely, of course. The Pig Man would always be there. Hollenbeck would always be there. But Kett couldn't see them anymore. When he looked at Billie all he saw was the woman he'd fallen so desperately in love with.

"What?" she asked, smiling.

"Just you," he replied. He tugged on the collar of his charcoal jumper, already too hot. He wondered if he should have worn shorts and trainers instead of jeans and boots but he couldn't face going in to get changed.

"And them," she said, misunderstanding. "Your mum's not going to know what hit her."

"'*My, what lovely granddaughters I have*,'" he said in a croaky falsetto. "'*Argh, get them off me!*'"

"'*Why is this one stealing my purse?*'" added Billie.

"'*Why is the little one farting on my head?*'" said Kett.

"'*How many times can that one go for a poo?*'"

And they were both laughing.

"What are you talking about?" asked Alice, leaning through the gap in the chairs.

"Nothing," said Kett. "Is the chinchilla definitely in her cage? I don't want her eating all the shoes again."

"Yeah," said Alice, not very convincingly. "Where are we going?"

"Like I said, it's just a trip. It won't be for long."

"Can I have your phone?"

"Haven't you got your iPad?"

"I need to be online for *Roblox*," she said. "The iPad doesn't work."

He almost said no, but decided the battle wasn't worth it. He pulled out his phone and loaded the app, handing it over.

"I want it!" Evie demanded.

"I want it!" Moira echoed.

"Hush up," he said. "You can take turns. And if you're good there might be some cake in it for you."

"Cake!" Moira said, breaking into a smile.

"Did your mum ever bake you a cake?" Billie asked as Kett backed the Volvo up, nudging it out of the space.

"Nope. But a lot can change in twenty years."

He eased them down their narrow road, pulling out into traffic. It was already well after ten and most of the cars were queued on the opposite side of the street as they fought for the Saturday parking spaces. He turned off the inner ring road as soon as he could, zigzagging through the quiet residential streets until he reached the A11. The world had shrugged off its winter coat and missed Spring entirely, the tarmac shimmering and the temperature on the dash already reading nineteen degrees. Despite the bricks that sat in his stomach at the thought of seeing his mother again, he was feeling weirdly optimistic.

"Do you think *she's* changed?" Billie asked over the thrum of the tyres, the old Volvo rattling.

He opened his mouth to answer before realising he didn't have one. So much time had passed that he couldn't really remember what his mum had been like. He didn't know how many of his memories were real, and how many he'd fabricated in the years that followed their final meeting. But there were some things he couldn't forget.

Some things he couldn't forgive, too.

"No," he said after a moment. "I don't think she will have changed. Some people don't, do they?"

"I hope she has," Billie said, her bare foot wedged in the corner where the dash met the door, her head resting on her knee. Billie had never met his mum, of course, but she'd heard the stories. "For your sake. For theirs, too."

Kett checked the mirror, seeing Alice trying to keep the phone out of Moira's grasping hands, Evie's big eyes full of the passing countryside. He hadn't told them who they'd be meeting because he didn't want to get their hopes up. Grammies were supposed to be fun and full of love. If Mary Kett was any of those things then he'd tell them who she was. If she wasn't, it was better that they didn't have their hearts broken.

His heart had already been broken once. He wasn't sure she could hurt him again.

"Good to be out of the city, though," Billie said. She flicked on the radio, scrolling through the stations until she found *Future FM*. Jimi Hendrix was singing and she turned it up, tapping on her knee with both hands.

"It is," said Kett, smiling. And it *was*. Norwich hadn't exactly provided a host of happy memories since he'd moved here last year, and there was something about roaring down the dual carriageway with the sun blazing through the windows that was liberating. He felt *free*. There seemed to be sunshine inside him too and he put his foot down, taking the car up to seventy. Hendrix gave way to the Foo Fighters, then to a band he didn't recognise but the kids did, all three of them howling along tunelessly. Billie smiled at him and he smiled back, something almost dreamlike about the mirages that rippled the road, about the liquid sunshine that pooled on the yellow fields. It seemed as if they reached Thetford too soon, as if they'd slipped through time, or as if he had woken from an impossible sleep.

"Whytetail?" Billie said, pointing to a battered sign as they exited Thetford. Kett frowned, glancing at the satnav which was telling them to keep going south. It was too late to turn and he followed the road as it wound through flowering verges, past blossoming meadows and woodlands which seemed to puff their chests proudly. He hadn't seen the countryside like this for so long, caught in the mad grip of Spring. It seemed as if he had lived inside one long, unbroken winter.

They found another sign a few minutes later, and this one too was at odds with the satnav. He ignored his instincts, following the screen as it took them on a wide arc and over a low bridge.

"Are we nearly there?" Evie asked, and Kett looked back to see her squirming.

"I told you to go before we left," he said.

"I did."

"She didn't," said Alice.

"I did!" she shot back. "The poo didn't come out. It went back in."

"It went back *in*?" Kett said, meeting Billie's eye. "How?"

"It just did!" she replied, her cheeks blazing.

She was saved further interrogation when the car rounded another corner, passing a sign that said, '*Whytetail, Please Drive Carefully*'. It was hard not to, because just past the sign was a speed bump the size of Ben Nevis, the Volvo thumping over it before Kett had a chance to slow down.

"I think that might have knocked the poo back out," said Alice, cackling. Evie smacked her, starting a flurry of shouts and slaps.

"Enough!" Kett said. "We're here."

Both sides of the street were crowded with new, red-brick houses and white-rendered bungalows that gave way to a newsagent, a butcher and a cafe. A handful of people hugged the narrow pavements, old women with trollies and kids wobbling on their bikes. Kett slowed to a crawl, scanning the rooftops and seeing no sign of a church. There was no sign of anything, in fact, and after less than a minute they passed another sign saying, '*Thanks for visiting.*'

"Weird," he said, driving for half a mile before finding a track to turn around in. He took them back, the sun in his eyes, and pulled the Volvo up beside the little shop. A *Walls Ice Cream* sign sat outside the door, squeaking in a breeze that Kett couldn't feel through the open window. "Hang on."

"Ice cream!" Evie shouted, echoed by her little sister.

"I'll see what I can do."

He opened the door, climbing into the heat and waiting for a family to laugh their way past before he stepped inside the shop. It was a typical village newsagent, every item imaginable somehow crammed onto the dusty shelves, the air full of the smell of old paper and some-thing else, something a little rotten. An old man stood behind the counter, hiking up a pair of faded green corduroys that looked far too big for him. He was wearing a baggy tank top over a dirty white shirt and there was something about his face that seemed just as loose. He had to be in his late seventies, every movement laden with discomfort. As Kett crossed the shop he realised the smell was coming from the man, like he hadn't washed since Christmas.

"*G'morn*," he said with a weary nod. His Norfolk accent was as thick as they came. "Lost?"

"How did you know that?" Kett asked.

"Can read a face, and yours is lost. Let me guess, you're looking for Whytetail."

"The church?"

"You're in the wrong place," said the man, wiping his wet eyes with a napkin.

"This isn't Whytetail?"

"It is now, but it weren't always. If it's the church you're after then you're looking for the old village. Mile away as the crow flies but you have to double back because of the river. Take a left, it's not far."

"You're sure?" Kett asked, and the man nodded, his chin ballooning.

"You won't find much there. Not been much there for a *hunnert* years. Just the church and the old Clifford place, and a mill if you're happy to trek into the wild. Not much, unless it's the commune you're after?"

"Commune?"

"Some folk call it that, others aren't so kind. Either way, if you're looking for them folk and their hokey well—sorry, *holy* well—then double back, take a left."

"Thanks," Kett said. He scanned the shelves of chocolate bars and grabbed a Twix, only to drop it. It had melted, the insides liquid.

"Three for two," the man said.

"I'll pass." Kett rapped his knuckles on the counter before walking away. "Turn around, then take a left?"

"Uyuh," the man said. "And you wanna watch yourself with that lot."

Kett stopped, looking back. The man wiped his eyes with his handkerchief again, his face looking like meat that was sliding off the bone.

"Why?" he asked.

"Religious nutters."

When it was clear that was all he was getting, Kett walked out of the shop into the sun. Billie stared up at him from inside the car, the kids gazing out of the darkness with big, bright eyes. It looked like night inside the Volvo, like the sun hadn't risen, and for a reason he couldn't fathom, he shuddered. He opened the door and climbed in, rubbing the goosebumps from his arms.

"What?" Billie said, reading him the way she always did.

"Nothing."

"Ice cream?" Alice asked, looking up from his phone.

"They didn't have any."

Kett started the engine and pulled out. The same people walked down the streets, and all of them seemed to watch him go. He felt Billie's hand on his arm, a gentle squeeze.

"It's nothing," he said. "Wrong village."

He drove back the way they'd come, taking the first left and finding himself on a road that wound for more than a mile, a single solitary farmhouse the only sign of life. It seemed like an age later that he turned another corner and plunged into the shade of a crowd of overhanging trees. The road here looked like it had been strafed by the RAF, cratered with enormous holes, and the kids bounced in the back like whack-a-moles, all of them groaning and giggling, their faces suddenly glowing as they broke back into the sun.

Kett blinked, the day too bright like it meant to blind them to what lay ahead. A sign proclaimed that he had arrived once again in Whytetail, and at first he thought he'd somehow driven back into the same village. But the houses here were long dead, some rotted to their shells, others burned. Kett slowed down, rounding a corner to see a little line of shops. These too had been gutted, just skeletal shapes that rose from ruptured graves of brambles and long grass. Songbirds disappeared into the overgrown gardens as the car growled past, the air silent.

"Where are we?" Billie said. Her smile had vanished too, another startled bird. The kids had fallen silent, all of them staring out of the windows.

"I don't like it here," said Alice.

"Me neither," Kett said.

The sun still blazed, the sky flawless, but something in the stillness of the village, in its fairy tale squalor, was making his skin crawl. He kept his speed low, driving down the empty street and past another audience of crooked trees only to slam on the brakes hard enough to make the big car thump to a halt.

Ahead was a church that seemed far too big for a little village like this, its stone almost black against the brightness of the day. The shadow of its blunt, square tower sat fat on the road, reaching for the car.

And standing there in that finger of darkness, as if she'd known they were about to arrive, was Mary Kett.

CHAPTER FOUR

THERE WAS NOWHERE TO PULL OVER, BUT KETT DIDN'T think the neglected road saw any traffic at all so he cut the engine and sat there in a silence so deep he might have been underwater. His mum didn't move, as still as one of the weathered statues that sat in the graveyard of the church. As *old* as one of those statues, too. So much older than he'd expected her to be—her back bent, her hair short and grey, the lines chiselled into the stone of her face.

Then, like a fairground automaton, her head juddered up and her pale eyes seemed to see him there.

Kett's chest burned, but it was only when Billie squeezed his arm that he realised he was holding his breath. He let it out gently, inhaling again and feeling like there was no air left in the world. The silence had spread to the car, the kids sensing something that made them wary.

"Gently does it," Billie said quietly. "Take it slow. This was never going to be easy."

Kett nodded, his head swimming. He hadn't realised how much it would affect him, seeing her again. Because there was his mum, the same mum who'd tucked the blankets beneath his chin every single night, who'd kissed him on the forehead before school, who'd wrapped him straight-jacket tight in the days, the weeks, the months that followed his dad's death. The same mum who'd rarely smiled but who had laughed herself breathless the time he'd sat on the rhubarb crumble she'd left to cool on the kitchen bench. The same mum who'd hooked a duck at the Norfolk Show and won him his first plastic policeman's set—a little blue gun, a badge, a radio. He could still feel the snap of the gun as he pulled the trigger, the scrape of the plastic clip on his chest as his mum fixed the badge to his T-shirt.

The memories kept coming, too many of them, too fast, too loud, and he had to rest his head against the steering wheel and force himself not to scream.

He was not prepared for this at all. Not one bit.

"Daddy?" said Evie. "Who's that old lady?"

"It's a friend," Billie said, answering for him. Her hand still rested on his arm and it felt like the only thing stopping him from blowing out through the window, up into the cloudless sky. "Daddy needs to talk with her, but we're going to stretch our legs and have a look around."

"And watch Evie have a poo," said Alice.

"I don't need a poo!" Evie screamed back.

"Poos, too," Billie said. She leaned in. "There's no pressure, okay. You don't owe her anything."

Kett nodded, looking up. Mary was still standing there, the hem of her grey dress on the ground. She lifted her glasses off her nose, cleaning them on her dress the way she always had, and tucked a silver crucifix into the collar of her blouse. She took a step towards the car, freeing herself from the shadow of the church. There was more life in her now, as if she was warming up. She cupped a hand to her forehead and squinted, even though the sun was behind her.

Then her mouth opened, and although Kett couldn't hear her he could see his name on her lips.

Robert?

He climbed out of the car, stepping into a pothole that almost tripped him. He gripped the door until he found his balance, then pushed it gently shut. The world was still unbearably quiet, just the crunch of gravel beneath his mum's foot as she took another tentative step towards him.

"Robert?" she said again.

"Mum," he replied, forcing the word past the hot rock that sat in his throat. The emotion was enough to crush him, if he let it in, so he pushed it back and locked it tight the same way he had all those years ago when he'd walked away from her.

Mary looked like she was going to keep walking but instead she took a step back. Her hands wrung endlessly in front of her chest, contorting themselves into shapes. Kett scanned the overgrown graveyard, the hedgerows, the dark stained-glass windows of the church, wondering again if he'd made a mistake, if somehow Hollenbeck was waiting here for him. But there was no sign of life other than his mum. As breakable as he felt right now, he didn't sense danger here.

"You..." Mary said, her voice frail. "I thought you'd be here sooner."

"I'm here," he replied, ignoring the flare of anger that her words ignited. "We all are."

He looked back at the car. Mary followed his gaze and seemed to see Billie for the first time.

"My wife," Kett said when she didn't speak. "Billie. The girls are here too, although I haven't told them who you are."

"The girls?"

"My girls. Your granddaughters."

Her dark eyes studied the car, then studied him.

"You shouldn't have brought them," she said, and his anger swelled.

"I'm starting to think maybe I shouldn't have come at all. What is this, Mum? Why call me after all this time? Why bring me here?"

Mary opened her mouth, gulping air. She took another step back, swallowed once again by the shadow of the church. Kett grit his teeth, the anger unbearable, then he heard the Volvo's door open. Billie walked to his side, hesitant, like she didn't want to scare off a wild animal. She slid his phone back into his pocket and pushed her arm through his. The smile she offered Mary was brighter than the sun.

"Hi," she said. "I'm Billie. I've been looking forward to meeting you."

"You have?" Mary said.

She stopped retreating, looking over her shoulder at the church. Her hands were still working furiously, as if they were trying to untangle an invisible rope. The kids had got over whatever spell this place had cast on them, screaming bloody murder from inside the car. It was actually rocking.

"Do you mind if they come out?" Billie said. "It's been a bit of a drive. We're happy to take a walk while you and Robbie catch up."

There was something so effortless in the way she spoke, something that seemed to put his mum at ease. Mary nodded, her brow knitted, her hands twisting. For the first time Kett wondered if she was all there, if maybe the decades hadn't been kind to her. Something seemed to be missing, as if she'd been hollowed out—physically and mentally. He thought of puppets, wooden heads and strings.

"Of course," she said after a moment. "The yard is perfectly pleasant, and if you walk that way you'll find *our* church. They'll be starting choir practice soon, and they will make you feel very welcome."

"Thank you," said Billie. She squeezed Kett's arm then let go, and he had to stop himself from reaching out and pulling her back. He watched her walk to the car and open the back door, then he turned and studied his mum as the kids emerged. Her face seemed to carry the weight of a hundred different emotions all at once and finally her hands stopped moving. She put her fingers to her mouth, her eyes full of tears as Moira appeared, held in Billie's arms, then Alice, and finally Evie. The girls gave their grandmother a suspicious look before hustling their mother with a barrage of questions.

"You'll be okay?" Billie asked, and he nodded. She switched Moira to her other arm. "I love you."

"I love you," he replied.

"Don't go past the wooden church," Mary said. "Don't go down to the river. Please. Not yet. This is a sacred place, and they won't like it."

"We won't," Billie said, throwing Kett a bemused look before turning and leading the girls away. They pushed through a gap in the hedge, Evie's voice clarion loud as she screamed at Alice.

"I haven't pooed myself!"

Kett breathed a laugh through his nose. Mary was watching them go, her fingers still resting on her lips.

"They're amazing girls," he said to her. "A pain in the arse, but amazing."

"You shouldn't have brought them, Robert," she said. He opened his mouth in anger again but before he could speak she held up a trembling hand. "Not because I don't want to see them, not because I don't... don't want to get to know them. God knows how much I've missed you, Robert.

He truly does. But because I called you here for another reason. I called you here because I need your help. *We* need your help."

She looked at the church again, at the tower which seemed far too tall and far too black, like a hand held up to stop the sun. She watched it as if it might suddenly come to life, a giant rising from the earth.

"What's going on, Mum?" Kett asked.

"Something has happened," she said, speaking to the church. "They're dead."

The shadow seemed to grow, seemed to swallow the day and freeze the air. Kett leaned forward, unsure if he'd heard her right. But she said it again.

"They're dead."

"Who's dead, Mum?"

"Caitlyn and Liam."

"I don't know who they are."

He heard Alice laugh and the sound of it seemed too far away. He searched for them but it was like the graveyard had opened up and swallowed them whole.

"Mum," he said. "What's going on?"

She turned away from the church but she didn't look at him, studying the road as if reading her lines in the tarmac.

"Robert, they were killed. We found them yesterday morning. It was awful."

Kett held up his hand.

"Hang on, you're saying two people are dead? Murdered? Mum, I'm not police anymore, I told you that on the phone. If—"

"We can't go to the police," she said. Her hands started their mad dance again, flexing in front of her chest. "That's why I asked you. That's why I was so glad to hear that you weren't. We can't go to the police."

"Why?"

Nothing. The silence of the countryside was overwhelming. There was something monstrous about it.

"Why?" he said again.

"I... You should speak to somebody else."

"I'm speaking to you. If you tell me why you can't call the police, then I'll consider helping you."

"I really can't," she said. "I'm sorry."

"Then so am I," Kett replied.

She looked at him, her expression full of desperation.

"A baby is missing."

Despite the heat, Kett felt his skin crinkle into goosebumps. Mary shook her head, the words flowing from her now like she'd been uncorked.

"Caitlyn and Liam had a child, a baby boy. Adam. He's only two weeks old. He's missing, Robert. The man who killed his mother and father took him and we don't know where he is."

"When was this, *exactly*?" Kett said.

"It happened yesterday, or maybe Thursday night. We don't know when. Reginald's wife took them flowers yesterday morning at seven and she found the door open. They were... they were butchered. I don't know a better word for it. The baby wasn't there and there was blood in its crib."

"Mum, listen to me," Kett said, taking a step towards her. "Listen very carefully. You need to call the police. When a child is taken there is usually a very small window where we can get them back, and in order to do that, we need as many people looking for him as possible. We've lost, what, twenty-four hours already? More. Call them now and I'll help. If you don't, you'll never see that boy again. Do you understand?"

"No," she said. "We can't. There was a note."

"What did it say?"

"I don't know. I can't remember all the words. But the killer made himself very clear. If we call the police, the boy will die."

It was Kett who was shaking his head now.

"Will you help, Robert?" Mary said. "He's a dear, sweet boy. He's a child of God. A miracle. An innocent. Please."

A missing child. He'd been here before, so many times. And he'd never walked away, not once.

He wasn't about to start now.

"I'll help," he said. "But you have to listen to me. You have to do everything I tell you to."

Mary nodded, her smile almost a grimace.

"And Mum, you keep saying we. Who are you talking about?"

She frowned, as if it was the stupidest question in the world. Then she looked over her shoulder at the church.

"Them, of course."

And Kett saw them standing there by the open door, a congregation of ghostly faces in a sea of shadow. They hadn't been there a moment ago, he was sure of it. And yet there were so many of them—twenty, maybe, men and women and children—he didn't know how they could have assembled without him seeing.

"My family, Robert," said Mary, sadly. "My family."

CHAPTER FIVE

It was darker inside the church than it had any right to be, shadows pooling in the corners where they grew slowly stagnant. It was colder too, as if the building was refrigerated. It should have been welcome, after the heat outside. But there was nothing welcoming about this place.

Kett hesitated in the doorway, grateful at last for his jumper. He rested one hand on the ancient stone as he peered inside. The people who had gathered in the church's shadow were now lined up in the dark interior, their features barely visible. Kett had counted five men as he'd followed his mum from the road, all conservatively dressed and dour, reminding him of the Amish. There were seven women and five children, all older than his own and all impeccably behaved. He didn't think he'd heard a single word from any of them as they rushed inside and stood behind their parents.

A touch on his elbow, so brief he wasn't sure if he'd imagined it. Mary stood next to him, gesturing at the door with mousy little movements. He still didn't move, because there was something about the church that made him feel uncomfortable, something that set off a warning in his gut. He couldn't figure out what it was.

"Mary," said one of the men, the tallest and oldest of them. His low voice travelled through the church like thunder and Kett recognised it. It was the man he'd heard on the phone when he'd spoken to his mum yesterday. "Whenever you're ready."

Mary touched his arm again, warily, as if every movement might trigger some kind of reaction from him. He relented, walking inside, gripped by the impossible cold. Out of the sun, his eyes quickly adapted. It wasn't as dark in here as he'd assumed, fingers of sickly light pushing through the leaded glass and pooling on the floor. The biggest window boasted a few remaining panels of stained glass but the others had been boarded over. The nave was empty, no pews, just a collection of mismatched chairs and sofas and trellis tables. The walls were bare, not so much as a crucifix mounted on the pitted stone—although an old fashioned corded phone had been crookedly mounted by the door.

"This is him?" said the man. He was in his late seventies or early eighties, Kett guessed, but he was a big guy. Six-four, maybe, stood slightly bent with his hands clasped behind his back. There was something in the way he held himself that made it clear he was in pain but doing his best not to show it. Beneath a full head of snow-white hair his face was long and thin, his nose like an eagle's beak, and something in the intensity of his eyes made Kett feel both reassured and wary. A giant brass cross peeked out from the collar of his white shirt.

"Kett," Kett said. "Robbie. You are?"

"This is Reginald," Mary answered, but the man held up a huge hand and his mum seemed to suck the word back in.

"I'll take it from here," the man said. His words were confident and clipped, his voice remarkably deep. It reminded Kett of Christopher Lee, and visions of *Dracula* filled his head. The man broke ranks and walked across the nave, the same hand held out on an arm that seemed too long. Kett wasn't exactly short, but he found himself looking up at him the way a child might. "Reginald Cairns. I'm the Pastor here at Whytetail."

Kett shook the man's hand, his palm as soft as leather. Cairns held on for a moment longer than he needed to, those blue eyes like drills. Kett was the one who pulled free, taking a step back to put some distance between them. In doing so he bumped into his mum, reaching out to her instinctively. His heart was going like the clappers and he couldn't work out why.

"The Pastor," he said after a moment, looking at the bare walls. "Something tells me this isn't your run of the mill church. Deconsecrated?"

Cairns shared a glance with Mary.

"I didn't tell him," she said quietly.

Cairns cleared his throat, clasping his hands behind his back again. There was a smell to the man, a pungent medicinal scent that wasn't unpleasant.

"We are a religious community, although our religion is not the same as that practised in other parts of the country."

"I don't care," Kett said, his voice batting off the walls, rising to the shadowed rafters like a trapped bird. "Mary says two people have died, that a baby is missing. I'm not a police officer anymore, Mr Cairns, but unless you provide me with a very good reason why I shouldn't, then in about sixty seconds I'm going to call my colleagues and get a Task Force down here."

"If you do that, the baby will die," Cairns said. He

looked over his shoulder and nodded once. Another member of the congregation broke free and trotted over—a man who was just as tall as Cairns. He was in his forties, perhaps, although there was something childlike in his slack expression. He was wearing a baggy white shirt, like Cairns, but there was muscle underneath. He gave Kett a nervous look then handed the Pastor a piece of crumpled paper.

"Please tell me that isn't the note," Kett said.

Cairns offered it to him and Kett shook his head. He pointed to the nearest table.

"Put it there. How many people have touched this?"

"I couldn't say," the Pastor replied. He walked to the table with those same big, lumbering steps, putting the paper down then running a big hand over it. "We're a close community, undergoing a period of profound shared grief. I cannot tell you who has touched it."

"For fuck's sake," Kett muttered beneath his breath.

He leant over the table, studying the note. The paper looked like it might once have been part of a bag, ripped in two, and it was marbled with old blood. The writing was big, angry, urgent. Six lines of it, each one angled more severely than the last. It was hard to read all of the words because the ink had been smudged.

"'*You knit me together in my mother's womb,*'" he read aloud. "'*Now suffer for it. He shall not know his mother or his father. He shall only know his...*'"

"Failure," Cairns offered. "It's spelled wrong."

"'*His failure. I have no reason to keep him alive. Come after me, call the police, and...*'"

Kett stopped, knowing that there were children listening. Cairns showed no such restraint.

"'*And I will spill every last drop of his blood, and the dirt will drink it up,*'" the Pastor said, his words echoing. They seemed to leach into Kett's head, into his skin, making him shiver. He read the note again then turned to Cairns.

"The two people who died. Where are they?"

Cairns swallowed, his enormous Adam's apple bobbing. "They're safe," he said.

"Safe?" Kett shook his head. "What are you talking about?"

"Safe. We have a facility. We tend to our own dead."

Kett glanced at his mum but her eyes tracked the stone floor, full of something that might have been fear, or shame.

"I need to see them," Kett said. "Do you have any idea who wrote this note? Any idea who might have wanted to hurt them?"

"No," said Cairns. "It's an outsider. Nobody here would ever commit such a crime, such a *sin*."

"I need a list of everyone in the community," Kett said. "Men, women, children. Anyone who comes anywhere near this place. Deliveries, cleaners, whatever. I need it now. And I'll need to talk to everyone here."

"Does this mean you'll help us?" Cairns said.

"I'll help you find the child," Kett said. "But we do it my way, and I can't do it by myself."

He checked his watch to see that it was almost midday.

"We've lost so much time. I'll need to bring in some help."

"We can't call the police," Cairns said, and this time it was Kett who silenced him with a hand.

"If you want this baby back, you have to trust me. Whoever did this doesn't want to hurt the child, or they already would have. They either need Adam for leverage or for something else. I'm not saying they *won't* hurt him, but I don't think that's their plan. If we're going to find him we need to be careful, and we need to be quick."

Cairns swallowed again, offering that same terse nod.

"We just want to find our son," he said.

"Give me five minutes." Kett pulled his phone from his pocket. "Mum, a word."

Mary Kett looked at Cairns as if asking for permission and he nodded to her. Kett walked outside, the day wrapping him in a heat that felt almost tropical compared to the church. He shuddered, scanning the graveyard, looking for his kids and not finding them.

"You could have warned me," he said, turning to her. "There's a killer, Mum, and you didn't think to mention it? My kids are here. I thought..."

He rubbed his temples, feeling the first dull peals of a migraine. What did he think? That she'd called him because she missed him? That she'd called him because she wanted to see him, because she loved him? Because she wanted to apologise for what had happened? He studied the misery in her face, the reluctance to meet his eye.

"I'm..." she said, but if there was another word there she didn't seem to have the power to bring it up.

Kett swore silently as he walked away, calling Billie. He didn't hear the sound of her phone from anywhere nearby, but after a couple of rings she picked up, the line full of Moira's screams.

"You okay?" she asked.

"I got this completely wrong," he said, still walking. "This isn't a reunion, it's a murder."

"A *what*?"

"Two people, parents. Their baby is missing and there are specific instructions not to call the police."

"Jesus," Billie said. "Moomoo, just please be quiet for a second."

The crying quietened, Billie's voice louder.

"Is it safe?"

"I don't know," Kett said. "There's something about this place I don't like. Something... I don't know, *wrong.*"

"You're under a lot of pressure, Robbie. It's never going to feel normal."

"Maybe. Just be careful, okay?"

"Always," she said, the word heavy with worry.

Kett hung up, squinting back at the church. It rose from the yard like a gravestone, as if a Titan had been buried here amongst the mortal men. The sun seemed to sit right on the top of the tower, caught there.

He turned away, blinking splashes of light across the countryside as he called Clare. The Superintendent answered after three rings, and he sounded breathless.

"I told you, they're too tight in the crotch," he said. "I'm not sitting there for three hours with my bollocks in a mousetrap."

"Uh..."

"If he wasn't such a tossing peacock then we could all wear a normal bloody suit, it's his bloody fault. Why should my crotchal area suffer?"

"Uh, Clare?" Kett said. "I'm pretty sure this isn't who you think it is."

"Kett?" Clare said. "Tossing hell, I thought you were my wife. She's been calling all morning about the wedding."

"The wedding?" he said, remembering Clare's oldest son. "Steve's?"

"He's putting us in these godawful tossing cock suits."

"What kind of wedding *is* this?"

"I swear to God you couldn't fit a hamster's hairy bollocks in them, let alone mine."

"That's a visual I am never going to be able to get out of

my head," Kett said, shuddering again. "Look, sir, something's happened."

Clare grunted, and Kett took that as a sign to carry on—quietly, though, because he knew he was breaking the kidnapper's rules.

Call the police and I will spill every last drop of his blood, and the dirt will drink it up.

"I got a call from my mother. She's living in a place called Whytetail."

"I know it," Clare said. "*Of* it, at least."

"Two people have been killed. A baby has been kidnapped."

"What?" spluttered Clare. "When?"

"Yesterday morning, maybe Thursday night."

"Christ, Kett, this could only happen to you. I'll mobilise a—"

"Wait, there was a note. Any police presence and the kid dies."

"You believe it?"

"I think it's a risk we can't take," said Kett. "I'm here, I can get things started, discreetly. But I can't do it alone."

"I'll send Savage. Porter too. I'm coming down there, Kett."

He opened his mouth to tell the Super not to, then closed it.

"Fine," he said. "But no Uniforms. And try not to look like a copper."

"I'll wear my wedding suit," Clare said. "Crotchal compression or not, no police in their right mind would be caught dead in an outfit like this."

"We need all eyes on this from a distance. CCTV, traffic cameras, everything. If somebody's moving a child we're running out of time to track them."

"If?" Clare said. "You think there's a chance the killer's still there?"

Kett scanned the graveyard, seeing his mother standing once again in the shadow of the church, like she couldn't escape it. Somewhere close by, a song started—something choral that seemed to haunt the quiet summer air. He took a deep breath, smelling grass, smelling blossom, feeling almost drunk on it.

Whytetail had been a hard place to find.

He got the impression it was a harder place to leave.

"I don't know," he said. "Something tells me they might not have gone far."

CHAPTER SIX

THERE WAS NO WAY THE BASTARD WAS GOING TO GET away.

DC Kate Savage vaulted the railing, the drop on the other side further than she'd thought. She landed badly, her ankle almost turning. Her grandfather's lucky whistle bounced out of her shirt collar, swinging wildly as she started running again. Further down the ramp a man was sprinting into the underpass that led beneath the main road, heading for Chapelfield Gardens.

"Stop!" Savage yelled, and she would have added something else if she'd had the breath for it. She'd chased the dealer down two streets, almost losing him in the flats that sat next to the school. He was a sneaky little git, and fast too.

"Duke, you there?" Savage shouted into her radio.

"Where?" came the reply.

"What do you mean, *where*?" Savage said. "Where do you think I mean?"

"Here?"

Savage lowered the radio as she reached the bottom of the ramp, tucking the whistle back into her shirt. There was a mirror mounted here, scarred with graffiti and almost entirely covered with stickers. The man was still running and Savage skittered around the corner.

"He's in the underpass, heading for Chapelfield."

"I'm on it," Duke said.

The man burst clear of the underpass, caught by the sun.

"Stop!" Savage yelled, wishing she had Colin the dog with her.

She doubled down, the echo of her pounding feet filling the low underpass, the air full of the stench of piss. She had no idea how the guy was running so fast considering he was off his head. A shout from the park, a cry of distress.

"St—"

Savage sprinted out of the underpass only for something to slam into her, as big as a car. She hit the ground hard, rolling into the bushes. She'd made a fist before she noticed the uniform and the beard.

It was PC Duke.

It's me, you idiot, she tried to say. There hadn't been much air left in her lungs before he'd collided with her, and what was left had been punched clean out.

"Shit, sorry," Duke said, offering her a hand. She took it, grunting her way back to her feet.

Savage pointed into the park.

"Get him," she groaned, still winded.

"Oh, right, yeah."

Duke broke into a run, shouting. Savage braced her hands on her knees, trying to suck in air. There was a rumble of feet as DI Keith Dunst practically fell into the underpass, wheezing like an accordion. He half ran and half limped to Savage, his big mouth gulping for air.

"Where... is... he?" he asked.

Savage pointed up the slope into the park, and for a moment both of them stood there trying to get their breath back.

"Couple of *bona fide* Robocops, eh?" Savage said.

"I'm old," Dunst replied. "What's your excuse?"

"Got hit by a bear. Come on."

They jogged into the park together to see a cluster of uniformed police standing over their suspect. Duke was slapping the cuffs on him and he flashed Savage a grin as she made her way over.

"Don't know what you're so happy about," she said, rubbing her ribs.

The grin vanished.

"Sorry," Duke said again.

"You read him his rights?" Savage asked, and Duke nodded. "Then get him out of here."

Duke and another Uniform hauled the man to his feet and gave him a hefty shove towards the road. Savage followed them through the growing, wide-eyed crowds, slowing her breathing, enjoying the warmth of the sun on her face for as long as it took her to reach the gate. Traffic roared and grunted along the road she'd just passed beneath, the intoxicating smell of blossom replaced by the equally intoxicating stench of exhaust fumes. The man was loaded unceremoniously into the back of an IRV and he shot Savage a filthy look through the window.

"I'll get you next time, bitch."

"Not if Duke gets me first," she replied, smiling at the man's frown of confusion as the car pulled away.

"Sorry," the big PC said a third time. He took off his hat and scratched his shaved head, then used the same hand to wipe the sweat from his brow. "Let me make it up to you?"

"I'm pretty sure the whole Neanderthal tactic of

knocking women out before a date doesn't work anymore," Savage said, looking down the street and seeing a familiar tank-like Mercedes 280. "Hang on."

If there was any doubt that it was the Superintendent's car it died when the driver's door opened and Colin Clare unfolded his lanky frame from it. Savage actually felt her jaw drop when she saw what he was wearing—a salmon pink satin suit complete with a ruffled white shirt and a bow-tie that was almost as big as his face. The trousers were, without a shadow of a doubt, the tightest trousers she had ever seen—hugging his bottom half like a pair of cyclist's Lycra leggings. Savage wasn't sure where to look, although it was almost impossible to look anywhere else.

"Oh, Jesus, sir, a little warning would have been nice?"

"What?" Clare grunted.

"The trousers, sir," she said, tilting her head up to the sky, wondering if it would be better to stare at the sun for a few minutes.

"They need some... adjusting," muttered Clare.

"Yeah, and so do the trousers," Savage said.

There was the sound of a window winding down and Savage looked back at the car to see Porter leaning out of the passenger side. He was grinning like an idiot, but his eyes were streaming.

"You crying, sir?" she asked him.

"Pollen," he said, nodding at the park. "That shit's everywhere. But to be honest I don't mind, because it means everything is blurry and I don't have to look at those trousers. You ever seen anything like it?"

"Never have, never want to again."

"It gets worse when he sits down."

"That's enough," Clare roared. "Savage, I need you in the car. Something's happened."

"Double homicide," said Porter, wiping his eyes.

"Shoot," Savage said, walking to the Mercedes. Porter leaned back and opened the door for her and she slid into the familiar fug of fresh pine and teenage BO. "Where?"

"Whytetail," said Porter. "South Norfolk. You know it?"

"Heard of it, sir," she said. "That's the village that moved, right? The whole thing upped and shifted itself two miles down the road a hundred years or so ago. There's a, uh, well? Or something. Holy. My granddad used to talk about it."

"I've said it before and I'll say it again, Savage, you're a regular encyclopaedia," Porter said. "All we know is that a couple were murdered there Thursday night or early yesterday morning. Their baby's missing."

"Oh no," Savage said. "Why are we just now hearing about it?"

"It's Robbie," Porter said. "His mum lives there. She asked for his help."

"Asked the *police* for help, right?"

"No, just us," Clare said from outside, one hand down the front of his trousers as he attempted to loosen them. "Kidnapper has threatened to kill the boy if the police are called in. We're picking Franklin up on the way, but other than that we're on our own."

He climbed into the car and both Porter and Savage winced.

"Told you it was worse when he sat down," said Porter.

Clare shot him a look that might have stopped his heart dead.

"Just us," the Super said again, starting the engine. "And the clock's ticking."

CHAPTER SEVEN

IT WAS LIKE WALKING INTO A DREAM, KETT THOUGHT, especially with the air full of distant, singing voices.

Pastor Cairns led the way through the graveyard, keeping to a meandering path that had been cut through the knee-high grass. Some of the stones still stood but most had been laid flat, the names and dates scratched into oblivion by centuries of wind and rain.

Wildflowers grew tall, mostly dandelions as bright as suns but also bluebells and snowdrops and little clusters of forget-me-nots that seemed to lift themselves in worship. Cow parsley sprouted everywhere, twice as tall as he was. The smell of the place was overwhelming, and so was the heat—so fierce it seemed to make the whole world shimmer.

Kett tugged at his jumper, wanting to take it off but hesitating, because for some reason he thought it would make him look weak in front of these people.

These people.

They followed like a flock of pigeons chasing a trail of crumbs, his mum behind him and the folk from the church behind her. A mayflower procession. They'd looked grey in the half-light of the nave and it was worse out here, like they'd slipped from a black and white film. There was no colour at all in their uniform of black trousers and white shirts. Even the kids were dressed the same, the girls in knee-length dresses. The young ones were as quiet as if their jaws had been wired shut, all of them watching Kett with a frightening intensity.

The adults watched too, and he didn't know what to make of their expressions. Some, like the big man who'd passed Cairns the note, were wary, their concern etched into the lines of their faces. Others bore something that looked more like mistrust, possibly even fear. Whatever it was, it was making him feel like he'd chugged a pint of icy water.

"Mr Cairns," he said.

"That's *Pastor*," the man replied. "If you please."

"What exactly is this place?"

They were reaching the end of the graveyard, a giant hawthorn hedge bursting with white flowers shielding whatever lay beyond. There was a gap in it, barely wider than he was, and here the Pastor stopped. He seemed to consider the hedge for a moment, his jaw bulging, before looking back.

"This is Whytetail," he said. His blue eyes were watery, old, but there was a fierceness to them. "Or the Commune of Our Lady of the Water. It is a community of found souls. Do not judge, Mr Kett."

That's DCI, Kett almost said, before remembering. He swallowed, his throat made of sandpaper.

"We've existed in this place for a very long time. Not everybody likes us being here, but we have endured, and we will continue to do so. You may find yourself a home amongst us too, one day, beside your mother. You seem lost, Mr Kett. As lost as she was when we took her in."

Kett looked back at his mum, seeing her study the ground with an expression of abject misery. Some part of him reacted with a hot flush of sympathy, a tug on his heart that he wasn't expecting. She met his eye and he turned away, back to the Pastor.

"CCTV? Security?"

"We don't need it," said Cairns, sniffing with defiance when the stupidity of his words became apparent. "We're very low-tech. No cameras, no phones other than the one in the church. Nothing electric at all, apart from our lights, of course, and the radio."

"Cars?" Kett asked. "Any vehicles missing? Anything the kidnapper could have taken?"

"We are asked to surrender our cars when we arrive," Cairns said. "We have a Land Rover that makes runs to the nearby village for supplies, but it's very much still here."

Kett sighed.

"You say not everyone likes you being here. Who are you talking about?"

Cairns breathed out a slow, controlled sigh. He pushed through the hedge, swallowed whole. Kett approached cautiously, turning side on but still feeling the scrape of the barbs as he walked into the shade. It was cold here, the narrow space reminding him of a coffin, and for a second he felt the panic of claustrophobia. Then he emerged from the other side and drew a deep breath of Spring-scented air.

Ahead of him was an immense expanse of meadow which sloped gently down towards thick woodland, and past that a river. At least two dozen identical buildings sat here, wooden cabins with no discernible order or pattern to where they'd been placed. To the left, halfway down the hill, was a larger one. It reminded Kett of a Scandinavian church, its steeple much shorter and much pointier than that of the building they'd just left. He was almost certain that the singing was coming from there.

He scanned the village, searching for his family and not finding them.

More people milled between the buildings, kids running and laughing. It gave Kett no small sense of relief to see them. Two other men were walking up from the wooden church, and they definitely *weren't* laughing.

"Your lot, mostly," said Cairns, and Kett frowned at him until he remembered the question he'd just asked.

"The police don't like you being here?"

"The authorities," Cairns said. "We're self-governed, self-policed, self-funded, and yet somehow we're labelled a community of concern."

"You can't just call yourself self-policed," Kett said. "It doesn't work that way."

"*He* works that way," the man replied, and a glance at the sky made it clear who he was talking about.

The two other men reached the group, their faces sour. Unlike the people Kett had met in the church, these two were dressed in jeans and white T-shirts. One was portly and bald, his head shaped like a baked potato. The other was short and wiry, his mad blond hair shaped like a haystack.

"What's this?" spat the bald man in a brash Yorkshire accent.

"This is Mary's boy, Tom," said Cairns. "He's going to help us."

"We agreed, no help," the man said, glaring at Kett. "No police. The letter said so."

"He's not police," said Cairns.

"Summer will be very disappointed," the man said. "She'll be furious."

The bald guy turned and stropped away, his haystack-headed friend running after him.

"Who was that?" Kett asked.

"Oh, ignore him," said Cairns. "Tom Faulkner. He's not a fan of outsiders, as you may have gathered."

"And who's Summer?"

"My wife," said Cairns. "You'll meet her soon. Like I said, ignore Tom. Summer will be happy to see you here. Family is everything to her, and we know that yours is in great need of healing."

Kett gave his mum a sideways glance as she appeared through the hedge but she didn't see it. How much had she told them about their past? About his childhood, his father? Her face seemed to open as she walked back into the sun, her back straightening and her chest lifting as she took a giant breath. He didn't feel her joy. He couldn't work out why this place was getting to him, why it had slipped beneath his skin like a hawthorn barb.

And he hadn't even seen the dead yet.

"Where did it happen?" he asked.

"Down in the old—"

"Wait," said Kett, gesturing at the crowd as it birthed its way from the hedge and continued to gawk at him. "Do these people need to be here?"

"We are a—"

"Community, I know," Kett said. He turned to his audience. "I'll tell you what, if you were at the scene when

Caitlyn and Liam were killed, you can hang around. If not, feel free to bugger off."

Mary Kett gasped. Several of the others looked at Cairns, and it was only when the Pastor waved his hand that they dispersed. Free of the moment, the kids broke into a run, laughing. Mary started to go, then stopped, then started again, staring back only once at Kett as if she couldn't quite believe it was him. Only the big man from the church stayed behind, jamming his hands into the pockets of his dark trousers to signal that he had no intention of leaving.

"I'd like it if Paul could stay," Cairns said. "He's my right-hand man."

"Paul?" Kett asked, and the man looked at the Pastor.

"You need him to remind you of your name?" Kett asked.

"Paul P-Palmer," the man said with a nervous stutter. His voice was about an octave higher than Kett had been expecting, as childlike as his expression. He licked his fat lips—lips that had been chewed to pieces, judging by the scabs and the dried blood. His face was round and blunt, his widow's peak shining but the rest of his hair clinging on in bushy black clumps. Out here, with the sun in front of him, it was clearer than ever just how big a guy he was. He'd have given Porter a run for his money in the gym.

"Were you there when they were killed?" Kett asked, and Palmer shook his head slowly, like he was watching a tennis match.

"He was the first to arrive after my wife found them," Cairns said. "He dealt with the bodies."

"Right," said Kett. "Dealt with, as in moved them out of the crime scene?"

"We cannot permit the dead to linger," said Cairns.

"Not here. You can see them, just as they were when we found them."

"Right. So let me ask you again, where did it happen?"

"In their residence," said Cairns, not moving.

"One of these?"

Kett looked at the little cabins. They reminded him of the holiday park in Elsham where the four kids had gone missing, and he had to close his eyes against a rush of vertigo as he remembered leaning over the cliff and seeing the churning sea below.

"No," said Cairns, and Kett opened his eyes to see the man staring down the hill towards the wooden church. "As new parents, they resided in the Manor."

"Which is..." Kett prompted, fast losing his patience. Cairns cleared his throat, his reluctance written into every line of his furrowed brow. "Look, *Mr* Cairns. You are the one who asked me to come. I would be more than happy— I'd be *ecstatic*, to be honest—to walk through that hedge, get in my car, and never look back. So how about you start making this a little easier?"

Cairns coughed again, grimacing as he tried to straighten his back.

"It's Pastor," he said quietly.

"Is it, though?" said Kett. "Take me to the Manor. Now."

Cairns bristled. It was obvious he wasn't used to taking orders. But after a moment of consideration, he steered his crooked body around and began to stride down the hill. The grass was knee-high and thick with flowers but there were paths here, made of loose pea shingle and secured by wire mesh. Cairns nodded to the people he passed and they nodded back, most stopping what they were doing and lowering their heads in reverence. Even the kids quietened as they watched him go, their expressions wary, as if he was the headmaster in a school.

The wooden church loomed up before them, far bigger than it had seemed from the top of the hill. The choral singing broke off as they approached, then began again, floating from the open door with unnerving intensity. Whoever was performing in there, they were good. It reminded Kett of the times he'd gone to watch his mum sing in the cathedral, the same layered, harmonious sound, the same ethereal beauty. He rubbed the goosebumps from his skin, pausing for a moment. Cairns and Palmer had walked a little further before they realised he was no longer with them.

"This way, Mr Kett," Palmer said.

"Just a minute."

He made his way up a small set of wooden steps and stopped at the door. Unlike the stone church he'd just left, this one was hospital-bright thanks to the rows of big, clear windows down both of its long walls. A group of twenty or so people stood at the far end, lost in their music. A woman in a long, white dress conducted them, and even as Kett watched she shushed them into silence.

"And again," he heard her say, and there was a collective breath before the singing began. The sound of it was almost liquid, it filled every single inch of space.

Kett turned his attention to the rows of empty pews— empty, that was, except for Billie and his three girls. They sat together halfway to the choir, as still as if they had been sculpted there. Even Alice, who couldn't sit for a second without fidgeting, was rapt. It should have been a good thing but Kett didn't feel it. It reminded him of the fairy tales he read to his kids, like they were under some kind of spell.

Or like this was a dream, he thought again.

You're being ridiculous, he told himself.

He turned and walked down the stairs, leaving them to it. Cairns and Palmer were waiting for him, and both looked nervous.

"They're good," Kett said. "The choir."

This, at least, made the big Pastor smile.

"We're quite famous for it," he said. "Ama is a wonderful conductor and teacher. We were on *Songs of Praise* last year. You might have seen us?"

"No," Kett said. "Not my cup of tea, I'm afraid. Lead on."

Cairns shuffled behind the church into a large circle of mowed grass. Right in the middle of it was a wooden statue, as tall as a totem pole. Kett could make out a crudely carved face, a wide, round middle, but that was it. On the other side of the circle was a regiment of cypress trees, dozens of them, and past them a brick wall that looked like it had weathered a few centuries.

"Whytetail wasn't always a holy commune," Cairns said. "It started as a country estate. Whytetail Manor was home to the Clifford Family, until the last of them died. After that, it went into disrepair."

"1905," added Palmer, although he gave no clue what he was referring to.

"For a while it was famous here. You've heard of the well, have you not?"

"Nope," said Kett.

"The Well of Our Lady," he said. "Lord and Lady Clifford witnessed a miracle there at the end of the Nineteenth Century. They received a blessing from God. It's why this place is sacred. It's why we see so many miracles here."

"Right."

"My wife's great-grandfather bought the land a hundred

years ago and started building this place," Cairns went on. "It has rested with us ever since."

"What about the old village?" Kett asked, thinking of the abandoned houses he'd seen.

"It grew up around the estate," Cairns said. "But after the Cliffords died out and the land was sold, people moved away. I told you, they don't like us. Godless folk rarely do. Just before the Great War the whole village moved two miles down the road. Rebuilt, resettled, called it Whytetail too."

"Helpful," Kett said.

"The houses you passed earlier are only the fringe of the old village. The rest lie on the other side of the river and have sadly passed into terrible ruin. But we have done our best to keep the beating heart of the estate alive."

Cairns led the way into the shadow of the whispering trees, the heat of the day vanishing almost immediately. He was struggling now, limping hard, his right hand grasping, and Kett wondered if the man usually walked with a stick or a frame. They passed beneath a brick archway wide enough for a cart and Kett found himself in an open courtyard. Right in front of him was a large, white manor house with a Dutch gable roof. It had seen better days, the render peeling away and several of the windows like glassless, gaping mouths. It didn't exactly look fit for human habitation.

"The dead couple lived *here*?" Kett said. "With a newborn?"

Cairns and Palmer shared a look, but Kett couldn't read it.

"They did," Cairns said, his voice hoarse like his batteries were about to die. "All our miracles live here, until we can be sure they are ready."

"Ready for what?" Kett asked.

"I'll show you," Cairns said, hanging his head. "But please, Mr Kett, I ask you again, don't judge us."

He walked away, and Kett thought it again, how much this felt like a dream.

Or a *nightmare*.

CHAPTER EIGHT

Cairns led the way down the side of the Manor, bracing his hand on the crumbling wall every now and again to stop himself from keeling over. They seemed as old as each other, the man and the house, and Kett wondered how long they both had left before they fell down and didn't get up again.

"This is the original Clifford residence," Cairns said, his rich baritone echoing back to him. "They didn't last long here. After the miracle they were driven away. Ignorant minds believed them to be cursed, not blessed."

"Right," said Kett again, growing tired of the bullshit.

The windows of the ground floor were all either broken or hidden behind plywood boards, thick tongues of ivy probing the toothless gums. A pair of black doors sat at the top of a staircase, sealed with a chain as big as an arm, but Cairns and Palmer walked right past. They reached the end of the building and turned the corner, entering another cobbled courtyard with a run of smaller buildings on the opposite side. This wing of the house seemed in better condition, its big windows intact, the sun reflecting off the walls so brightly that Kett had to shield his eyes with his hand.

"Cursed," Cairns said again.

"I heard you," Kett said. "I just don't care. Through there?"

He pointed past the two men to an open door, a servant's entrance, by the look of it. Cairns nodded but he didn't start walking again. He leaned on the wall, screwing his eyes shut, his breaths shallow and ragged.

"Are you okay?" Kett asked him, and he managed a flick of his hand.

"I'll take you," said Palmer, walking through the door.

Kett followed him, glancing back at Cairns to see that what little colour he had in his face had leached out, leaving him as white as the wall he leant against.

Kett stepped through the door into the chill of the house, his shoes clacking on the flagstones. There was no sign of Palmer, and he wasn't in either of the small storerooms that led from the narrow corridor. Kett carried on, finding himself in an enormous kitchen. It was old, for sure —a range cooker, a butler's sink—but it was clean, and judging by the smell of bread it was very much in use. Palmer stood by a door on the far side, glowering with impatience.

"He'll be alright?" Kett asked.

"Reg? Yeah. He has these turns. He'll be fine in a minute or so. He'll meet us there."

Palmer waited for Kett to catch up before walking on, entering another narrow corridor. There were four doors here, all open, and when Kett walked past the first he saw a young couple sitting on a bed, a baby in their arms. He stopped, offering them a nod. The man nodded back but the woman stared firmly at the floor. The baby—she must have been six months old—twisted her head and studied him with big, curious eyes.

"This way," Palmer said, and Kett ignored him.

"Hey," he said to the baby, waving his hand. "How're you doing?"

The child gurgled.

"Mr Kett," Palmer said.

"How old?" he asked the man.

"Four," came the reply, so quiet that Kett had to lean through the door.

"Four months? She's big. Beautiful. What's her name?"

At this, the woman looked up. She was in her twenties and wearing a cream dress that dropped all the way to her calves. She smiled at Kett, then at the girl.

"Alice," she said, and Kett laughed.

"I've got an Alice too. Lovely name. Were you here on Thursday night? Friday morning?"

He was aware that Palmer had walked to his side, close enough that he could feel his heavy breath on his neck.

"You'll have a chance to talk with everyone later," he said.

"I'm talking to them now," Kett said, resisting every urge to give the big man a shove. "Unless there's a reason I shouldn't?"

No reply, but the man didn't move.

"What are your names?"

"I'm Josh," said the man. "This is Gayle. Cadieux."

"You were here on Thursday night?" Kett asked again, and the young guy nodded. "You hear anything? See anything?"

"No," he said. "The building is old, the walls are pretty thick. I didn't hear anything, other than the crying."

"Crying?"

"The baby. Never stopped screaming."

"Josh," hissed Gayle. A warning.

"You know why the baby cried so much?" asked Kett.

"It's what they do," said Josh. "Alice here cried the same. Easier to comfort, though. I think Caitlyn struggled with it. Liam never gave her much help."

"I think it was that thing they get," said Gayle. "Colic."

"Oh, yeah," said Kett. "I know all about that. Our youngest had it. Didn't stop screaming for weeks. I don't know how any of us got through it."

"It's what *we* do," said Josh. "Right? Parents. We get through it because we don't have any choice."

Kett nodded.

"You remember when the crying stopped?"

Both of them shook their heads. He scanned the room, seeing little in the way of personal items—a crucifix on the wall, a chest of drawers with a changing mat on top. A poker had been propped against the wall beside the bed, but there was no fireplace.

"What's that for?" Kett asked, nodding at it. Josh turned to look, frowning as if he hadn't noticed it before.

"Rats," he said.

"*Rats?* Here?"

"It doesn't happen often," said Gayle, almost as if she was apologising to him. "But when it's this hot we leave the doors open at night, and they sometimes come up from the basement."

"Rats?" Kett said to Palmer, and the man just shrugged.

"Right." Kett returned his attention to the young couple. "So you knew Caitlyn and Liam?"

"Sure," said Josh. "They were already here when we arrived."

"We were pregnant a little while together," said Gayle, one hand to her stomach. "It was nice to have somebody to moan about it all with. It's terrible, what happened to them, what happened to little Adam."

Josh put an arm around her, pulling her close, and she leaned into him. Alice wobbled on her lap, tugging at the buttons on her dress.

"Do you have any idea who might have wanted to hurt them?" Kett asked. "Who might have wanted to take the baby?"

"Outsiders," Gayle said, swatting away a bluebottle that had flown into the room. "Nobody here would do such an awful thing. This is a good place."

"Well, if you think of anything, come find me."

They nodded and Kett left them to it. Palmer stood back, seemingly relieved, and carried on walking.

"How many people are living in the building?" Kett asked.

"Oh, you'd need to speak with Reg about that."

"Because you don't know, or you don't want to tell me?"

He stopped at the last door on the right. It was open, and when Kett looked inside he saw a room identical to the one he'd just passed.

Identical, that was, except for the blood and the flies.

"Jesus Christ," said Kett, putting the back of his hand to his mouth. He wasn't squeamish—twenty years on the job immunised you to pretty much everything—but there was something about the scene that made his stomach feel like it was about to cramp.

The room was so bare it was almost spartan. A metal bed sat opposite the door, the blankets half on the floor.

The mattress had to be an old one because there was a hollow in the middle. Blood had pooled there and partially dried, the wooden beams of the ceiling reflected in its waxy skin. More blood covered the flagstone floor, so many footprints in it that it looked like the instruction card for a dance routine. Flies waltzed over it, hundreds of them, fat and swollen. Kett peered around the door and when he saw the crib he felt as though he was about to vomit up his heart.

There was no baby in it, of course, but the bright white linen was streaked with blood.

And where a young boy had once slept sat a dead rabbit.

"Christ," Kett said again. It was cool in here but that didn't stop the stench of death. It sat in the back of his throat, as thick as a butcher's bin. More flies crawled on the rabbit's face, over its open eyes, vanishing into the crooked cavern of its throat.

Palmer stepped into the room and Kett grabbed his arm, hauling him back. The big man shook himself free, ready to argue, but Kett pushed into him and forced him back.

"Nobody goes in," he said. "Not one fucking person. Do you hear me?"

Palmer licked his lips, then nodded slowly.

"You left the door open?" Kett asked. "How many people have been in that room?"

Palmer didn't answer, he just stared at Kett with a vacant expression. Kett looked down the corridor to the room he'd just left. It was close enough that he could hear the young couple talking, the chirrups of their baby girl.

"And you're letting that couple stay there?" he said, his voice lower. "There's a child, for fuck's sake."

"Those are the rules we live by," came Cairns' voice, followed shortly by the man himself. He limped through the kitchen door, still looking half dead. "Don't take it out on Paul here. He must follow them as the rest of us do."

"It's the scene of a crime," Kett said. "Two murders. You can't just let people piss around in there. I'll need a list of everyone who went in, anything that was touched."

"There's no need for a list," said Cairns. "It was myself, my wife, and Paul. Nobody else would enter."

"You need to move the couple and their child. This is no place for them."

"No," said Cairns. "Please do what you can. Aside from the dead, nothing has been touched."

Kett sucked air in through his teeth, then turned back to the room. He didn't have any gloves or shoe-covers with him but it wasn't like he could disturb the crime scene any more than the other men had. He entered carefully, avoiding the Rorschach blots of blood. The only window was a horizontal slit of frosted glass above the bed but the bright, bare bulb made every inch of space glow.

"Caitlyn and Liam," he said. "What were their surnames."

"Brown," Cairns said. "Both. They were married."

"How old?"

On either side of the bed was a small metal table. A glass of water sat on one, next to a slim gold watch and a pair of black glasses. The other was bare. To the left of the door was a chest of drawers, every drawer open and clothes vomited to the floor. There was blood on the shirts and dresses, on the handles too. Kett leaned closer and saw that the top drawer was empty.

A framed photograph sat on the top of the unit, Caitlyn and Liam and their newborn baby in a hospital bed, everyone still bloody, her face bearing the same look of terror and wonder that Billie's had when she'd given birth to

Alice. They were a handsome couple, him fit and well-groomed, his hair already more silver than black. Her hair was a strikingly bright shade of red, so many freckles on her face it looked like somebody had hurled a handful of dirt at her.

"You said there were no cameras here?"

"We relax the rules on certain occasions worth celebrating and remembering," Cairns replied. "A birth being one of them."

"How old were they?" he asked again.

"I'd have to check," said Cairns. "Liam was thirty-six, I know that much. Caitlyn was a little older."

"How did you find them yesterday morning?"

"Summer found them."

Kett turned to the two men who crowded in the doorway.

"Where were the bodies?" Kett said.

"In the b-bed," Palmer replied. "Least, *he* was."

"Which side?"

Palmer nodded to the side closest to the chest of drawers.

"There. It weren't pretty."

"Could you see how he was killed?"

"Knife was still in him," Palmer said.

"Where?"

"In the bed."

"No. Where in *him*?"

Palmer swallowed noisily, then pointed to his own throat.

"Where's the knife now?"

Another look at Cairns.

"It's not a hard question. Where's the knife?"

"I washed it," said Palmer.

"You *washed* it?" Kett growled. "*Why?*"

Palmer's mouth opened but nothing came out.

"Right, what about Caitlyn? She was in the bed too?"

"Half of her," Palmer answered. "Legs. Top half was on the floor, like she'd fallen."

Kett turned to the other side of the room, to the crib that sat there. It was an old one, carved from dark mahogany. The sheets were new, though, stained with blood so bright it didn't look real. A darker pool of blood covered the space between the crib and the bed, and it was easy enough to guess what had happened.

"She was reaching for the crib?" Kett asked.

"I guess," said Palmer. "Yeah, she could have been. Reached for it and fell out of the bed, maybe?"

"Did you see how she was injured?"

The sound of a shrug, and when he looked back Palmer was shaking his head. He was drenched in sweat.

"Nothing?"

"Just blood," the big man said. "All over her and under her."

There was a wardrobe in one corner of the room and a sink in the other, but nothing else. The only decoration was a metal crucifix on the wall above the sink, as dull as lead. Kett turned back to the crib, to the dead rabbit that seemed to meet his eye. Its body was a ruin but its white tail looked as clean and as soft as a cuddly toy.

"You know what that's about? The rabbit?"

Both men shook their heads.

"Was in there when I got here," said Palmer. "Pulled from a brace we caught earlier in the week."

"Shot?"

"Yeah," the man said. "Crossbow. Tom hunts them."

"Tom Faulkner? The bald Northern guy?"

"Yeah, a few of the other men too. We eat them."

"And the note was found in the crib?"

Palmer nodded.

"Where, exactly?"

He saw Cairns and Palmer look at each other, and the impatience gnawed at him.

"In it," Palmer said.

"Yes, you said. It was in the—"

"In the rabbit," the man went on. "In its body cavity."

Kett ducked to look beneath the bed, his chest releasing a scream of pain. There was nothing there except dust, but he stayed down until he got his breath back, easing himself back to his feet and turning to the door instead.

"There's no lock," he said.

"We don't need them here," Cairns replied. "What harm could..."

And the words died on his lips.

"Is there a lock on the door we came in through, from outside?"

"No," said Cairns.

It wouldn't have mattered if there was, Kett realised. Half the windows in the house had been smashed. Anyone could have got in.

"Who lives in this building? Who uses it?"

"Just the new parents," Cairns replied. "It's purely for them. It's a sacred space, a calm space."

"You've got two churches out there and *this* is a sacred space?" Kett scanned the room again then turned to him. "Why?"

"The Cliffords lived here when they were visited by the Lord, and now so do our blessed couples."

"Let's go back a bit," Kett tried again. "How many people live here in the Manor? Parents?"

"Just six, at the moment," Cairns said. "Well, four now, I suppose."

"Four parents? And their children?"

"That would make seven, in total, yes," Cairns conceded. "We have a set of twins."

Kett wondered if he could hear one now, the faintest of cries echoing down the narrow corridor.

"But we all use the kitchen," said Palmer. "Everyone in the community. Only one we have."

He wanted to press the men but they crowded the entrance to the room, boxing him in, and he couldn't shake the idea that one of them was about to grab the door and pull it shut. He took a step towards them, resting his elbow against the door, his pulse so fast and so loud it was a wonder nobody else could hear it.

"I'll need to speak with them all," he said. "And I'll need to speak with your wife, too."

"Of course," said Cairns, but he made no show of moving. Kett took another step, almost face to face with the men. Past the smell of the blood and the stench of the rabbit he could smell it again, that medical scent. A lotion of some kind.

"Let me through," he said.

Cairns didn't move and Palmer's scowl became a loose, idiot smile. The panic was like a kettle coming to boil, Kett's fist already bunched.

"Move," he said.

And they did.

"A moment," said Cairns, teetering back as if he was about to fall. He hit the far wall of the corridor, wincing.

Kett stepped out of the room, his head swimming.

"Where—" he started, only to be cut off by his phone—

the clarion cry of the *Mexican Hat Dance* more out of place here than it had ever been. He answered it without looking.

"Kett?" said Clare. "We're here, where are you?"

"I'll come and meet you," he said, and what he managed to keep to himself was, *Thank fuck.*

CHAPTER NINE

I<small>T WASN'T EXACTLY A WARM WELCOME</small>, S<small>AVAGE</small> thought.

Not cold either. Just *weird*.

She leaned on the bonnet of Clare's Mercedes, trying to pull her unruly hair into a ponytail. It was almost long enough, now, although strands fell loose and tickled the side of her face. They'd parked behind Kett's Volvo because there was no way they were getting past it, the narrow country road completely blocked. It didn't matter, because there was nowhere to go after this, the maps showing a dead-end about half a mile further down.

In front of them sat a church that seemed far too big for a village this size, the shadow of its tower so dark it looked like a ravine had opened up in the earth. The hot air swam with music, a choir of some kind.

Two men watched them from the other side of the large graveyard, one bald, the other trying to make up for it with sandy-coloured hair that seemed to reach for the heavens. Their arms were folded over broad chests, their faces glum.

Savage realised she was playing with her lucky silver

whistle and tucked it back into her T-shirt. She was wearing her gym leggings and trainers, everything black.

"Bit creepy, this," said Emily Franklin as she climbed out of the back of the car. Like the rest of them, the young pathologist had been instructed to wear something informal, because they were undercover, but Savage had never seen her in anything else. She wore a pair of denim shorts and a T-shirt emblazoned with the Juicy Fruit logo. On her back was a *Trolls* rucksack, and she looked about fourteen years old. A pair of flip-flops flip-flopped as she walked to Savage's side. She spotted the men and waved, but they didn't wave back.

"Can I stay in the car?" asked Porter through the open window. His eyes were red and puffy from the pollen and he sniffed wetly like somebody who'd just been jilted at the altar. Savage laughed, pulling her phone out to see that she didn't have a signal here.

"Come on," she muttered. "You got service, Emily?"

Franklin checked her phone and nodded.

"Kett's here," said Porter.

The former DCI was pulling himself through a slim gap in the hedge that surrounded the cemetery. He was wearing jeans and a dark grey jumper, of all things, even though it had to be pushing thirty degrees. He broke into a jog, then thought better of it, his face creased with pain and damp with sweat by the time he reached them.

"Hey," he said. "Looking good. You decide against the dog?"

Savage nodded. She'd been tempted to bring Colin along for the ride to make them look even less like they were on the job, but the little dog didn't cope well in the sun.

Kett frowned through the sun-drenched windscreen.

"Pete, I thought I said try not to look like a policeman?"

"I don't," Porter replied. He cranked the door and clambered out, adjusting his suit jacket. "This isn't my normal suit."

"But it's still a *suit*," Kett said, shaking his head.

"It's a cheap suit."

"It looks exactly like your other suits," said Kett, and Porter's mouth dropped like he'd been insulted.

"It's from *Marks and Spencer's*," he hissed. "My other suits are Tom Ford!"

Clare's door opened, the lanky Superintendent groaning as he unfolded himself from the car in his salmon-pink wedding suit. He'd taken off the bowtie, but he still looked utterly ridiculous. Savage saw the moment Kett's eyes dropped, then widened.

"Oh," he said. "I was not expecting them, sir."

"Them?" Clare barked back.

"I mean *that*," Kett said, no idea where to look. "The suit."

Clare was doing his best to adjust his trousers but they seemed to have shrunk even further in the heat of the car, the pink satin almost painted on.

"Why am I thinking of the word cameltoe?" Kett said.

Porter unleashed a laugh that echoed back from the wall of the church.

"I have no idea what you're talking about, but I would ask you to remove your attention from my crotchal area," Clare said, mincing as best he could to the back of the car. "Fiona ordered these tossing trousers."

"Ah, that's what they are," Kett said, and Savage put a hand over her mouth to hold the laugh there.

"They're too damned tight, I can barely walk."

"At least nobody's going to mistake you for police, sir," Kett said, turning to Porter. "Unlike this numptie."

"It's a cheap suit!"

"Wait up," said Clare, opening the boot. He pulled out a canvas sack big enough to hide a body in. What he dug from the sack was worse.

"My turn to wash the kit this week," Clare said, throwing a ball of cloth to Porter. The DI caught it, letting it unfold to reveal a bright yellow football shirt.

"No, sir," he said.

"It'll fit. Sally's a big girl."

Porter's bottom lip shot out but he laid the shirt on the bonnet of the car and proceeded to undress. It was a tight fit, but not unflattering. He flexed an arm and Savage was amazed the short sleeve didn't split.

"Right," said Clare. "As far as anyone has to know we're looking at the church for a wedding. I'm the father of the bride. Savage, you're the lucky woman. Porter, husband to be. Emily, maid of honour. Kett, I have no idea."

"Flower girl," said Porter with a wink.

"Why do I have to be the bride?" Savage asked. "I don't want to marry Pete, especially in that T-shirt."

Porter pouted at her.

"No offence."

"Well I don't want to marry him either," Franklin said. "Offence intended."

"I'll marry you, Pete," Kett said, and Porter pulled a face.

"Enough!" roared Clare. "Kate, you're marrying Pete, end of story. Robbie, fill us in."

"I'll do it on the way, if that's okay, sir?" Kett said.

He stripped off his jumper, carrying it to his car and stowing it on the passenger seat. As he walked back, smoothing down his white polo shirt, he studied the two men by the hedge.

"This place is definitely *off*."

"In what way?" Savage asked as she pushed herself off the car. Kett walked slowly, leading the way.

"I don't know. It's a closed community, very sheltered. The man in charge, Reginald Cairns, calls himself a Pastor but I don't think it's an official title. The two dead are Caitlyn and Liam Brown, both in their late thirties. She'd just given birth, a couple of weeks ago. He was stabbed in bed, she died half in and half out of it, although I don't know how she was killed. They moved the bodies."

"They *what*?" Clare spluttered.

"Cairns ordered it, and a man called Paul Palmer moved them out of the room to their own morgue."

"They have a morgue?" Franklin said, rubbing her hands together. "Goody."

"Did you tell them that's against the law?" Clare asked, and Kett shook his head.

"I don't think they give a shit. This place is truly off the grid. No phones, no internet, no TV. Room's full of blood but it's contaminated. Cairns says only three people have been in since the murders but I don't trust him. Half the village could have been in there."

"Any sign of the baby?" Savage asked.

"No. The killer—at least, I *think* it was the killer—left a dead rabbit in the crib, along with the note. They're making a point, I just don't know what it is yet."

"We're running out of time if we want him back," said Clare.

They were approaching the hedge, and a third man appeared—a big guy with a face like an angry pig. He glanced nervously at the other two men and watched the party approach with small, dark eyes.

"That's Palmer," Kett said quietly. "I think he needs

Cairns to tell him when to take a piss. The bald Northerner is Tom Faulkner, nasty piece of work. No idea about the haystack. They're not going to like the fact that you've turned up. I get the impression Cairns is a control freak, wants everything under his thumb. It's going to be harder for him to boss us around if we're all here."

"You like him for it?" Porter asked.

"Cairns?" Kett popped his lips. "I don't know. He's old, infirm, but he's a big man and I get the impression he's quick to anger. If he did do it, he didn't do it alone. He's got an extra pair of hands for that. Palmer."

Kett nodded at the big man as he called his name, but Palmer didn't reply. He dug his hands into the pockets of his dark trousers and studied them like a sullen schoolboy, making no effort to move out of their way.

"I'm not doing this again," Kett said to him. "Move, or we can make everyone's life a little easier and haul you down to the station. Right, sir?"

He looked back at Clare, who was tugging on his trousers and muttering quiet obscenities.

"Sir?"

Clare looked up in shock, his belt still clasped in both hands.

"Right," he said, oblivious. "Yes?"

"They're here to help," Kett said to the big man. "They're here to bring Adam home. Let us in."

Palmer looked back as if to seek Cairn's approval. But he was alone, and eventually he shuffled to one side. The other men moved back too, neither of them speaking. Kett pushed into the narrow gap in the hedge, followed by Franklin and then Porter. Clare waved Savage in before him and she walked into the opening, barbs probing her face, her bare arms.

They emerged onto a sloping meadow covered in wooden chalets and drowning in sunshine. It resembled something from the *The Sound of Music* and she had to stop herself from humming the theme tune. At the bottom of the hill the river shone like a burning filament, leaving a sun-bright scar on her retinas. She blinked it away as she walked, flashes of white littering the landscape, chased away every time she looked for them.

"You know about this place, right?" she said. "Whyte-tail. The village that moved."

"Yeah," said Kett. "Cairns told me."

"He told you about the babies?"

Kett glanced back at her. A couple of young girls sped past, kicking a ball, one of them almost running into the back of Porter's legs. They giggled away, disappearing behind one of the buildings.

"There's a legend," she went on. "Granddad told me. Back in the late Nineteenth Century this place was owned by the Cliffords. Not a very nice family, all things considered. According to the stories, they couldn't conceive a child."

Savage glanced at Porter to see his face fall. He kicked at the dirt, looking away before she could mouth an apology.

"So they asked God to help them. Lord Clifford had a vision. Apparently, God told him he needed to dig a well. So he did, and the angels rewarded him with a child."

"Savage, put a sock in it," said Clare.

"Sorry, sir," she said. "Where do you want us?"

Clare looked at Kett, and Kett stared down the hill.

"Savage, Porter, head down to the old Manor house. It's where the crime scene is, so check it out while you're there, see if you can find something. Make sure you search the whole building top to bottom, okay?"

"Sir," said Savage, nodding.

"Boss, I think it might be best if you talk to Cairns. He's old and grumpy, I think you'll be on the same page."

Clare nodded, then frowned.

Kett scratched his beard and looked at Franklin.

"Emily, come with me. We've got some dead people to talk to."

CHAPTER TEN

It wasn't a morgue. It was an outhouse.

At least that's what Kett *thought* it was, as he traipsed along the path towards a squat brick, toilet-shaped building. It boasted an ornate wooden door and two miniature towers that mirrored the one on the stone church. It was almost lost in a forest of nettles, thick cords of bramble wrapped around its base and ivy reaching for the tiled roof. Like so much else here, there was something reminiscent of a fairy tale in the building, a place for people to sleep for a century or more.

Or a place for the dead to rest.

"This is it," said Palmer.

The big man was out of breath after the walk, even though it had been largely downhill, and he rested his hands on his hips as he sucked in air. They were east of the main complex, a good twenty-minute walk away and deep into the woodland that edged the river. Kett could hear the rush of water from nearby, but that was it. It was almost perfectly still and perfectly silent here.

"This is your morgue?" said Franklin as she caught up,

the snap of her flip-flops finally silenced. She bent down, rubbing her hands over her legs and feet. The bare skin there had already risen into painful welts from the nettles, and her expression made it perfectly clear she wished she'd worn something more suitable. She grumbled her next words low enough that only Kett would hear them. "It's a bit shit."

"What is it?" Kett asked. "This place?"

Whatever it was, it would be roasting in there. It was early afternoon and the sun was relentless, burning right through the canopy. He was surprised he couldn't smell the dead from out here.

Palmer stood straight, wiping a hand over his sweaty face. He looked at the building for a moment as if he couldn't remember. Flies approached the man, curious, batting off his face and neck, resting on the damp patches beneath his arms. He made no effort to shake them away.

"Ice house," he said after what felt like forever.

"An ice house?" said Kett. "What the hell is that?"

"A house, for ice," explained Franklin, rolling her eyes. "Old estates had them so they could keep ice in the summer."

"You still keep ice in here?" Kett asked hopefully, and Palmer shook his head.

"But the temperature stays low. Best place to keep the dead, we've found."

"You've had a lot of dead?"

"No more'n our fair share," the man said. "No more'n we deserve."

"What's that supposed to mean?" asked Kett.

The trees swayed overhead in a sudden gust of wind, letting the sunlight through. Kett had to turn away to save his eyes, and if Palmer responded to his question he missed it. By the time he looked again the man had walked to the door and was using an enormous key to unlock it.

"So there are some locks here, then," Kett said, to no response. "Anyone else touch the bodies?"

"Just me," Palmer replied. "I don't fear the d-dead."

He grabbed the brass ring in one hand and tugged half a dozen times before the door came loose.

"I can't believe you were stupid enough to move them," Franklin said, flip-flopping past Kett. "You do know that's a crime, right?"

"Leaving them in their own blood and filth would have been a crime," Palmer said, shooting the pathologist an angry look. "Leaving them like that would have been a sin. They deserved better than that. They deserved rest."

Franklin looked like she was going to say something else but instead she lifted a hand to her mouth as the smell broke free of the building. Kett took shallow breaths through his mouth but it was still overpowering—not rot, because it was too soon for that. Just *death*, the unmistakable sweet-meat stench of something that had once been alive and now wasn't.

Palmer took a stumbling step back as if he hadn't been expecting it. He looked at Kett with an expression that bordered on panic, as if he was about to cry for help. He flicked his hand at the door as if trying to fight off a ghost, then stuttered a few half-formed words.

"In there, w-watch yourself, it's a big drop."

Franklin opened her rucksack and pulled out a forensic apron and a mask. She slipped on a pair of latex gloves then pulled out another set, offering them to Kett.

"No thanks," he said. "I'm not planning on touching anything."

"Your loss," she said, her voice muffled. "You got a torch?"

"Only on my phone."

He flicked it on, shining it over Franklin's shoulder as she walked to the open ice house door. Past her, Kett saw that the building contained a single room that had been dug deep into the soil—maybe five feet beneath the surface. The floor was paved with a circular pattern of bricks, a small drain in the middle.

Two corpses rested there, dressed in matching blue pyjamas and stiff with blood.

Their eyes were open.

"You didn't think to cover them up?" Franklin asked, and there was anger in her voice.

If Palmer heard her he made no attempt to reply. Franklin muttered a series of curses then shuffled around and climbed onto the wooden ladder. Her foot must have slipped because she squawked like a parrot as she gripped the rung. Kett offered her a hand but she knocked it back with a fierce glare, taking it slow until she reached the floor below.

Kett stepped into the ice house, planting one foot on the ladder, his eyes swimming with the sheer thickness of the smell. He started to descend then stopped, looking at the big man who was framed in the doorway. The panic of claustrophobia gripped him hard.

"If you so much as touch this door while we're down there," he said, "It'll be the last thing you ever do. That's a promise. Understood?"

Palmer held up both of his big hands, licking those chapped, swollen lips. Kett eyeballed him for a moment more then backed carefully down the rungs, his body screaming with the effort. The smell of the dead had gone right to his head, as if drums were beating in there. The ground was there before he was ready for it, his back jarring and the phone slipping from his hand.

"Shit," he said, picking it up and doing his best to ignore the wetness of the screen.

"Bet you wish you'd said yes to the gloves now, eh?" said Franklin.

"Bet you wish you weren't wearing flip-flops," he shot back.

The pathologist pulled a lamp from her bag and switched it on, filling the space with yellow light. Kett heard a shifting sound overhead, a chittering, and his heart was in his mouth as he looked up, half expecting to see a ghost there. There wasn't, but the rafters crawled with bats, dozens of them, their eyes bright. When Kett turned back to the floor he saw that it was covered in guano.

"Gross," he said, wiping his phone on his jeans.

Franklin ignored him. She was crouched next to the body of Liam Brown, her gloved hands probing the wound in his neck. Kett started to kneel beside her but the pain forced him back up again. He leaned on the wall instead, massaging his chest with his free hand.

"Fairly easy, this one," Franklin said. "A three-centimetre wound in his neck, looks like it punched through the left sternomastoid muscle then nicked the..."

She leaned in, her fingers exploring.

"I'd guess the left internal jugular and the external carotid. It's hard to tell, because numbnuts up there moved the body. There was a lot of blood?"

"Yeah," said Kett, the smell making him feel light-headed. It was cooler in here than outside, but not by much. "Palmer said he found the knife in his throat. Lodged there. Pulled it out himself and washed it."

"Washed it?" the pathologist said. "Why the fuck would he do that?"

"My words exactly."

"That's annoying. Because look, see these?"

She was pointing to the man's neck, and beneath the sheen of blood Kett saw a number of smaller wounds.

"Hesitation marks?" he said.

"There's at least four of them, light injuries that suggest the killer was unsure. I say killer, but these marks are very common when somebody commits suicide by knife. I've seen it a few times."

She acted it out, four tentative jabs then a monstrous thrust into her own throat. Kett winced.

"It's a possibility," he said. "Are you thinking Liam killed Caitlyn and then himself?"

Franklin sighed and then shrugged.

"Without prints, it's hard to say. But find out if he was left-handed. It's unlikely that a right-handed person would inflict a wound like this on himself."

"And it doesn't explain what happened to the baby," said Kett.

Franklin examined Liam's hands. There was blood on both of them, dried beneath his nails and between his fingers. She unbuttoned his pyjama shirt, exploring the pale expanse of his chest and ribs.

"No sign of any further injury," she said.

She did a duck-walk over the grate so that she was squatting next to Caitlyn. Kett angled the beam of his torch on the woman's face, on those awful, open eyes. Her copper hair hadn't lost any of its vibrancy in death, those freckles darker now. Franklin snapped off her gloves and pulled on a fresh pair, walking her fingers over Caitlyn's cheeks, her neck, then up to her head. It was only when they vanished into her red hair that Kett noticed the blood that matted it.

"Ouch," Franklin said. "Shit."

"Knife?" Kett asked.

"No, there's a crater here, in the side of her skull. Deep. Somebody hit her extremely hard."

She stared at the ceiling as she moved her hand, her face a mask of concentration.

"Just once. I'm guessing something with an eight-to-ten-centimetre diameter. Hard to tell the shape, maybe a hammer."

Kett shuddered, hearing the sound of it as if he was right back there in the Pig Man's house, the fire roaring.

"Poker?" he asked, remembering the one he'd seen.

"No. Something with a bigger surface area. I can't say for sure."

"Palmer said she was half in the bed, half out. I think she was trying to get to the crib."

"Which side was it on?" Franklin asked. "The crib?"

"Her side of the bed, right-hand side as you're looking at it from the door, left as you're lying in it."

"Makes sense. She lunges out of the bed, somebody cracks her on the right side of her skull. She probably didn't know anything about it. Did you tell me what position the male was in? I can't remember."

"On his back," Kett said. "According to Palmer, anyway."

"Makes sense. Wound goes straight down. No defensive wounds on his hands that I can see, just blood. I think he was sleeping on his back, killer drove the knife down. He woke up, grabbed his neck, but he'd have been dead in seconds. The female tried to escape, or tried to get to her baby, got her feet caught in the blankets or something.

The killer had time to walk around the bed and bludgeon her."

"Why didn't the killer use the knife on Caitlyn?" Kett asked. Franklin clucked her tongue as she considered the question.

"My guess is that he lost his weapon," she said. "He punched it in hard, it could easily have penetrated the vertebrae, lodged itself there. Hard to get a grip when it's covered in blood. Plus, Liam's hands are on the handle, he's stopping the killer from pulling it out. He has to use another weapon. Was there anything missing in the room?"

"I'm not sure," Kett said. "I get the feeling they wouldn't have told me even if there was."

She looked at Caitlyn and frowned.

"Most of the blood here seems to have come from her wound. I don't see the kind of splatter that would have come from Liam's injuries. Not if she was lying next to him."

"She was killed first?" Kett asked.

"I'll need my lab before I can say for sure."

"Time of death?" Kett asked. Franklin shrugged.

"Hard to tell, with the heat and the movement of the bodies. I'd estimate that they both died around thirty-two to thirty-five hours ago. Maybe between two and five yesterday morning. But that window is pretty big."

Franklin stood up, groaning dramatically as she straightened her back.

"What a mess," she said. "I'll get them back to the morgue, discreetly. I'll know more after I've had them on my table."

Kett nodded and turned to the ladder. Franklin's voice drew him back.

"There is, of course, another explanation for why he was stabbed and she was bludgeoned."

"Yeah?"

"Yeah," said Franklin, her eyes bright. "Have you considered that there might have been two killers in the room?"

CHAPTER ELEVEN

SOMEBODY SEEMED TO HAVE CRANKED UP THE thermostat on this side of the enormous hedge, because Savage was sweating buckets by the time she was halfway down the hill. It was hotter than she'd ever known it to be this time of year, the heat almost suffocating. She ran a finger along the collar of her T-shirt to pull it away from her throat, trying to work a little air in as she, Porter and Clare followed the sound of singing.

They weren't alone. The two men from the churchyard were walking behind them, close enough to hear everything they said, but far enough that they could pass it off as coincidence. They were both in their thirties, or early forties perhaps, and the one with the hair had the dead-eyed hunger of an addict—or former addict, at least. All they'd done in the way of communicating was nod in the direction of the wooden church that sat beside the little chalets.

"This *heat*," said Porter, his cheeks blazing, his eyes streaming. He flapped his arms, imitating a bird trying to take off. Savage had absolutely no idea what he was doing.

As they walked, the choir grew louder. They were obviously rehearsing because every now and again they'd tail off and restart. It was a beautiful sound, something mesmerising in that rise and fall of voices, in those remarkable, haunting harmonies. It made it seem as if nothing here was real, and despite the beauty in the music, it wasn't necessarily a good feeling.

They were a stone's throw from the building when the door opened and a familiar face appeared. Billie Kett walked into the sun, Moira in her arms. Evie traipsed out after her with a face like thunder, then Alice, one finger jammed so far up her nose that Savage half expected to see the tip protruding from her ear. Billie saw them and offered a frazzled smile.

"Hey," said Porter. "Fancy meeting you here."

"Pete!" yelled Alice, running down the steps, only pulling her finger free to hug the big DI. "We were listening to them singing but then we had to leave because Moira was singing too and she's really loud."

"That she is," said Porter, ruffling her hair. "Surprised to see you lot here."

"Robbie didn't know what was going on until we'd arrived," said Billie, struggling with Moira. She nodded to Clare as he walked past, her eyes almost popping out of her head as she watched him walk up the stairs.

"He does know about those trousers, right?" she said. "You can see..."

"Everything," Savage said with a shudder. "He knows."

"This whole thing was a bit of an ambush," Billie went on. "You know his mum's here, right?"

"Yeah," Savage said. "Haven't met her yet."

"You can't miss her. She's the spit of her grandkids. Doesn't look a lot like Robbie, though."

Moira attempted to throw herself out of Billie's arms, almost succeeding.

"How's it going?" Billie asked over the top of the girl's sweaty head. "You've seen Robbie?"

"Yeah," said Savage and Porter together. The DI gestured for Savage to continue and she did. "It's a nasty one, and this place... I don't know."

She glanced at the two men, who were hanging back but only just.

"Feels weird, right?" Billie said. "I'm going to take them home, we're just waiting to say goodbye."

"I don't want to go home!" Evie said, stamping her foot on the grass.

"Savage, Porter, get up here!" Clare appeared in the door of the church, his briefcase clamped to his chest. He waved them on with his free hand.

"Gotta go," Savage said. "Be careful."

"I was about to say the same to you," Billie said. "Good luck."

"Bye, Uncle Pete!" Alice called after them. "I love you!"

"Love you too, kiddo," Porter replied, grinning.

He ran up the steps, Savage right behind him. With the door open, the singing was so loud it almost didn't seem real.

"What's up, sir?" she said.

"Just hurry up," the boss replied, holding the door open for them.

Inside, the church was bigger than it looked, taller too. Light streamed through the windows, illuminating the empty pews and, further down, a raised platform beneath the open tower. Twenty people stood there and sung their hearts out, their faces full of joy. It reminded Savage of the times her mum had taken her to church when she was a kid, the entire congregation on their feet, singing and clapping.

This was a different kind of music, but it carried the same power.

Then, just like that, it stopped, leaving a dreamlike echo of sound inside Savage's head.

"Thank you, Ama," said a croaking voice from the other end of the church. An old man walked through a door clutching a sheaf of papers, his free hand on the wall to steady himself as he limped. He pushed himself into the middle of the room, staggering towards the nearest pew and almost not making it. The woman conducting the choir ran to help him take his seat.

"Pastor Cairns?" said Clare, his brash voice the antithesis of what had come before it. He strode up the centre aisle, the boards creaking beneath his feet. The building felt like a boat, Savage thought. An ark of some kind. Clare dropped his briefcase onto the nearest pew when he reached the old man, sticking his hand out with such urgency that Cairns flinched like he was under attack. "Colin Clare."

The singers were walking out of the door at the back, chatting to each other. Clare waited until they'd gone before leaning in with a dramatic whisper.

"I'm a *Superintendent*. I'm here for the *case*."

"Thank you," Cairns said, with no small amount of distaste. He glanced at Porter and Savage. "I really don't think we need you all here. The note specifically said not to involve the police. I just wanted Mary's son to help, and if you had any respect for—"

"A child is missing, Mr Cairns," Savage said. "Take it as a sign of our utmost respect that it's just us, and not the entire force."

Clare waved her down, gently.

"We'd like to use this place as a command centre," he said. "We'll need space to conduct interviews."

"The old church would be a better location, this one—"

"Is right where we need it to be," Clare said. "We'll be discreet."

He tugged on his pink trousers in the most indiscreet manner possible, then nodded to the documents in Cairns' hand.

"Are they for us?"

The old Pastor stared at them for a moment as if he couldn't remember, then nodded. He passed them over and Clare handed them to Savage. It was a plastic folder, and amongst the other papers inside were two passports. She perched on the nearest pew and shook them out beside her.

"Liam and Caitlyn's," Cairns said.

"Why do you have them?" asked Savage.

"We keep everything safe when people arrive here," the man explained, his face a mask of pain as if the words were sharp. "It's part of the agreement we have with our residents."

He cleared his throat.

"You must understand that many of them come from troubled waters. We are the island that saves them. When they are ready to leave, they may leave."

"And who decides that?" Porter asked.

Cairns looked at him, his eyes bright.

"They do."

"Did Caitlyn and Liam come from troubled waters?" Clare asked.

"No. They were good people. They came because they wanted a miracle. And they got one."

Savage opened the first passport and saw a woman's face—heavyset, pretty, freckled, her bright red hair pulled into a ponytail. She was as serious as everyone else was in a passport photograph, but something about her face made Savage think it didn't often see a smile. The date of birth made her thirty-nine years old, and she had a Norwich address. A quick flick through made it clear that she hadn't been one for adventures. Every page was blank.

"When did Caitlyn arrive here?" she asked.

Savage opened the second passport, looking for a photograph and not finding one. She flicked through it again, more slowly, seeing the place where the page had been cut out.

"She and her husband arrived together two years ago," Cairns said. "A little less than that. July 2018."

"And what brought them here? You say they wanted a miracle?"

"Yes," said Cairns. "They came seeking quiet worship, an escape. Liam had just lost his job as a teacher. Depression, I think. He was prone to maladies of the mind, wasn't close to his family. Neither was Caitlyn. They were deeply unhappy. They needed something new, and they found it here."

"Do you know what happened to his passport?" Savage asked, holding it up. Cairns frowned then shook his head.

"It must have been like that when they arrived. We don't touch them, we keep them locked away."

"Any other children?" Porter asked, strolling past the Pastor and onto the platform the choir had just departed. It wobbled beneath his shoes and Cairns looked worried, as if it might collapse.

"Caitlyn? No. The boy was her first. She and Liam had been trying for a child for some time. It's one of the reasons they ended up here, so that they could relax and try for a family. We have a reputation, I'm sure you know. This place has a history of producing little miracles."

"With the help of angels?" Savage asked, pulling a document from the folder. When nobody replied she glanced up to see them all looking at her. Clare's forehead was accordioned with disapproval. She held up a hand. "I'm sorry, I didn't mean any offence. I was talking about the legend. The Cliffords and their well."

Cairns' expression softened. He pointed to the chain around her neck, as if he expected to find a crucifix hanging there.

"Yes, the Well of Our Lady. Are you a believer?"

"My granddad loved the old stories. He was a local boy, kind of. Hemsby."

"Other side of the county," Cairns said, disappointed. "Other side of the world. Yes, the legend tells us that Lord and Lady Clifford asked the Holy Father for help in conceiving their child, and he answered their prayers by demanding that they pass, well, a *test* of sorts. He instructed them to tap the earth, to find holy water, and they did. The well that Lord Clifford dug is still here. The Well of Our Lady. The sacred water is one of the reasons we are so successful in our mission, although our true strength lies in good food, fresh air, friendship, rest and prayer. Lots of it. You'd be surprised how quickly those things bear fruit, even in the most barren of places."

He directed those last words at Porter, who stared back at him in surprise. It was a coincidence, of course, but here in the quiet church, it brought a rash of goosebumps to Savage's arm. She unfolded the sheet of paper to see that it was a birth certificate, brand new.

"Adam Reginald Brown," she read. "March 31st."

And here she paused again, breathing out a laugh.

"Same birthday as me," she said. "He was born here?"

"He took us by surprise," said Cairns. "Three weeks early. Luckily my wife was a midwife, although that was a long time ago. He was healthy, and we took him to hospital immediately. He and his parents stayed the night, mother and child were discharged the following day in perfect health."

There was nothing else of use on the birth certificate so she folded it up and returned it to the envelope, sliding everything into the plastic folder.

"Mind if we keep hold of these?" she asked.

"Just please return them as you found them."

"Everyone here knew about the baby?" Porter asked, sniffing wetly.

"Of course. It was a time of great celebration. Babies always are."

"Was anybody jealous of the child?" Savage said. "Anyone else who might have come here seeking a miracle but who hadn't been able to find one?"

"Absolutely not," said Cairns. "I know every soul in Whytetail and nobody would take a life, let alone steal a child from their rightful parents. I will personally vouch for every single person here, damn me for eternity if I'm wrong. This was not one of my flock. This was an outsider, I know that for a fact. Find him, and you will find the boy."

"With that much certainty, you must have an idea of who did this," said Porter. He jumped off the stage and the sound of it was like thunder.

The old man's mouth moved like he was chewing toffee, and his eyes scrolled back and forth across the floor. He shook his head.

"Just find him. That's all that matters. Find the child."

A knock at the door, and Savage turned to see an elderly

woman there. She was as drawn as Cairns was, as if her skin had been pulled too tight, but she offered a tired smile to the group as she walked into the church. Cairns seemed to relax when he saw her, his own smile much wider and much warmer than it had been before.

"My treasure," he said, with genuine affection.

"Reginald, are you okay?" The woman walked into the nave with a slow but dignified gait, her long, dark dress snapping at her bony ankles. She was carrying a wooden cane topped with a large brass sphere, although judging by the discomfort in her expression she should probably have been using it.

"I have been better, my love," Cairns said. "I have been better. Officers, this is my wife, Summer Cairns."

Summer stopped in front of her husband, and even though it obviously caused her immense pain she lowered herself onto her knees in front of him. She held out the cane with both hands, as if she was handing a monarch his staff.

"Oh, you found it," Cairns said. "I knew you would. You are a blessing."

He took the cane from her, the brass sphere catching the light. It was a globe, Savage thought, the size of a tennis ball. Cairns braced both hands on it, then manoeuvred himself out of the pew. A trickle of spit dripped from his mouth and he wiped it away quickly, as if ashamed. For a second it looked as if he might drop down again but through some Herculean force of will he stayed upright.

"With me, my love."

He staggered past, drumming out the rhythm of his walk with the tip of his cane. Summer grabbed the pew and tried to stand, her body trembling. Clare was there in a heartbeat, helping her up.

"Thank you," she said, studying him with eyes that

seemed sharper than the rest of her. "Did you get what you needed from my husband? He does go on. His mind isn't what it used to be, I'm afraid."

She leant in, her voice so quiet Savage could barely hear it.

"Don't take everything he says as the gospel truth."

"Then maybe you could tell us your side of the story," said Clare. "We're setting up an interview room right here, if you have the time?"

She patted his hand then shuffled after the Pastor.

"You trust him?" Porter asked in a whisper as he walked to Savage's side. "That man seems full of secrets."

Cairns hesitated as he reached the door, lifting his cane in a trembling hand. It dropped with a sound like a cannon going off, making Savage jump. He couldn't have heard Porter, there was no way. And yet somehow, he knew.

"There are no secrets in the eyes of God," he shouted over his shoulder. "Not for us. Not for anyone."

He cracked his cane on the floor, once, twice, three times, the sound of it batting around the church as if looking for a way to escape.

Then his wife took his arm, steering him into the sun.

"Savage, Porter, go check out the murder scene," Clare said when they were gone. "I guess we're about to find out if there are secrets here or not."

CHAPTER TWELVE

Kᴇᴛᴛ ʜᴇᴀʀᴅ ᴛʜᴇ sᴏᴜɴᴅ ᴏғ ᴘᴇᴏᴘʟᴇ ᴛᴀʟᴋɪɴɢ ᴀs ʜᴇ made his way back up the hill from the ice house, and by the time he'd neared the edge of the woods he realised they weren't just talking, they were *singing*. Franklin marched beside him, her face grim, and behind her Palmer did his best to keep up. The big man looked like he'd seen better days, his cheeks blazing spots of colour but the rest of his face as white as a sheet.

"What's going on?" Kett asked him.

"Lunch," he grunted.

"Sounds more like a party," Franklin said.

Breaking free of the trees, Kett saw the people of Whytetail weaving between the chalets in the direction of the wooden church. The adults were the ones doing the talking, but the kids were making most of the noise. They were singing a song that Kett had never heard before, a nursery rhyme of some kind. He caught the words *blackbird* and *blackberry* but the rest was lost in their tuneless, excited voices.

Curious, he followed them, the sun like a hand on his

back pushing him up the hill. The warmth of it eased the pain in his chest so much that he put his fingers there, feeling for the shard of Keefe's bullet. Everything seemed so much easier here, he thought. Even with the murdered couple, even with the missing child, even with the sense that they weren't welcome, the place hummed with a strange, undeniable peace.

A place of miracles.

"Paul!" came a cry, and a young boy came whirling out from behind a chalet, his grin almost bigger than his face. Palmer laughed as he scooped him up, holding him to his chest. In a heartbeat that dour expression vanished, the big man's smile making him look even more like a child.

"Staying out of mischief, Vincent?" Palmer asked.

"Never!" said the kid, and both of them laughed. Palmer lowered him gently to the ground.

"Go on, find your mum and dad."

The boy ran off and Palmer caught Kett's quizzical expression.

"I'm not always a miserable old fart," he said. "Just a bad time, is all. Kids, it runs right off them, don't it? Bad stuff."

"Do they know?" Kett asked, pausing to let the man catch up. Franklin stomped past, her legs covered with fresh nettle stings, her flip-flops like castanets.

"About the killings?" Palmer said. "Yeah, we don't have no secrets here, not from them, not from anyone. They know about death, they know it's not the end. Caitlyn and Liam were loved here. They'll be missed. But we'll see them again and the kids know it."

The big man looked up at the sky, and in doing so missed his footing. He stumbled, managing to catch himself.

"You been here long?" Kett asked him.

"Longer'n anywhere else. Never saw a reason to leave. Nobody ever does."

"Must be something good worth staying for," Kett said.

"Ask your mother. She says she's never really been at peace, not until she got here."

It hurt to hear that, like a pressed bruise. He'd never thought of his mum as happy or unhappy growing up, children rarely did. Only later had he realised how sad she had seemed, how closed off to him and the rest of the world. Even before his dad had passed—and he had to be careful thinking of him, because those memories cut like knives— she'd never been one for unearned smiles or hugs, and her reserve of kind words had been shallow.

They were approaching the end of the cluster of chalets, the wooden church in view. Some of the men were hefting large wooden trellis tables and heavy benches up from the Manor, setting them out in the carefully mowed circle around the strange wooden totem he'd seen earlier. Others were carrying trays laden with bread and cheese, glass jugs brimming with water and cut fruit. People were taking their seats, the air full of laughter as the children ducked beneath the tables and vaulted the benches.

"Feels like a celebration," Kett said. Palmer shook his head.

"We eat together every day, and out here when we can. I suppose every day is a celebration of sorts, the good days and the bad. Join us."

Kett wasn't sure if it was a question or an order. Palmer started to lumber away.

"Hey, Paul, one more question," said Kett. "Liam Brown. Was he right or left-handed?"

Palmer looked at his own hands as if they might hold the answer, then he turned to the sky, swallowing noisily.

"Right," he said.

Kett caught up with Franklin, spotting Savage and Porter walking up from the direction of the Manor. He waved and they made their way over. By the time they'd reached him Clare had appeared from the church, the Super penguin-walking down the steps with a face like a man who had his bollocks in a vice.

"Manor is clear, sir," Savage said when Clare had reached them. "One locked door we'll need to get through. Had a peek through the keyhole and it looks empty. No crying babies."

"And they definitely didn't want us in there," Porter added. "Any news from the dead?"

"Definitely dead," said Kett.

"And definitely murder," Franklin added. "Her, at least. Jury's still out on him."

"No, Liam was right-handed," Kett said. "Palmer just said so."

"Then murder it is," Franklin said with a dramatic flourish.

"How'd you get on with Cairns?" Kett asked. He spotted the old Pastor in the crowd, leaning on a brass-topped cane. "He have that with him when you spoke to him?"

"The cane?" said Porter. "His wife brought it over. Why?"

"Caitlyn Brown was bludgeoned to death, one blow, with an object about this size," Franklin said, holding up a bunched fist. "I thought it might be a sledgehammer or an ornament. A cane like that would do it."

Even as they watched, Cairns teetered and almost fell. It took a couple of passing guys to keep him upright and they manoeuvred him to the nearest bench.

"I can't figure him out," Porter said. "But this place is well shady."

"*Well shady* being a well-known police term," Clare said with a disapproving look.

"Cairns thinks an outsider took the child," said Savage. "Want me to start knocking on doors in the village?"

Kett nodded before remembering it wasn't his call.

"Not yet," said Clare. "I think we start here."

"Why aren't they looking for him?" Kett asked. "There's a baby missing and they're having a party. I don't get it."

He was answered by a cackle of laughter. Alice was running out of one of the wooden chalets, jumping up and down and spinning like a loon. Behind her came Billie, then Mary Kett, who had to edge out of the door carefully because she was holding hands with both Evie and Moira. It gave his heart a mighty kick to see her with them, and he wasn't sure why. Lost time, perhaps. Such a waste.

"Dad!" Alice screeched, breaking into a galumphing run. "Dad, she's our *gran*! Did you know that? Our gran!"

Kett breathed out slowly, bracing himself as she thumped into him. He hugged her then let go, his chest throbbing.

"Our gran," Alice said, beaming. "I didn't think we had one. Did you know?"

"Yeah," Kett said, pushing her hair out of her eyes. "I had an idea. You okay?"

They were all heading over, Mary's face flushed but her eyes bright. Billie said something to her and she smiled—the first smile he'd seen on his mum's face in so long. It made him think of those other smiles, the ones from childhood that he'd somehow managed to forget, and when the kick in his heart came again he recognised it as guilt.

"Dad!" Evie said, using her free hand to wave. "We've got a gran!"

"Gan!" added Moira.

Billie mouthed the word *sorry* but he waved it away. It had to have come out sooner or later.

"How's that all going?" Savage asked.

Kett started to reply but he was cut off by the sound of drums, then recorders. A small marching band made up of children waddled out from the brick archway that led to the Manor, each of them seemingly playing a different tune to the rest. They marched past the cypress trees and up the path, followed by four women and a man, each pushing a trolley laden with trays of food and drink. Cairns began to clap along to the rhythm of the drums, everyone else joining in. Alice whirled into the middle of it all, delighted. Kett wanted to tell her to stop but he didn't think she'd listen.

Besides, it didn't go on for long. The band reached the benches and ended with a flourish of mismatched notes, somebody's recorder squeaking and loosing a round of laughter in the crowd. Cairns waited for the trolleys to come to a halt before struggling up, his knuckles blanched on the head of his cane. Everyone fell utterly silent as he lifted his free hand.

Everyone except for Alice, that was.

"Food!" she yelled, loud enough for the word to echo back from the wooden church. "Dad, can we? Dad?"

Kett waved her down with both hands, but Cairns was laughing.

"You are most welcome to join us," he said, his voice cracked and broken but laden with kindness. "All of you. Call me your friend and I shall welcome you to my table, in the presence of Our Lady of the Water."

Here, Cairns looked at the totem in the middle of the

circle, and Kett finally understood what it was: a woman close to giving birth. The Virgin Mary.

He heard Porter's stomach grumble.

"Be rude not to, right?" the big DI said.

"You forgetting there's a baby missing, sir?" Savage said quietly. "Because I think they all have."

"Thank you," Kett said, making no move to join the others. "Before you eat, do you mind if we ask you a few questions?"

Cairns frowned, then nodded. He sat down rather abruptly, as if his legs had given way beneath him, then nodded again. An older woman with long, grey hair held his hand, pulling it onto her lap in a way that left no doubt she was his wife.

Kett moved closer to the group, waiting for the children in the band to join their families. Mary led his girls to an empty bench on the right and they sat down together, Billie crouching beside Moira to stop her from toppling off. He didn't really want them here, but he couldn't exactly chase them off without a hurricane of tantrums.

Everyone looked at him and he studied them for a moment, counting. Thirty-four adults in the community, eleven children—including the baby he'd met earlier. Most were sitting down but he noticed Tom Faulkner, the bald guy, standing towards the back. Haystack hair was there too, and so were another couple of men. They looked bored.

"My name is Robert Kett," he said after a moment. "I'm sure you all know by now that I'm Mary's son."

He glanced at his mum to see that her smile had vanished.

"I understand this is a difficult time, but we need to act fast. Is everyone here? Everyone in the community?"

There was a current of movement as heads turned left and right and nodded.

"This is all of us," Cairns croaked. "Although Caitlyn and Liam Brown are no longer with us, and Adam is sadly absent. Their baby."

I hadn't forgotten, Kett thought, seeing their bodies caked in bat shit, their glassy eyes open.

"There's nobody else?" he went on. "Cooks? Gardeners? Cleaners? Everyone is here?"

"We do the work ourselves," Cairns said. "This is every last resident at Whytetail."

"Who was the last person to see the child?" Kett asked.

The woman sitting next to Cairns put her hand up.

"That's Summer," Savage whispered in his ear. "Pastor's wife."

"When did you last see him?" Kett asked.

"Thursday night," she replied, her voice much stronger than her husband's. "Took them their supper at about half-past eight."

"At or about?"

"About," she said. "We don't have clocks here, other than the one up in the old church. We don't like to be governed by time."

Porter scoffed. Kett shot him a warning before turning back to her.

"And they were fine? The child was there?"

"He was in his crib," she said. "Liam was working the fields but Caitlyn was there."

"And she was happy?"

Summer nodded, her lips tight.

"But the child was upset. Adam often was. Colic, we think. There's not much you can do for it, other than let it pass."

"Who was with Liam on Thursday?" Kett asked.

Palmer put his hand up and so did another couple of men, Haystack included.

"We were all tending the fields," Palmer said. "Stopped about half eight, maybe nine."

"Late to be working, isn't it?"

"We work later in the spring, until sundown. Parted ways right over there and Liam went back to the Manor."

"And nobody else here saw him after that?" Kett asked.

The woman from the room down the hall from Caitlyn's—Gayle—put up her hand. She had her baby cradled in her arms, fast asleep.

"I saw him pass by, waved to him. But he didn't see me."

"Did you hear anything after that?"

"Just the crying, poor lad."

"Thank you," Kett said, puffing out a breath. "Anyone else?"

Nothing, other than a hushed demand from Billie telling Alice to sit down. Porter sneezed loud enough to make several members of the community jump in fright.

"What about phones? Cameras? I know they're not allowed, but if any of you have one I'd like for you to check it, see if you caught something. Look closely."

Cairns shook his head.

"As I said, we don't like to be governed by technology, either. There are no mobile devices here, no cameras or computers, no phones other than the one in the old church."

Kett glanced at Clare, who was fast turning the same colour as his suit in the heat. The Super stepped forward, more than a few eyebrows rising in the crowd as they took in his figure-hugging trousers.

"We're setting up in the church," he said, hitching a thumb at the wooden building behind him. "We'll need to speak with everyone here, individually. Pastor Cairns, if you could organise them that would be much appreciated."

The old man nodded, although he didn't look too happy about it. From somewhere further up the hill Kett could hear what sounded like a chainsaw, faint but persistent.

"I don't think I need to remind you that a child is missing," Kett said. "And we're fast losing any hope of finding him."

The noise was getting louder, and the crowd was growing skittish. Kett looked back, searching for the source of it, seeing nothing past the chalets.

"What is that?" Savage asked.

A growl—not a chainsaw, he realised, but an engine.

"Stay calm," Cairns said. "Remember, we do not fight."

"*Fight?*" Kett said. "What are you—"

And he had to stop as a truck roared into view, barrelling down the hill.

CHAPTER THIRTEEN

I T WAS A NISSAN NAVARA, AN OLDER MODEL WITH BIG
wheels and bigger suspension.

And it had to have been doing forty miles an hour as it
carved a path through the long grass.

"Christ!" Kett said, watching it bounce over the path
before thumping past another chalet. The engine gunned as
it sped down the hill, heading for the river. The windows
were open and Kett could make out at least four people
inside—big grins, wild eyes.

"Stay where you are," Cairns said, but his baritone was
almost lost behind the swell of panic in the crowd. Some
people on the edge of the group were moving towards the
chalets, others were gathering in the middle by the totem
pole.

"Who the tossing hell is that?" Clare said.

The truck was turning, its wheels kicking up clods of
dirt as it spun in a wide circle. It hit a bump, rocking so
much that it looked like it might topple over.

Then it began to accelerate up the hill.

Right towards them.

"Billie!" Kett yelled, moving towards her. "Get the girls up."

Alice had caught onto the mood of the group, her hands in her hair. She looked like she might bolt but Billie took her arm, grounding her. The truck was still gaining speed, fifty miles an hour now. The sun was behind it and Kett could see two faces in the dark windscreen, both men. They looked like they were laughing.

"Stop!" Porter shouted, running past Kett.

The men didn't respond, other than to push the truck harder. It had reached the outer edge of chalets now and it would be on them in seconds. There was nowhere to hide out here and people knew it, deserting the circle like startled animals even as Cairns tried to calm them down.

"Stop the fucking car!" Porter yelled, pointing a finger at them.

There was no way the driver could have heard him. He wrenched the wheel, the truck kicking up gravel as it skidded over another path. It snapped a washing line, scattering clothes, then crumpled a bike that had been lying on the grass.

A swell of rage washed through Kett, hotter than the sun. His girls had been right there, just minutes ago. The truck would have killed all three of them. It was moving around the group, the men inside jeering out of the windows. Somebody in the back stuck something out of the window and with a whoosh a firework shot free, angling up —thankfully—over the heads of the crowd and exploding with a crackle.

"Who are they?" Kett yelled.

Cairns was too far away so Kett jogged to him, almost bowling over a couple who were running the other way.

"Who the fuck is that?"

"Nobody," Cairns said. "They don't mean any harm. They won't hurt us. Just stop panicking, stop running. We don't fight!"

Kett had no idea if the Pastor was talking to him or to his flock. Either way, his words dried up after a second or two, the colour fading from his cheeks like somebody was draining the blood right out of him. He slumped, then slid off the bench, a dead weight with glassy eyes.

"Oh, Reginald, no," said his wife, crouching beside him.

There was no time to help him. The truck had turned a full circle around the green, vanishing behind the chalets again. From the sound of it, it was heading back downhill towards the woods and the river. Kett glanced over to make sure his girls were okay, all of them clinging to their mother in the shadow of the totem. Billie nodded at him.

Go get them.

"Come on," Kett said, breaking into a run, one hand on his aching chest.

Porter appeared beside him then Savage overtook them both, her arms and legs like pistons. Clare began to run too, an awkward, straight-legged gait that made him look like he had a ferret in his pants, but after a couple of seconds he stopped and waved them on. The only member of the community to follow was Palmer, who was surprisingly fast.

"Who is that?" Kett asked him when they were free of the crowd.

"Folk from over the way," he said, his breaths like bellows. "No good."

The truck had vanished into the woods but Kett could still hear it, the sound distorted by the heavy canopy. Halfway down the hill he had to slow to a walk, the agony in his chest making it impossible to get air in. Palmer stopped running as well, the big man plastered with sweat. Savage and Porter were oblivious, almost at the treeline.

"They ever hurt anyone here?" Kett asked. Palmer shook his head, coughing hard, his lungs full of gunk.

"Just... bullies," he said. "Show-offs."

"What does Cairns mean when he says you don't fight?"

"Exactly that. Fighting's a sin. We turn the other cheek."

"And you're okay with that?"

He shrugged, but his expression said he almost certainly wasn't.

Kett stepped into the shadow of the first line of trees, taking a moment to appreciate the shade. The truck's engine was idling now, somewhere close. Kett heard a door slam, a shout. Laughter, lots of it. Savage was waiting for him, Porter just ahead of her.

"Right there," Porter said. "What do you want to do?"

Kett knew exactly what he wanted to do, but he swallowed the anger down like it was heartburn. He walked to Porter's side and followed the big man's finger through the trees. Sure enough, there were the truck's headlights, full beam despite the sun. There was no sign of the men through the thick foliage.

"They ever armed?" Kett asked when Palmer had caught up.

"No," he said, but the word was barely out of his mouth when gunfire cut through the air. Kett glanced at Savage and she shook her head.

"More fireworks," she said.

The pop came again, then a crackle of small explosives and the sharp smell of gunpowder. There was a clap of wings as a handful of pigeons took flight, something bigger darting through the undergrowth to Kett's right.

"We should just leave them," Palmer said. "They go away after a while."

The men were laughing, an ugly kind of laughter, a *drunken* kind.

"Fuck that," Kett said.

He pushed past Porter, escaping the trees onto a gravel track. He followed it round, the river appearing like a strip of phosphorous, blindingly bright. He had to hold his hand up to his face to stop it burning clear through his retinas, and he heard the men before he could see them.

"Here come the wankers!"

More laughter, and Kett lowered his hand, blinking splashes of light across the woods and the water. There weren't four men, there were five, all in their twenties boasting neat hair and tribal tattoos. They were wearing black boots, black T-shirts, black shorts—combat gear, although it was pretty obvious they weren't soldiers. The truck was emblazoned with RS *Plastering* and a mobile number.

"What do you twats want?" the same voice said. One of the men stepped forward, a can of Fosters in his hand. He wasn't the biggest of the lot but he was toned, veins bulging in his forearms beneath the bands of his tattoos. His hair was immaculate, his face too.

Kett felt Porter walk up beside him, sniffing.

"You *crying*?" said the man.

"It's the pollen," said Porter, wiping his eyes.

"Sure. Why don't you fuck off indoors then?"

Then Savage was there, the men leering at her.

"*You* don't have to fuck off, love."

Savage didn't reply but Kett could feel her bristling.

"Please..." started Palmer, and the men all burst out laughing.

"P-P-P-Paul P-P-P-Palmer!" said the same man, his voice slurred in a cruel imitation. "P-p-p-please fuck off or I'll p-p-p-piss my p-p-p-pants."

They were like hyenas, their teeth bared as they howled with delight. One of the other men threw an empty can at Palmer, although it missed him by some way. He didn't react, his back hunched like an old dog, his face full of quiet fury.

"Right, son, that's enough," said Porter, sounding far too much like police. Kett put a hand on his arm, gently.

"You boys look like you're lost," Kett said, eyeballing them all in turn.

"You look like *you're* fucking lost," another of the men replied, leaning on the side of the truck.

"Who the fuck are you, anyway?" the first guy said. "Not seen your sorry arse around here before. Thought this place was full to the brim with cripples and cunts."

They laughed again but it was quieter now. There was something dangerous about it. Two of the men were moving away from the truck, flanking the one in front. A third was sliding another slim firework from the trailer bed, a lighter in his free hand. Another one lobbed his beer can and it hit the ground inches from Kett's feet, spraying beer as it rolled into the bushes.

"I wouldn't do that if I were you," Kett said.

"Yeah?" the beer-thrower replied. "What you gonna do about it? Pray for me?"

Kett ignored him, speaking to the first guy.

"You know there are kids here, right? You could have killed one, driving like that."

The man shrugged.

"Wouldn't be no great loss, would it? One less fucking Whytetail retard."

The fuse had been lit, Kett could hear the hiss of it inside his head. This time it was Savage who rested her fingers on his arm, just for a second.

"Leave it, guys," Palmer said.

"Leave it, guys," echoed a blond guy at the back, followed by a high-pitched giggle. "Go on, Roly, put him in his place."

The first guy, Roly, was thinking about it, Kett could see it in the way he squared his shoulders and balled his fists. His eyes were big and dark and he wondered if he'd been indulging in more than drink. Porter was half a step in front of Kett now, and even in his yellow football shirt and with hay fever tears in his eyes he cut an imposing figure.

"Go on, Roly," said the same guy. The others were goading too, another beer can sailing over Kett's shoulder.

"Yeah," said Porter, his voice quiet and dangerous. "Go on, Roly."

Roly blinked, jutting his jaw out, unsure.

"You lot live in the village?" Kett asked.

"Fuck do you care?" asked Roly.

"Know anything about a baby that went missing from here yesterday?"

Roly frowned.

"You what?"

"A baby," Kett said. "Taken from his room. You seen anything? Heard anything?"

"You sound like a copper," said one of the men, one who hadn't spoken yet. He was shorter than the others but he was built like a brick shithouse. His black tattoos didn't end at the wrist like the other men's, they leaked onto his hands and down his fingers—a lion's head and a bear's. He turned his attention to Palmer. "You *seriously* talking to the police?"

Palmer stuttered something but Kett spoke over him.

"Why do you say that?"

Roly had started pacing like a boxer in the ring, shaking his hands out. The guy with the firework was snapping the lighter on and off, on and off. Kett wanted to tell him to stop but he knew it would confirm their fears that he was police.

"Fucking police in Whytetail," the short guy said. He was livid. "You don't know the shit you're in, Palmer. You're gonna get it now."

"I'm not police," Kett said. "So answer my question. A baby."

"If he's not a copper fucking have him," said the short guy.

"Yeah," said Roly, his confidence back. "Me and you, you quaking old fuck. How about it?"

"Don't," said Savage.

"I wouldn't normally bother," Kett said. "But this guy is seriously getting on my tits."

He took a couple of steps towards Roly, trying to work the knots of pain from his chest. He *did* look like an old man, but right now that was an advantage. Cocky little shits like Roly never looked too closely.

"Boss?" said Porter.

"Just stay back," Kett said. "This won't take long."

Roly was in full-on warrior mode now, fists clenched beneath his chin, bouncing on the balls of his feet. He was fit, that much was clear, and there was nothing in his face that suggested he meant to take it easy. Kett moved slowly, his own arms raised.

"Still say they're police," said the short guy.

"You're wrong," Kett said. He was half a dozen yards away from Roly now, close enough to smell the stench of cologne, sweat and stale beer.

"Prove it," the guy said.

"Sure," Kett replied.

He straightened, ignoring the stabbing pain behind his ribs. Then he fixed Roly with a look. Not just any look, but *that* look—a look that came from twenty years on the job, from handling murderers and rapists and kidnappers and all the other scum of the earth, a look that came from sinking a hammer into the back of the Pig Man's head, that came from hauling his girls out of the inferno of Bingo's house. Roly saw it, and it was like he'd been struck by an invisible fist. His eyes widened, his stance faltered.

"Oh fuck," he said.

The man threw a punch but he was already defeated and Kett stepped calmly out of the way. Roly staggered, caught off-balance, and Kett grabbed him by the scruff of his T-shirt.

"I'm not fucking police," he growled in his ear.

Then he drove his knee into Roly's crotch.

It was like he'd filleted every bone out of the young man's body, Roly folding into him with a soft grunt. Everyone on the track groaned in sympathy, except for Porter, who loosed a cannon shot of a laugh. Kett stood back and let Roly fall, then he knelt down between his legs, the same knee landing hard in his groin. The noise he made this time was more like an opera singer performing an aria.

"A baby," Kett said, batting Roly's hands away when he tried to strike him.

"Roly?" said the short guy, stepping forward. Porter intercepted him.

"You think your mate had it bad, then keep coming," he said.

The man looked at Savage but she, too, was ready for a

fight, her body wound tight. After a second or two he stood down, wiping the back of his hand over his nose.

Kett ground his knee into Roly's crotch, the young man squirming in agony.

"I'm going to ask you one more time," he said. "Then I'm going to stick one of those fireworks down the front of your trousers and light it. Understand?"

Roly nodded, his eyes streaming.

"Is there anyone in the village with a new baby, a kid they shouldn't have?"

"I don't know," he wheezed. "I don't know."

"What about the rest of you?" Kett asked, looking up. "A boy, two weeks old, known as Adam."

Nobody replied, and Kett adjusted his weight until Roly squawked like a chicken.

"Enid," said the blond guy at the back. "You could ask her."

Kett didn't miss the way the short man looked at him when he said the name, like he couldn't believe it had dropped out of his mouth.

"Who's Enid?"

"Nobody," the kid replied, quietly.

He looked past Kett, into the woods, and Kett turned to see two other men standing there. One was Tom Faulkner, and he didn't recognise the other. They held back as if afraid of getting involved.

"Nobody," the kid said again. "Forget it."

"Enid?" Kett asked Roly.

"Pub," the kid spat.

Kett lifted his knee and Roly wound himself into a ball, groaning like he was about to puke. Kett patted him gently on the head.

"See, that wasn't so hard."

He started to push himself up then thought better of it, leaning in.

"I ever see you here again, I ever hear you call a child that word again, I ever so much as see your mobile number on a flier dropped through a door, then I won't just kneel on them. I'll cut them off. Understand?"

Kett didn't think he'd ever seen anyone nod with such enthusiasm. He stood, trying not to let the pain show. His pulse machine-gunned in his skull, the edges of his vision flickering.

"Now piss off," he said. "The lot of you."

CHAPTER FOURTEEN

KETT WAITED FOR THE MEN TO CLIMB BACK INTO THE truck, their tails firmly between their legs. It was all Roly could do to curl up in the back seat, and the blond man took the wheel, the Nissan trundling along the path at all of five miles an hour. Even when it turned out of sight the engine remained quiet until, after a few seconds, it faded away completely.

Kett doubled over, his hands on his knees. His head was swimming, the pain in his chest like he'd been shot all over again.

"Probably shouldn't have done that," he said.

"At least there's no danger of them thinking we're police," said Savage. "I could have sworn I heard his bollocks pop."

Kett winced, managing a laugh.

"Deserved it," Porter said. "Bunch of twats. Hey, Palmer, this happen often?"

Palmer shook his head, but it was a lie. All three of them studied him until he gave up.

"More often, recently. I don't know why. There's always

been bad blood between us and the village. Goes back a hundred years or more. But these young men, they're worse. They drive over and let off fireworks, dig up our crops, let the pigs out and chase them off. They'll be back, and they'll be furious."

"Let them come," Kett said. "I wasn't lying. You know this Enid person?"

Faulkner was stepping out of the trees, uncertain.

"Yeah," Palmer said, wiping the sweat from his forehead. "Everyone knows her. Works in the pub. She brings supplies for us sometimes. Gossip, yeah, but she's better than the rest of them up there."

"Paul," said Faulkner, and there was no mistaking the warning in his tone. Palmer whirled around, his big fists bunched.

"You don't like it, Tom, then maybe you should do something about it," he said. "You know it's only a matter of time before they hurt somebody, deliberate or not."

"It's *our* business," Faulkner said, glaring at Kett. "Not theirs. Come on."

He beckoned for Palmer to come to him and the big man did, huffing his way up to the woods.

"Want me to go speak to Enid?" Savage said when the three men had walked into the trees.

"No," Kett replied. "Porter, can you go?"

"Sure," the DI said. "After lunch, right?"

"What?"

"Lunch," Porter said. "They're serving it up the hill. Right now. As we speak. *Lunch.*"

"Fine," Kett said. "After lunch."

"And me, sir?" Savage asked.

"You're with me," said Kett. "There's something I need you to do."

BY THE TIME they'd made their way back up the hill, order had been restored. Most of the community were back on their benches in the circle of short grass, and food was being served from the trays. The air of festivity had gone, though, replaced by a nervous quiet. Even Cairns seemed subdued, pacing between the tables as best he could. He caught sight of Kett and frowned.

"Go eat," Kett said to Porter. "But make it fast. I need you in the village."

"Sure," Porter said, breaking into a run and heading for the bench where Mary and Billie and the girls were sitting. Billie gave Kett a look and he lifted a hand to show that he was okay. Alice and Moira were ripping through a pile of rolls as if they hadn't eaten in a week, Evie hoarding an entire basket of bread beneath the table. Clare was with them and he limped over.

"Problem sorted?" the Super asked, spraying crumbs. Kett nodded.

"Men from the village, just troublemakers. Palmer says there's bad blood. They don't fight back here. Makes them an easy target."

"For bullying," Clare said.

"And kidnapping," Kett added. "If this was an outsider, like Cairns thinks, then maybe they knew the community wouldn't put up much of a fight. The men gave us a name of somebody in the village who might know something. But..."

"But what?"

"I don't know. There's bad blood between the village and the community but it feels like there's bad blood here too. Faulkner, the chap with the bald head. I think he's battling something out with Palmer. Like they're fighting for top dog."

"Place like this is always going to have arseholes like them," Clare said. "I think the answer's outside. Who's the contact in the village?"

"Enid. No surname. She works in the pub. Porter's going to check it out when he's eaten."

"He can check it out now," Clare said. "Porter, sling your tossing hook. Take the Merc."

"But it's—"

"Now!"

He threw his keys and they landed on the ground some way off. Panicked, the DI managed to grab a roll and some cheese before scooping up the keys and scampering away. Kett watched him go, the heat broiling his thoughts inside the cauldron of his skull. He checked his watch. Time was running out.

"Right," Kett said. "We need to start the interviews."

"I'm on it," said Clare. "Where are you heading next?"

"Back to the room where the Browns were murdered. I need Savage's eyes. Something doesn't feel right about the Manor."

Pastor Cairns was limping around the group, looking about a century older than he had that morning. The brass head of his walking stick caught the light, exploding like fireworks.

"We need to see if that cane is our murder weapon," Kett said.

"I'll do what I can," Clare replied.

Summer Cairns was approaching, looking as flustered as her husband.

"Mr Kett," she said. "May I have a word?"

"In a bit." Kett moved away. "I won't be long."

"Where are you going?" she called after him.

Kett didn't answer, walking around the edge of the benches. Savage trotted to catch up with him. Summer was looking from side to side, desperate now, trying to get the attention of some of the men. Faulkner was responding, making his way over, but Clare intercepted him with a question.

"Wait," Summer shouted to Kett.

"You think they're hiding something?" Savage asked when they'd broken free of the group.

"Maybe. Both Cairns and his wife strike me as people who don't like it when things get out of their control."

"True. And it's weird how they seem more upset about us being here than they do about two murders and a kidnapped baby."

"Yeah."

Kett glanced over his shoulder to see Cairns slumped against one of the tables. He looked like he was about to fall but somebody managed to prop him up, guiding him onto a bench. Summer had given up and was hobbling to his side.

Kett left them to it, quick marching through the line of cypress trees and under the brick archway into the grounds of the Manor. It was deserted here, only the birds and the flies watching as they crunched their way down the side of the building. They walked past the boarded front door and around the corner into the courtyard.

"Go check the stables," Kett said, nodding at the building opposite.

"Sir," Savage said, running over the moss-covered cobbles.

Kett made his way past the door he'd entered through earlier, heading for the far side of the building. The courtyard turned into a track, which ended at a chained gate.

Even from here he could see that the padlock had rusted solid. It hadn't been opened in years. The brick wall contained the building, eight feet tall and difficult to scale—maybe impossible to scale with a baby in your arms.

"Nothing," Savage said as she ran back. "Storage, but no sign of anything illegal."

"Whoever took the baby would have needed to head back the way we came to reach the road," Kett said. "Up the hill and past the chalets. Somebody must have heard something."

Savage nodded, but she was frowning at something over Kett's shoulder. He turned, staring down the side of the building.

"What?" he asked.

"That cable," Savage said, pointing.

Sure enough, there was a thick, black cable running up the side of the Manor, entering through the wall of the first floor.

"Phone?" Kett said.

"Too thick. That's for internet."

"Cairns told us there was no internet here," Kett said. "You searched the building, right?"

"Briefly. Enough to know there's no baby in there. Cairns kept us busy in the church so there wasn't time for a full sweep, and I got the distinct impression they didn't want me in there."

"Let's get to it, then."

They doubled back, reaching the side door at the same time Palmer lumbered into sight.

"You can't be back here," he said.

"Why?" Kett asked. "I thought you needed help finding a missing baby."

"He's not in there," Palmer said.

"You sure about that?"

The man licked his lips.

"If Cairns doesn't want me here, he needs to tell me that himself," Kett said. "Why don't you go fetch him."

"I can't, he's had a turn. But he asked me not to let you wander, especially here. It's a sacred place. I'm asking you to respect his wishes."

"I'm as respectful as they come," Kett said.

He stepped through the door. It was freezing in here despite the heat outside, the kitchen as quiet as a tomb. He ignored the door he'd walked through earlier, which led to the rooms for the new parents, heading for the other one instead. It was unlocked and it opened into a wide corridor with a curved staircase. It was damp in here, blooms of mould on the white walls. Kett took the stairs carefully because he wasn't sure if the rotting wood could hold his weight.

"You're not supposed to go up there," Palmer called out.

The galleried landing was in worse shape still, the wall-paper hanging in strips, chunks of ceiling knocked loose like old teeth. All of the doors were open, leading into sad, empty rooms bare of everything except a trickle of sunlight.

All except one at the far end.

"Please," Palmer said.

Kett glanced back down the stairs to see him standing there—not angry but scared. Savage stood behind him.

"What's up here?" Kett asked him.

"That's where I found the locked door," said Savage.

"It's the Pastor's quarters," Palmer said. "His private space."

"He told me nobody else lived in the Manor," Kett said, and Palmer's mouth flexed wordlessly.

Kett walked to the door and tried the handle, only to

find it locked. He tested it with his shoulder but despite the damp and the rot it was a solid door that had weathered centuries. He wasn't sure even his size eleven boot would shift it. He returned to the stairs.

"Where's the key?"

Palmer stood there, wide-eyed and lost.

"Find it," Kett told him. "Now."

He nodded, scampering away.

"Keep an eye on him," Kett told Savage, and she vanished back towards the kitchen.

What the hell is going on here? Kett asked himself, and he was answered by the sound of his phone. He pulled it from his pocket, surprised to see how low the battery was. He never should have let Alice play *Roblox* in the car, it drained the juice like nothing else.

"Kett," he said as he answered it.

"I know it is," came Franklin's reply. "Because I dialled your number. It would be weird if somebody else answered."

"What do you need, Emily?"

"I need you back here. Because there is no doubt in my mind that our good Pastor's cane is what left a crater in Caitlyn Brown's skull."

CHAPTER FIFTEEN

Porter stuffed the last of the bread roll into his mouth, mourning his meagre lunch as he jogged back into the overgrown graveyard. The old stone church seemed to have grown even taller, as if it was trying to peek over the enormous hedge to see what was going on inside Whytetail.

"Not sure you want to know," he told it.

Clare's ugly Mercedes had no remote locking, and when he jammed the key into the lock it didn't seem to want to let him in. He jiggled it and it eventually relented, the door opening to release a fug of pine scent and BO.

"Ugh."

He slid inside, the heat unbearable, the leather seat actually scalding his arse cheeks. Still, it was good to be out of the fresh air. The pollen in this place was thicker than ever, he could almost see it battering on the windows, trying to climb into his sinuses. He wiped his eyes, squeezing his nose, everything leaking.

He started the engine and the old car seemed to groan, but when he tested the accelerator he could feel the power there. He almost turned around to head for the village but after a second or two he switched the engine off instead, clambering back out. He walked past Kett's Volvo and followed the road on foot. It swept in a wide arc to the left, towards the river, the towering hedge locking the community well out of sight. After a few minutes the road ended as if the countryside had simply risen up and swallowed it.

By the time he'd walked back to the car a couple of the men from the community had appeared, watching him from the graveyard like a pair of sour-faced gargoyles.

"Fuckers," he said quietly with a smile and wave as he got into the Mercedes.

To his disappointment, the Super's collection of greasy music tapes had absolutely no smooth jazz at all. So he performed what turned out to be a thirteen-point turn then gunned it.

He followed the road back slowly, scanning the enormous fields for any sign of life, searching the stretches of thick woodland that separated them. The countryside was lost in a mad riot of green, everything growing. It was playing havoc with his sinuses, his eyes like running taps and his skull stuffed with cotton wool and itching powder. His head felt about three times bigger than it usually did.

It was impossible to make out much at all through the thick vegetation. There were no people, no tractors, no roads splitting off from the one he was driving on. It was like this place was the end of the world, utterly forgotten. He didn't see a single building until five minutes after he'd left the church in his rearview mirror.

It was a farmhouse that had seen better days and he stopped the car at the end of a long, weed-strewn dirt driveway, leaving the engine running. The house was in such a bad state of repair that he might have dismissed it as being abandoned if it hadn't been for the brand-new Citroen van parked outside the front door. He wrestled the wheel around, the big car turning like an ocean liner and flattening a bed of lavender as it fought its way down the drive. Porter parked behind the Citroen and got out, almost drowning in the superheated, pollen-drenched air.

"I fucking hate the countryside," he muttered as he walked to the house.

There was a small porch, and when he walked into its shade he saw the camera there, facing the road, a small, blue light blinking.

"You beauty."

He knocked, and it was only when he heard the sound of a key in the lock that he remembered he wasn't supposed to let anyone know he was police. The door opened a crack, the security chain snapping, to reveal a woman in her fifties, white shirt and denim dungarees, her hair tied back with a multi-coloured bandana. She looked Porter up and down through the gap but didn't say anything.

"Uh..." said Porter, racking his brains. He tugged at the collar of the football shirt, trying to circulate some air.

"Yes?" the woman said.

"I've lost my... dog?" said Porter. "I got out of the car to let him have a wee and he bolted. I don't know which way he went."

"You seem very upset about it," she said, her expression full of sympathy.

"It's..." he started, about to explain his hay fever. He decided against it. "Yes, very upset."

The woman seemed to relax, staring past Porter onto the road.

"Haven't seen a dog," she said. "What kind?"

"Uh... a little one," Porter said. "Fluffy. White."

"Pomeranian?"

Porter nodded.

"What's he called?"

"Uh... Fluffikins?" Porter said. "My, uh, wife named him."

"Yeah, right. That's what they all say."

She shut the door and Porter heard the chain being pulled back. When it opened again it swung all the way, revealing a bright hallway full to the brim with paintings, sculptures and knickknacks. Porter's eyes almost popped out of his head when he saw a crude human figure halfway down that looked as if it had been made from Plaster of Paris.

"It can't be," he said, pointing to it. "Is that a James Preston?"

The woman glanced back, then broke into a smile.

"You're a collector?" she said.

"Kind of," Porter said, trying not to think about Blake Masefield, his murdered brother, his arsehole father.

"I bought it last year. I love his work."

"It's..." Porter said, searching for a word but not finding one. "Look, I hate to ask."

"Morag," said the woman, giving Porter another up and down. "Call me Morag."

"Morag. I saw the camera. Is there any chance I could take a look and see if..."

He hesitated, trying to remember what the hell he'd called his imaginary dog.

"Little Flifflebags ran this way."

Morag pursed her lips, unsure.

"What were you doing driving up this way?" she asked after a moment. "You're not anything to do with those weirdos over at the commune, are you?"

Porter shook his head.

"Commune?"

"Whytetail, the old village. It's the only other place along this road. It's a cult, I think. Although they'd never admit that."

"You speak with them much?" Porter asked.

"Not if I can help it. My place isn't exactly Silicon Valley but I don't trust anyone who says they don't use technology at all. No phones, no internet, not even a kettle, if you can believe it."

"What do they do all day?" Porter asked, leaning on the doorframe.

"Exactly," she said. "Orgies and moon worship, if you ask me."

Porter grimaced, trying not to picture Cairns and Kett's mother romping in the moonlight and finding that he couldn't picture anything else.

"You think they do anything illegal there?" he asked, trying not to sound like a copper. Morag shrugged.

"I don't think they're that interesting, to be honest. Perhaps if they *were* having orgies and whatnot I'd take more of an interest."

She gazed at Porter's broad chest, grinned at him, then broke into a wheezing laugh at his nervous expression.

"I'm joking," she said, walking down the corridor and turning right into the first room. "Computer's in here. Watch your feet."

He followed her into a small living room, the ceiling lined with dark beams. Artworks in various stages covered the carpeted floor and the room stank of paint, turpentine and cigarettes. A large kitchen table sat against the far wall, liquid sunshine pooling on it from the large window. A laptop sat in the middle of an impressive collection of full ashtrays, smoke rising from two of them.

"You alone?" Porter asked, kicking himself when Morag gave him a suspicious glance. "Just wondered if anyone else might have seen... Floofaboof."

"Oh, no, it's just me." Morag brushed ash from the seat of a wooden chair then sat down, logging into the laptop with a series of slow, uncertain pokes. It took four attempts before she managed it. "Bought this place after my divorce. Only thing I could afford with what the dickhead hadn't spent of our life savings."

"You're an artist?"

"I am. Very much an amateur. Oils, watercolours, the occasional bit of pottery. I made these."

She gave the nearest ashtray a nudge with a yellow finger.

"Kiln out the back. Second hand but still nearly broke me. I can show you if you like?"

"I'm fine," Porter said. "I'd just like to find... Farflebarf."

"Then take a seat."

Morag looked up and patted her lap, as if she meant for Porter to sit on it. Then she laughed like a drain and made way for him.

"Thanks," Porter said, taking the chair.

"When did your dog run off?"

"Uh... yesterday morning," he said. "Very early. It's been a terrible time for all of us. Worse still for... Fooflebutt."

"Floofaboof?" Morag said.

"Yeah, Floofleboot."

He found the camera app and opened it, scrolling slowly back through the timeline and seeing himself retreating from the door to his car.

"Don't often get strangers calling," said Morag, far too close. "All the way out here."

Porter cleared his throat, seeing Roly's truck coming to and fro, Clare's car driving backwards and Kett's Volvo reversing towards Norwich. He took it slowly when the screen darkened into night, seeing absolutely nothing there other than the occasional bright-eyed fox.

"It's so quiet out here," Morag said, the words right in his ear. "Nothing to disturb us."

Porter tapped his wedding ring on the table a little more urgently than he needed to. He kept scrubbing back, seeing a postal van but literally nothing else on the road to Whyte-tail. Morag appeared a few times, fetching items out of her car and plucking a few weeds from the driveway.

"I sometimes do yoga out there," she said. "Just to warn you."

"Right," said Porter. "I'll—"

"In my birthday suit," she whispered, close enough for Porter's knees to crack against the underside of the desk. He tried to shuffle away but the chair didn't have wheels.

The footage descended into night again and Porter slowed right down. It had been clear and the moon was three-quarters full, so he could see the road and the drive-way. He leant in, searching the shadows, looking for a car, for a person. The only sign of movement came at 01:26am—the slightest of flickers on the edge of the screen. Porter let it play a handful of times but he couldn't make any sense of it. It could have been an animal, a tree in the wind, maybe even a scattering of malfunctioning pixels. He kept going until he saw the daylight of Thursday evening, then stopped.

"Nothing," he said.

"I'm so sorry," Morag replied. "I'm sure he'll show up. Dogs always do. You can stay for a while, if you like. I'll put the kettle on."

Porter felt her finger run up his back and he leapt out of the chair like he'd been bitten.

"That's really kind of you," he said. "But I'd better be going. Thank you, Morag, I really appreciate the help."

"Of course," she said, laughing again. "You sure you don't want to stay?"

"Not this time." He retreated, almost knocking over Preston's limbless statue. "Fluffnuts needs me. Sorry."

"Good luck," Morag said as he tripped through the front door. "Come back whenever you need to."

He walked into the sun, his heart tripping. He climbed into the Mercedes, shutting the door then pushing down the lock when he saw Morag appear in the doorway. He waved to her, sneezed, then pulled out his phone to call Kett.

"Kett," the former DCI said.

"I know," Porter replied. "Who else is it going to be?"

"Why do people keep saying that?" said Kett. "Make it quick, Alice chewed up my battery this morning. You at the pub?"

"Not yet. I made a stop along the way. House just down the road from the church, camera on the door. There's nothing on it the night that the baby was taken. No cars, no people. There's only one road out of Whytetail, Robbie."

Porter started the engine, sticking the big car into reverse.

"I don't think our baby has gone far."

CHAPTER SIXTEEN

THERE WAS TROUBLE IN PARADISE.

Big trouble.

As soon as Kett walked through the Manor's brick archway and out into the meadow he heard shouting. The community was clustered around the wooden totem, everyone talking at once. It didn't take long to work out that Clare was right in the middle of it all, the Super's northern tones louder than anyone else's. Kett struggled up the hill, the sunlight burning a hole into his retinas, blinding him until he reached the crowd.

"Back off, he's not going to get any better out here," Clare boomed.

"He doesn't need an ambulance," a woman's voice answered. "He needs rest."

They were talking about Cairns, who was now lying on the ground, his eyes closed. Mary Kett was standing over him, holding up one of the picnic blankets to shield his face from the sun. She gave Kett a look that was one part worried to two parts angry. He looked past her, trying to find his wife and kids. They were nowhere to be seen.

"That's not up to him or you," Clare said. "The man needs a hospital."

"It happens all the time," Summer said. "He'll be as right as rain in a moment."

He didn't look as right as rain. He looked dead. *Long* dead.

Clare caught sight of Kett and pointed to the wooden church. Kett nodded, cutting around the back of the angry mob and walking up the steps. The door was open and Emily Franklin leaned against the back of a pew halfway down, her brow concertinaed with worry. Other than her, the church was empty, and Kett pushed the door shut behind him.

"This is getting bad," she said. "They're furious. I think you're asking for trouble unless you bring in some backup."

"I know. But my hands are tied. If the kidnapper's close we can't risk them thinking we're police."

"If the kidnapper is close then it's pretty obvious you're police."

"The cane," Kett said. "You've got it?"

Franklin nodded to the pew she was leaning against, and to the walking stick that lay across it.

"Grabbed it when the old man went down. Felt like the Artful Dodger or something."

Kett ducked beside it, seeing the fist-sized brass top—not a planet, as he had originally assumed, but a face.

"Two-sided," Franklin said. "There's a smile on one side, a frown on the other. Janus, maybe."

"Janice?" said Kett. "Who's that?"

"*Janus*, you anus," Franklin said. "Ancient Roman god, protector of doorways, I think. Or maybe just the sock and buskin."

Kett sighed, giving her an impatient stare.

"How did you qualify to become a police detective?" she shot back. "Sock and buskin, the twin faces of comedy and tragedy in theatre."

"Nothing funny about this, though," Kett said. "You think it's what killed Caitlyn Brown?"

"I can't say for certain without more tests, but it's the right size. The circumference of the tip of the cane is almost precisely the same as the circumference of the wound in Caitlyn's skull. It's the right length for an attack of that magnitude, too. It would have been like being hit with a sledgehammer. Go on, try it."

"Prints?" he asked.

"No," she said. "And you'll see why."

Kett picked the cane up, surprised by its weight. The shaft was dark wood, probably mahogany, and the head must have been solid brass. He twisted it around, the first face wearing a grin that was dead-eyed and sinister, the other one not so much frowning as screaming. Kett lifted it to his face and sniffed.

"Bleach," he said.

"It's been scrubbed clean. Savage mentioned that Summer Cairns gave the cane back to her husband, right here, after he lost it."

"Good work. Any word from the van?"

"It's on its way," Franklin said. "I asked for an ambulance rather than a morgue truck, so as not to give ourselves away. I have no idea how we'll get the bodies out of the icehouse and up to the road without anyone seeing us."

"You'll find a way," Kett said. "Can you call them for an ETA?"

"No. I had to lend my phone to Savage, she doesn't have a signal out here."

"Seriously?" Kett shook his head. "Okay. Take the cane with you when you leave with the bodies, I need to know for sure if that's our weapon. And I need to know today."

"And I need a please and thank you every now and again," she replied. "But it's not Christmas Day, is it?"

"Thank you. How's Cairns doing?"

"TIAs," Franklin said. "I'm sure of it. Transient ischaemic attacks. Mini strokes. My granddad had the same thing. Knocks you out for a few minutes and when you come around you have no idea who or where you are. It'll kill him, eventually."

"TIA?" Kett said. "Can that make you psychotic? Delusional?"

"Violent?" Franklin said. She chewed on it. "Maybe combined with dementia, paranoia. I don't know. My granddad never got violent but it's a possibility. You're thinking he had an episode, killed the two parents, took the child? If he did, there's a strong possibility he doesn't even remember it."

"He'd have been covered in blood," Kett said. "Drenched in it."

He looked at the cane, but it was Franklin who said what he was thinking.

"Maybe that isn't the only thing his wife cleaned up."

"She's protecting him," Kett said. He walked to the door, Franklin calling out behind him.

"I mean it. It's kicking off out there and I don't want to be alone when the shit hits the fan. I've seen enough horror films to know that religious communities like this fall apart fast, and with plenty of violence."

"This isn't a movie, Emily."

Kett opened the door, ready to step out into the sun and

almost leaping a clear foot off the ground when he saw Paul Palmer standing right there. The big man looked uneasy, his eyes squirrelling from Kett to Franklin then back again, his face greasy with sweat. His hands were clenched into fists but he looked less like somebody looking for a fight than somebody clinging onto the side of a boat during a storm.

"What's going on?" he said. "What are you doing in there?"

"How's Cairns?" Kett asked.

"He'll be okay," Palmer said. "He always is. He don't need no ambulance."

"Is he talking? I need to ask him some questions. Him and his wife."

"They didn't do nothing wrong," Palmer said, pleading like a child. "Whatever you think of them, of what happens here, they're not bad people. I know them. I know they're doing the Lord's work. We all are."

Kett pushed past him, clattering down the steps. Outside, the congregation was dispersing, families heading back to the cluster of chalets with downturned mouths and quiet children. Cairns sat on a bench, Kett's mum still holding a blanket to shield him from the sun. The old man's hand was inside the collar of his shirt, playing with the big crucifix that hung there. Only a few people remained, including Clare, Summer and a handful of the Whytetail men. Faulkner was there, Savage standing on his shadow. The DC saw him coming and nodded.

"Any luck with the key?" he asked when he was in earshot.

"I have it," Cairns replied, his voice like somebody scratching a fingernail down a gravestone. "Your policewoman told me you found the room. I have the key. There's only one."

"We need to look inside," Kett said. "Now."

"There's nothing in there," Cairns said.

"You sure?" Kett sat on the bench opposite the old man. "Can you tell me what happened just now?"

"He's in no mood for these games," said Summer, glaring at Kett like she was trying to crack his head open with the sheer power of thought.

"That makes two of us," said Kett. "Mr Cairns, I'll ask you again. What just happened?"

"I... I don't remember," he said, his rheumy eyes blinking at the grass. "I was standing here talking to my father, and he... And this man just fell..."

He pointed to the ground as if there had been somebody else lying there. Kett shared a look with Clare. There was no way on Earth that Cairns' father could be alive. The man was losing it.

"I have the key," Cairns said again.

"It's the sun," said Summer. "The unbearable heat. Please, he's not usually like this."

"What are you doing, Robert?" asked Mary, her arms trembling with the weight of the blanket. "This isn't why I asked you here."

"Was he like this on Thursday night, Friday morning?" Kett asked Summer. "Did he have a turn?"

"I won't let you talk to us like that," Summer said.

She looked at Faulkner, and the bald man stepped forward defensively. The other two men did the same, and there was no mistaking their intention.

"I'll have none of that," Clare said, pointing a finger at them. "Toss off, the lot of you."

They didn't respond, but they didn't come any closer.

"I'm not accusing anyone of anything," Kett said. "Believe me. But if you have a history of blacking out, Mr

Cairns, then I need to entertain the notion that you might have had something to do with what happened to Caitlyn and Liam and Adam. You may not remember it."

"He did not!" Summer said, her face knuckled with rage. "How dare you. Mary, end this, now, or... or find another place to live."

"I..." Mary said, almost choking on whatever she had been about to say next. Her thin arms dropped another few inches, a cap of sunlight claiming the top of Cairns' head. "*Please*, Robert."

"Give me the key," Kett said.

Mary started to plead again but Cairns lifted a hand—one which shook so much he might have been waving.

"I had nothing to do with what happened to my friends, my *family*. And I can prove it to you. I won't give you the key, but I will accompany you to my chambers. Paul?"

"I can—" Summer started, but Palmer bustled past her, forcing her to take a couple of steps back. He offered his hands to Cairns and the Pastor took both of them, his face a mask of agony as he pushed himself to his feet. A thunderous fart escaped him as he straightened.

"Oh dear," he said, everything trembling. "Oh dear me."

"Reginald," Summer said, more firmly this time. "Remember what is at stake here. Our home. Our very way of life. *Please*."

He ignored her, breaking into a shambling walk that made him look like a zombie.

"Make room," Clare ordered, speaking to Faulkner and his two friends. They retreated, all of them watching Palmer steer Cairns around the tables.

"It's okay," Cairns said to them. "It's okay."

"You should be ashamed of yourself," Summer spat. "He's done nothing wrong. He's a good man."

Kett walked past Savage and handed her his car keys.

"This is all getting a bit heated," he said. "Can you find Billie and the kids? It's probably time for them to leave."

"Sir," she said. She nodded towards Faulkner. "Sure you don't want some backup? I don't trust these guys one bit."

Kett shook his head. He didn't trust them either, which is why he wanted the kids well away.

"Just watch your back," said Savage.

Palmer and Cairns had found their stride, looking like a couple of men in a three-legged race as they cut through the long grass. Summer was attempting to follow as well but Clare was running interference, his big arms out as he tried to ask her some questions. Kett upped his speed, overtaking the men and passing through the archway into the shade of the big house. The man with haystack hair was there, leaning on the wall and chewing gum. He held out a hand to stop Kett in his tracks before pulling it back when Cairns came limping into the courtyard.

"It's okay," said Palmer. "Let him through."

"Not okay unless Tom says it is," Haystack said.

"Do what you're told, for once," Cairns snapped. "I'm still the Pastor here, Mark."

Haystack stepped back, allowing them to pass. Kett walked around the corner and through the door, grateful to be out of the sun.

"Are you going to tell me what's in the room?" he asked Cairns when he appeared.

"My private chamber," the man replied. "A place of peace and study."

"You told me nobody else lived in the building," Kett said as they entered the kitchen.

"They don't. At least, not often. I do stay the night,

every now and again, when the waters of my marriage aren't smooth."

"And you were staying there on Thursday night?"

Cairns didn't answer. He stopped, grimacing as he planted a hand on a countertop.

"Paul, can you be a good fellow and get me some water?"

Palmer nodded, letting go of the man and heading for the sink.

"I'll collect it on my way down," Cairns said. He looked at Kett. "Could you help me up the stairs?"

Kett hooked his arm beneath Cairns', taking his weight. The old Pastor was heavier than he looked and his quaking body made it difficult to hold onto him—as if he was trying to shake himself loose.

"Reg?" Palmer said from downstairs, as forlorn as an abandoned dog.

"Man the fort," Cairns said. "I'll be back."

They climbed at a snail's pace, making it to the top of the stairs a good two minutes later. Here, Cairns stopped, clawing in wheezing breaths. It wasn't his health that was causing him to hesitate, though.

"You mustn't judge me, Mr Kett," he said when he had recovered. "I am human, just like you."

"Judge you for what?" Kett replied. He adjusted his grip on the man, almost losing him down the stairs. Cairns teetered, twice as heavy now as he had been a few minutes ago, and it took a second or two for him to settle.

"My weakness."

They set off again, a broken train. When they reached the locked door Cairns put a hand inside his shirt and pulled out his necklace—the one that Kett had assumed was a crucifix. It wasn't a cross, it was a big iron key. He leaned into the door, fumbling the key in the lock with his long, crooked fingers until it clicked like a pistol being cocked.

"My weakness," he said again. "I knew it would be the end of me."

And with tears in his eyes, the old man opened the door.

CHAPTER SEVENTEEN

"How's it going down there? Plenty of fun in the sun?"

DI Keith Dunst broke into a wheezing laugh, as if he'd told the funniest joke ever. It quickly turned into a cough, loud enough that Savage had to hold Emily Franklin's phone away from her ear. She was standing in the shade of the giant hedge that separated Whytetail from the real world, the community bustling further down the hill. Most of the people had dispersed when Cairns and Kett had left, Kett's distressed mother almost running back to her cabin. But some of the men lingered, watching her from a distance with dark eyes.

"You should really stop smoking, sir," she said when Dunst had fallen silent.

"Pfft. Give it ten years and they'll tell you it's good for you again."

"Judging by the sound of that cough, ten years will be too late. What have you got for me?"

She heard the click of a computer behind Dunst's wheezes.

"Right, I'll start with Liam Brown. Born in '84. Grimsby. Pretty average life, no shocks and no surprises. Worked in Butlins after high school then did his degree down at Anglia Poly—art history, why on earth would you want to study the history of art?—before taking on a teaching role in Wisbech. Marshland. No arrests, not so much as a parking ticket or a speeding fine, but the school said he had some time off with depression and anxiety. Married Caitlyn Moore in 2013, at the Registry Office in Norwich. He's got no kids, other than Adam. Mum is dead, dad is in a home, he was... hang on... he was fifty-nine when he had Liam. That's some good going, although I haven't got the faintest idea why you'd want kids at that age. He's got a sister who lives down in Essex."

"They've been notified?" Savage asked.

"Uh-huh. Spoke to the sister myself. She was shocked, had no idea he'd had a child."

"Really?" said Savage. "Not close, then?"

"Apparently not. She'd met Caitlyn a couple of times, she liked her. Thought she was too old for Liam, though, even though there was just a handful of years in it. Caitlyn's a local girl, born and bred in Norwich. '81. Her parents are still local, they're going to ID the body as soon as we get it back."

"They knew about the baby?"

"Yeah, visited them in hospital after the birth. I don't think they're massively close, and they gave the impression they hadn't seen her as much as they'd have liked. But they were happy for her, and excited to be grandparents."

"They'll still be grandparents," Savage said. "We'll get Adam back."

Please, let us get him back.

"They didn't have many good words to say about

Whytetail," Dunst went on. "Thought it was some hippie shit. But they admitted something here had to have worked because Caitlyn had struggled for a while to get into the pudding club. They'd—"

"The *what*?"

"Pudding club," said Dunst. "Up the duff, bun in the oven. Pregnant. They'd tried IVF a few times. This pregnancy came out of the blue. They called it a miracle."

"Seems to be the word for it," said Savage. "Did they have any idea who might want to hurt their daughter? Who might have taken the baby?"

"Nah. Everyone loved her. I've spoken to her work, to her brothers, to a couple of friends and they all said the same thing. Caitlyn was a good person who'd finally found the one thing she really wanted in life. Only for some arse-hole to take it all away."

Savage breathed out a long sigh, pulling a leaf from the hedge and crushing it between her finger and thumb.

"Anything else?"

"Just that they kept the whole thing very quiet. Liam didn't have social media but Caitlyn had Facebook and Insta and neither have been updated this year. Last post from Caitlyn was a picture of an oven with a little heart in it. She says, hang on... *'Here's to the year of our dreams.'* She'd have been around three months pregnant."

"And there's nothing after that?"

"Nothing. No posts, no photos, no check-ins."

"There's not much in the way of a signal here," Savage said. "That's why I'm on Franklin's phone. Anything else, sir?"

"No," Dunst said. "How's Porter? Still weeping like a little girl?"

He roared another catarrh-drenched laugh and Savage

hung up, pocketing Franklin's phone as she made her way back down the hill. She heard the Kett kids before she saw them, the familiar mix of laughter and screams pouring out of one of the wooden chalets near the bottom of the hill. The door was open but she knocked anyway, greeted with the chanting verse of a song.

"You did a fart!"

"No, *you* did a fart!"

"He did a fart and she did a fart!"

More laughter, then Billie's voice.

"Girls, that's enough! Whatever will people think?"

Savage knocked again, a little louder, and somebody appeared in the tiny entrance hall. It was Mary, although it took Savage a moment to recognise her because it was the first time she'd seen the woman smile. She looked completely different to how she had just minutes ago, out by the wooden church. Younger, yes, but it was more than that. When she smiled, she looked exactly like Moira.

The smile didn't last for long.

"Are they back? Reginald and Robert?"

"I don't know, Mrs Kett," Savage said. "I've just come to speak with Billie."

"Oh. Then you'd better come in, I suppose."

Savage nodded a thanks as she stepped through the low door.

"Want me to take my shoes off?" she asked. Mary shook her head, leading Savage into a surprisingly large living area. Billie sat on one of two sofas and the three girls were doing a conga in the middle of the room, laughing their heads off. All three of them had stripped to their pants—or nappy, in Moira's case.

"Kate!" yelled Alice when she saw her. "We're having a naked party."

"Pants!" yelled Moira.

"Sorry," said Billie. "I tried to stop them. It's just so hot."

"I'm tempted to join them," Savage said.

"We can go down to the river, if they're hot," said Mary. "It's in the shade this time of day. And it will get us away from..."

She looked at the door, her fingers tying invisible knots in front of her chest.

"It's not usually like this. It's always so peaceful here. I wish you could see it. It will get better, I promise."

Savage smiled politely at her and turned to Billie.

"Can I have a word?"

"Sure," Billie said, pushing herself up. There was pain there still, Savage saw. The memory of what had happened to her at the hands of the Pig Man—as much in the furrows of her brow as the stiffness of her body. She braced a hand on the back of the sofa for a moment.

"Will you be okay with them for a second?" she asked Mary.

"I will," Kett's mum replied.

"She did a fart!" the girls chanted.

"Kate did a fart!" said Alice.

"Gran did a fart!" added Evie, and the three of them were howling. Even Mary had a smile on her face again, her eyes full of wonder, full of *love*.

Savage walked outside.

"How are they?" she asked when Billie caught up. "The girls. It's a lot for them."

"They seem fine. Happy. They've never had a grandparent before and she..."

Billie walked away from the door a little, as if she was worried about being overheard.

"You know, Robbie always talked about her as if she was

a monster—when he talked about her at all, that was. It wasn't often. But she's just... I don't know. She's just lost. Scared. Must have been hard, what happened with his dad."

"I don't know the story," said Savage.

"It's not my place to tell it. His dad was a drinker, a gambler. Fell in with some bad people and died in a bad way. I think Robbie always blamed his mum for it, never really spoke to her afterwards. He blamed himself, too, of course. Robbie was the one who found him, found his dad after... I mean, how do you get over that? There's no other family so Mary found her own, here. But maybe it will be good for her to get to know the girls. Get to know Robbie again."

"That's why I wanted to talk," said Savage. "Kett wants me to take you home. Things are getting weird. Heated."

"You found the baby?" Billie asked. Savage shook her head.

"But I think we're getting closer to finding out what happened. Kett's with the Pastor now, and if he's about to discover what I think he is, it might get nasty."

"Okay," Billie said. "I'll get the girls. You've got a car?"

"I've got yours."

Billie vanished back through the door, and a few seconds later the laughter turned to groans of disappointment—and a scream of defiance from Alice. Savage could hear Mary, too, trying to argue, asking them to stay. She left them to it, closing her eyes and letting the sunshine fall on her face, her neck. Even with the noise from the girls, it was so peaceful here, so quiet. She felt as if she could lie down and sleep for a month, like some storybook princess.

She came to with a sudden rush of vertigo, as if she had

actually fallen asleep. She was surprised to see Mary there, staring at her from the darkness of her chalet.

"You don't have to take them," she said. "They're not in any danger here."

"Not my call," Savage replied. "And I'm not sure you can guarantee that, Mrs Kett."

The woman stepped to the door, blinking against the sun.

"Did you know about Cairns' condition?" Savage asked her. "The mini-strokes? Does he ever do things out of character?"

"He's a good man," Mary said, walking through the door and scuffing the sole of her shoe on the frame, almost tripping. "He wants the best for all of us. There's not an unkind bone in his body."

"I'm not saying there is. But conditions like that can make you forget yourself. Can make you aggressive, sometimes violent."

"Not him," Mary said. "Not ever. I've never seen it, and I see him every day. All they do is cut him down, cut the legs out from under him. It's not fair, to see a great man like that afflicted with such a cruel disease. But he's not dangerous. He helps people. I can show you, if you like?"

"Another time, perhaps," Savage said. She sighed, something pulling at threads in her head. "Show me how?"

The smile was almost back on Mary's face.

"Don't leave," she said, disappearing inside the cabin. "Wait for me."

She was replaced by Billie, who had Moira in her arms. The girl was sobbing, her face puffy. Evie appeared too, grabbing her mum's legs and almost knocking her over. Behind them, Alice was screaming about not wanting to go. They were both dressed again.

"Come here," Savage said, holding her hands out to Evie. The four-year-old ran over and Savage scooped her up, groaning with the weight of her. "What have they been feeding you? Buses?"

"Come on, Alice," Billie said.

"We're going to look at something first, apparently," Savage said.

But Mary must have already told her because she appeared in the doorway holding Alice's hand. Alice's top half was bare and she was clutching her T-shirt to her chest in protest.

"It's not far," Mary said. "It's worth it."

"What is, Gran?" Evie said.

"A miracle," Mary replied. "Come on."

She closed the chalet door behind her, although she didn't lock it, setting off down the hill at some pace. Savage switched Evie to her other arm, the girl clinging on with sweaty hands. They escaped the cluster of chalets into the brute strength of the sun, heading through the knee-high grass towards the trees where they'd confronted the men in the truck. Halfway there Moira started struggling and Billie put her down, the littlest Kett running hell for leather down the slope before gravity pulled her into a careening somersault. She disappeared into the grass, her laughter like birdsong. Evie threw herself out of Savage's arms, and before long all three of them were rolling down the meadow.

"Idiots," Billie muttered, but she was smiling.

"I'm so happy they like it here," Mary said. "Everyone does. There's nowhere in the world quite like it."

She paused for a moment to let Savage catch up.

"Does Robbie like it?" she asked. "I was so hoping he would."

"I couldn't say," Savage said. "Where are we going?"

"You'll see."

She was angling off to the right towards a different section of woods, patting her leg in the direction of the children as if they were dogs. The smile was back, bigger than ever.

"Know anything about this?" Billie asked, and Savage shook her head. Despite the sun, despite the chorus of the birds and the soft breeze and the smell of the wildflowers and the nearby gargle of the river, she couldn't convince herself that it was anything good.

Mary reached the treeline and walked along it for a couple of minutes. Then she stopped.

"I'm not supposed to show you this," she said. "Visitors aren't supposed to know how to find it. But it doesn't count if you're family, does it?"

She didn't wait for an answer, she just stepped into the trees. The shadows swayed, something oceanic about their dark currents. Savage glanced at Billie, one eyebrow raised as they followed. The girls chased them in, full of curiosity, full of life, tripping over each other and the tree roots as they explored.

"Careful now," Mary said. "There's water."

"Girls," added Billie, louder. "Come here, it might be deep."

They followed the sound of the running water, breaking through the final line of trees and almost blinded by the sun-soaked river. When Savage had scrubbed the flares from her vision, though, she realised they were standing on the edge of a wide, shallow body of water. It was maybe twenty metres across, not quite a lake but not a puddle either. The river flowed just behind it, separated by towering banks of bulrushes. A weeping willow grew on the southern shore of the water, casting shifting patterns of sunlight and shadow on the surface. They almost looked like people, like dancers.

"This is it?" Savage asked. "A pond?"

The water was beautiful, but she wasn't sure it had been worth the trip. Mary must have been expecting the response, because she laughed.

"This is the Well of Our Lady," she said. "Not a pond, young lady. A natural spring. It has sat here for a hundred years, ever since God told Lord Clifford to tap the earth and give the holy water to his wife. It gave them a child, you know? It helped them conceive."

"What's conceive?" Alice asked, frowning at her gran.

"That's a conversation for another day," Billie replied. "It's a spring? It looks more like an oxbow. From the river."

Mary was undeterred.

"It has powers, this place. I've seen it myself. Couples come here because of the holy properties of the water, and it grants them their children."

"I'm sorry, *what*?" Savage said.

"Please don't tell anyone I shared this. But I want you to see, because I want you to stay."

"Couples come here and what? Drink the water, get pregnant?"

"Pregnant?" Alice echoed, snorting a laugh. Evie and Moira were right at the water's edge, staring into its sun-tipped ripples.

"Careful," Billie said.

"Yeah, or you'll get pregnant!" Alice added.

Mary laughed again, but she was waving her hands at the girls to shoo them back.

"You can't touch, just look," she said. "And yes, I've seen couples afflicted and barren bathe in this pool with Pastor Cairns. I've seen them drink from it. Women who have never been able to have children. And something happens to them. The Lord grants them a miracle. I've seen it. I *believe* it."

She did, Savage saw. There was something in her expression that bordered on mania—an expression that Savage had already seen on too many people in Whytetail.

"Time to go," she said. "Girls, say goodbye to your granny. You'll see her again soon."

"We'll get ice cream on the way," Billie said, turning their groans into cheers.

"Please don't go," said Mary.

Alice slid her hand into Kate's, holding tight, and Billie lifted Moira again. Evie hung back for a second, lost in the movement of the water. Then she broke free and ran to her mother's side. Only Mary remained, her mouth a grim line of disappointment. Savage almost felt sorry for her, lost in this place.

Not sorry enough to stay, though.

She clambered up the hill, into the trees, looking back. From here she could see over the river, over those monstrous banks of bulrushes. On the other side was another meadow rising into more woodland, almost a mirror image of the ground they'd just walked along. Flowerbeds had been dug there, teeming with roses. Fifteen of them, all in a line.

"Mary," Savage called back. "What's over the river?"

"Nothing much," the woman replied sadly. "The Pastor and his wife grow flowers there, sometimes. She sells them, you know. Roses."

Savage nodded. She felt something cool in her fingers and realised she was playing with the whistle that hung around her neck. She hadn't even realised she was doing it. Tucking it away, she set off after the others.

Everyone has a secret, her granddad had told her. *You just need to learn to read them.*

She looked back once more as she went, thinking as she did that those banks of earth didn't just look like flowerbeds.

They looked like graves.

CHAPTER EIGHTEEN

THE ROOM WAS A CAVERN OF DARKNESS. NOT EVEN THE light from the landing seemed to want to trespass here, holding back like a frightened animal. Cairns started to limp through the door but Kett used a firm hand to hold him back, reaching into the cool interior until he found the switch.

"Please don't judge me," Cairns said again, weaker than ever.

A bulb blinked overhead as if startled awake. In those staccato flashes of light Kett saw a large room, the walls cracked, the window boarded over. There was a desk against the far wall, a straight-backed dark wood dining chair next to it. There was nothing else, and certainly no baby.

"What is this place?" he said when the light settled.

Cairns croaked a wordless reply, his gulping swallow the loudest sound in the entire building. Kett stepped into the room but he didn't go far. He didn't trust the man not to slam the door and lock him in. Cairns was doing a great job of looking weak but it could easily have been an act. There was strength in him, Kett was sure of it. Strength enough to run this community.

Maybe strength enough to put a crater in a woman's head with his cane, too.

"My private chamber," Cairns said.

"For what? What the hell goes on in here?"

"Solitude," the man said. "And sin."

Cairns grabbed Kett's arm for support as he passed— hard enough to leave a welt of pain. Kett followed him to the desk.

"I'm not a bad man, Mr Kett. But I am a weak one. And I am guilty."

"Of what?" Kett said. He was holding onto the phone in his pocket, ready to call it in.

"Of terrible things."

The old man reached for the drawer, sliding it open. Kett caught a flash of something heavy, something metallic.

"Stop," he said, his voice echoing around the room. "Step back."

Cairns didn't listen, working a hand into the drawer. Kett grabbed his wrist, feeling the wiry muscles beneath the loose fabric and looser skin. It took more effort than he thought it would to pull the man's hand away from the drawer.

"What's in there?"

"The end of me," Cairns said, finally giving way.

Kett pulled the drawer but it was stuck fast, the old desk fighting him. He jiggled it, and after a second or two it slid free and clattered to the floor. Cairns cried out like there had been a living thing inside, but all Kett could see was a silver HP laptop.

"I'm sorry," Cairns said.

Kett lifted the laptop and laid it gently on the desk,

opening the lid. He kept glancing at Cairns to make sure he wasn't about to attack, or run, but the old man had slumped into the wooden chair, his head practically between his knees.

"I thought you didn't allow these here," Kett said. "Computers, phones, technology."

"I don't," Cairns said.

"What's the password?"

"Summer, of course."

Kett typed the word into the box, then tried again with a capital S when it failed to open. The computer was an old one, the icons blinking onto the screen one by one. There weren't many, and nothing that seemed out of place: *Internet Explorer, Word, Excel.* Kett checked the network settings but there was no Wi-Fi here.

"You're online?" he asked, thinking about the cable. It was on this side of the house.

"Behind the desk," Cairns said.

Kett felt with his fingers, finding the connection and clicking it into the Ethernet port.

"So what's the big secret? What's on here?"

He didn't really need to ask, did he? Men were men, after all. He double-clicked on the Internet Explorer link, a browser juddering onto the screen. Then he clicked the *History* tab.

"Wow," he said, scanning the list of websites. "You have been a busy guy, Reg."

The Pastor's head sank even lower between his bony knees, his spine a ridge of standing stones beneath his shirt.

"You do realise you can't just fold yourself up and disappear?"

"I can try," said the old man, his voice muffled.

Kett checked the dates in the browser's history, finding

nothing on Thursday night but plenty on Friday morning, starting early. The websites all looked like they were from an adult forum, and sure enough when Kett clicked one he found himself staring at a group of scantily clad women with big hair and bigger cleavages. The laptop was a time machine, and it had gone back to somewhere in the Seventies.

"Busty Bronwyn's Big Boobed Boudoir?" Kett read, tripping over the words.

"That's enough," groaned Cairns.

The box for the username and password had filled automatically and Kett logged in. Sure enough, the Pastor's name was right there at the top of the screen—his nickname too.

"Reg the Revver?" Kett said. "What does that even mean?"

Kett heard footsteps from outside, looking back to see Superintendent Clare in the doorway. Paul Palmer was right behind him, peering past his shoulder with the expression of a child who's finally been allowed a glimpse into Santa's Workshop. It very quickly became a frown of disappointment.

"Pastor Cairns?" he said.

"Tell him to go away," said Cairns. "Please. They can't know."

"What've you found?" asked Clare. "Any sign of the baby?"

At this, Cairns looked up.

"The baby?"

"You were talking about your sins," Kett explained. "We thought—"

"I had nothing to do with the missing child," he said, his strength returning. "I swear to God. Nothing."

"What are you looking at?" Clare asked, walking to the desk.

"I'm honestly not sure. The Pastor's playlist, I think."

"What?" Clare said, shouldering his way between them. "Good lord, man, who the hell is Busty Bronwyn and why does she run a Big Boobed Boudoir?"

"What?" echoed Palmer from the door, his voice broken.

Cairns groaned again, sinking deeper.

"Please don't let him see."

"Click there," said Clare, jabbing the screen.

"Photos?" Kett said, doing as he was told.

"No. Tossing hell, Kett, why would I want to look at that?"

It was too late to stop it, the screen loading slowly to reveal an image that might have come from a 1970s issue of *Playboy*: a moustachioed man in a tight pink suit and a woman in a wedding dress that could have been made from one giant slab of meringue, lifting the hem provocatively.

"'*I do*,'" Kett said, reading the title. "'*So do me.*' Sir, I'm almost certain that's the same suit you're wearing right now."

"Don't be ridiculous," Clare shot back, pulling the jacket over his chest self-consciously.

"In fact, *he* looks a little like you. What did you say you did before you were a copper?"

"Kett," Clare growled.

The Superintendent barged past, taking control of the laptop and clicking on another link.

Your chat logs.

"Pastor?" said Palmer from the door. He'd taken a couple of steps into the room like a man pushing himself out to sea in a leaking boat. "What's going on?"

"Move back," Kett told him, feeling a sudden and inexplicable surge of sympathy for the old man. "Give us some space. I'll send for you when I need you."

Palmer looked relieved to have been excused, retreating through the door and out of sight. He hadn't gone far, though, because Kett could hear his wet, heavy breaths from the landing.

"You're in here a lot, Cairns," Clare said. "Practically every night by the look of it."

"I don't sleep well," Cairns said. "I wake early and it's so lonely."

Kett turned back to the screen, seeing a list of chat logs arranged by date and subject heading. Whatever sympathy he'd had for Cairns fast dissolved when he scanned the titles.

"*Old and tough seeks a young bit of muff?*" he said. "Christ, Cairns."

"No," the old man said from somewhere between his knees.

"*Are you ready to have your wrinkly old arse spanked?*" Clare added, his face screwed into a grimace. "Toss me off, that's disgusting."

"You're not helping," Kett muttered.

Cairns might have been weeping now.

"There's one that's just called *Cottage Cheese*," Clare said, and Kett actually gagged.

"Don't click on it," he said. "For God's sake, don't click on it."

Clare didn't. Instead, he opened another chat log, this one from yesterday morning. The conversation loaded painfully slowly, each line worse than the last. It went from just after two o'clock to almost seven, and at the bottom was a bill for the cost of the chat—almost two hundred pounds.

"According to Emily, that's when our couple was being murdered," Kett said. "I don't see many breaks in the dialogue."

"There are a couple," said Clare. "There, between '*Like a pink courgette*' and '*I'd rather have a marrow.*' Four minutes. And again, three minutes before '*I bet you've had the whole larder up you.*'"

They shuddered together.

"Not long enough," Kett said. "Not for what happened."

"It's a laptop, he could have taken it downstairs with him to Caitlyn's room. It's not like he had far to go."

"I didn't, I swear," said Cairns, looking up again. "I'm a bad man, you can see that. Just look. I... I haven't been able to stop for a long time. I'm a sinner. An addict. But my sins were here in this room, behind this locked door, and only here, and only this. I swear in front of the Almighty."

"You can just call me Superintendent," said Clare without any trace of irony.

"It's an ethernet connection," said Kett. "No wifi. He couldn't have taken it with him."

"Right. Does anyone else use this tossing computer?"

"This *what*?" Cairns said.

"The computer," Clare said, flapping his arms impatiently. "Does anyone else know it's here?"

"No," said Cairns. "Nobody knows. They think I come here to be at one with myself."

Kett and Clare shared a look, but Cairns didn't notice.

"To pray," he went on. "I lift my right hand to God."

"Nope," said Kett. "That right hand can stay where it is."

He stood straight, rubbing his aching back. There was literally nothing else in the room, something monasterial about its sparseness. The desk was an altar, and it was all too clear what Cairns had been worshipping.

"You were here yesterday morning, right when Caitlyn and Liam were being murdered. You're sure you didn't hear anything from downstairs?"

Cairns rested an elbow on the desk and shook his head.

"The walls are thick, and I don't hear as well as I once did. People know not to disturb me when I'm in here."

"Worth searching the Manor again, though," Kett said. "Just in case we missed something else."

"I'll do it," Clare replied. "I'll take Palmer. Are there any more locked doors?"

"Just this one," the old man replied. He closed his eyes, going limp, and Kett wondered whether he was having another episode. Then he rested his hand on the laptop, gently, as if he was saying goodbye to a loved one.

"Are you going to arrest me?" he asked.

"For chatting to Busty Bronwyn about her vegetable garden? No."

"You're going to tell the others?"

Kett sighed, thinking about his mum, about her love for the community. He'd seen her heart broken once, when his dad had died. He didn't want to see it again.

"I'll leave that up to you," he said.

He closed the laptop and tucked it under his arm, halfway to the door before he stopped.

"Cairns, you say people know not to disturb you when you're in here. How do they know?"

The man waved his hand at the door.

"I leave my hat at the top of the stairs," he said.

"Better than a sock on the door handle, I guess."

He took another couple of steps, something nagging at him.

"Your hat?" he said. "I haven't seen you wear one."

The Pastor felt the crown of his head as if to check.

"I don't know where it is," he said.

"You lost it? Was it there on Friday morning, when you were in here?"

"No, before then," said Cairns. "I... I remember not having it, because I had to leave something else."

"What?" said Kett, although he already knew. The old man confirmed it by looking at his feet, searching beneath the desk.

"My cane," he said. "I don't know what happens to the dratted thing. Every time I turn around it's disappeared."

"Like on Friday morning?" Kett said.

"Yes. Just like Friday. I left it at the top of the stairs when I went into my room, and when I opened the door again it was gone."

CHAPTER NINETEEN

There was only one pub in the village, but it was almost impossible to find.

Porter slowed the Mercedes to a crawl as he passed the last few houses, the road opening up immediately into fields. He cursed beneath his breath then reversed into a driveway. Even with the windows wound all the way down the smell in the car was overpowering, the collection of pine air fresheners enough to make him high. It was worse than the pollen, and he breathed through his mouth as he drove back the way he'd come.

New Whytetail couldn't have been more different to the old one. Houses and shops held hands along a quaint, winding central street—all climbing roses and big Georgian windows, even though none of the buildings looked old. He passed a bakery, his stomach grumbling, then a little shop. On the other side of the street was a café called Benny's, and it was only because he was looking at the menu as he passed that he spotted a narrow side road lost between two overgrown hedges. A faded sign pointed to the River Garden Public House.

Porter slammed on the brakes, earning an impatient honk from an Audi right behind him. He turned the wheel but Clare's car was a cruise liner and he had to keep reversing and pulling forward before he managed to squeeze into the gap. The Audi honked again.

"Fudging winker," Porter muttered quietly, before remembering that he wasn't supposed to look like a policeman.

"Eat a bag of dicks!" he yelled through his open window, flashing the young driver his middle finger.

The horn blared again as the Audi accelerated.

"Wanker," Porter muttered, easing the car up the narrow track. It quickly opened out into a car park, an ugly brick building squatting on the other side of it. There were no other cars here, just a Transit Van in the far corner, so he parked in the closest space to the door and climbed out.

The River Garden was the most badly named pub in existence, because there was no river here, and no garden. The front door was locked, despite it being well after three, so Porter followed the enormous car park around to the side, past a couple of fruit trees dead in their pots and a bin that reeked of rotting food. The business end of the pub had been fenced off but Porter peeked through the gate to see that the kitchen door was open. The smell here was a lot better, something roasting.

"Hello?" he called out.

No answer. He walked to the door and breathed in, salivating, his stomach playing a tune like a brass band. Past a small corridor and a toilet sat a kitchen, but this too looked deserted.

"Hello?"

He walked inside, happy to be out of the sun. Sure enough the industrial oven was on, a joint of beef sizzling inside it. Potatoes bubbled in a pan on the hob. Porter took the only other door he could see, finding himself in another whitewashed corridor. He was on the verge of calling out again when he walked past an open door and saw a young woman sitting in an armchair in a small lounge. She screamed, and Porter almost did too.

"Shit," he said, holding up his hands. "I'm really sorry. I was looking for the bar."

The woman—girl maybe, Porter thought—pulled her legs up beneath her chin, terrified.

"I'm really sorry," he said again, moving on. He could hear footsteps from elsewhere in the building now.

"What now?" came a woman's angry shout.

To his immense relief the next door opened into the pub proper, and he darted through the unmanned bar and onto a stool just as the voice called out again.

"Sylvie?"

"Hello?" Porter said. "I'm so sorry, that was my fault."

More footsteps, then another woman peered through the door. This one was older, streaks of grey in the dirty blonde curls that fell to her shoulders. She was wearing jeans and a blue polo and she was drying her hands on a towel. She lowered her head to stare at Porter over the top of her glasses.

"Where did you come from?"

"I tried the front," Porter said, looking over his shoulder. "Sorry, the kitchen door was open. I did call out."

"Hang on," said the woman, disappearing. He heard her speaking to the girl, the hiss of an argument. Then she was back again. "You after a drink? We don't open until five, there's just no business here, but I'm happy enough to make an exception."

"Just a water," Porter said, and the woman stared at him,

one eyebrow creeping up in expectation. "Oh, right. Give me a Coke then. Diet. A small one."

"Last of the big spenders," she said, taking a pint glass from the shelf. "Ice?"

"Yeah," Porter said, feeling the sweat bead on his brow. "Thanks. Any chance of food?"

"Not unless you're staying for a while. It's just gone in."

The woman scooped in some ice and used the hose to fill the glass, placing it on a beer mat.

"She okay?" Porter said.

"She's fine," the woman replied. "Shouldn't even be here. Should be at school, sixth form, but she's refusing to go. Friend trouble. Kids, eh? Don't know a good thing when they see it."

"She's your daughter?"

"She's seventeen," the woman said, glaring at Porter like he might have had other things in mind. He sipped his drink, the ice tapping against his teeth, the Coke a cold explosion in his stomach.

"You're Enid, right?" he said.

She nodded, bracing both hands on the bar and reminding him of a wrestler about to lunge.

"Who's asking?"

"Pete," he replied, offering a hand that she ignored. He drummed his fingers on the counter instead, no idea how to proceed.

"You're looking for me?" she asked.

"I'm looking for a baby."

"A baby?" To his surprise, she broke into a laugh. "No babies here, I'm afraid. Just roast beef."

"You haven't seen any babies around here? A boy, a couple of weeks old, maybe with somebody who doesn't look like his mother or father?"

"Son, you're making as much sense as a badger with a frog in its mouth," Enid said. "But if you want a baby, you're in the right place."

Porter felt his skin crinkle into goosebumps. The bar suddenly seemed too quiet, and too empty.

"How do you mean?" he asked when she didn't go on.

"Well, almost in the right place," she said. "You're looking for Whytetail, the old town, over the way. You got kids?"

"I..." Porter swallowed, shaking his head. "No."

"Trying for them?" Enid asked, like she was reading his mind. "How long?"

"Uh..." He drank another gulp of Coke, slamming the glass down a little too hard and slopping some over the top. "Sorry."

"Don't you worry," Enid said, wiping it with her towel. "No shame in it, Pete. Took me and Chris a fair long time to get our kids too. Some folk just get screwed out of all the luck. But there are ways and means, son. The world is full of little miracles, after all, especially for those with a little cash to spend."

She studied him, frowning at his lurid yellow football shirt.

"Which isn't everyone, I know."

"I'm not quite sure what you're getting at," Porter said.

"I'm saying that Whytetail might be the answer to your prayers, if you're happy to pay for it."

Porter sat forward on the stool, craning over the bar. He must have looked, for a second, a little too much like police because Enid moved back.

"You're saying I can *buy* a baby?"

At this, Enid burst into laughter again—hard enough for

a bubble of snot to pop from one nostril. She wiped it with the same towel, still chuckling.

"Are you for real?" she said. "You can't buy a bloody baby."

She leaned back, yelling into the corridor behind her.

"Chris, this man thinks he can buy a baby!"

If Chris was there, he didn't reply. Porter took another sip of his drink but the ice did nothing to calm his burning cheeks.

"It's not a supermarket," Enid said. "But it is a holy place."

"Right," said Porter, disappointed.

"Don't knock it. I've seen it with my own eyes. Couples of all shapes and sizes going to live up there, looking to start a family. Most of 'em do what you've done, they come in here because they can't find the place. I hear their stories. I hear the way they've struggled. Then they go up to Old Whytetail and nine, ten, eleven months later there's a wee'un. Miracles, all of them."

"How?" Porter asked.

"Something in the water, I think," Enid said, leaning on the counter. "Supposed to have healing properties an'all. The story is, the old family who lived there asked supernatural forces for help when they wanted a child, but that's just local talk. Jealous mouths. They were blessed, proper blessed, and so's anyone else who goes up there with an open heart and an open mind."

"And an open wallet?" Porter said.

Enid placed a warm, soft hand on top of his, squeezing gently.

"Folks gotta eat. And it's a small price to pay. Tell you what, I'll give you the drink for free. That's a couple of quid you can throw in the jar right there."

"Thanks," said Porter. "So I just go up there and ask for help?"

"Pastor Cairns is the man in charge," Enid said, finally letting go of him. "But you want to speak to his wife, Summer. She's the one who makes the big decisions. Tell them Enid sent you, tell them I vouch for you."

"I might just do that," Porter said. He finished off the Coke, stifled a belch with his fist, then slid off the stool.

"Thanks for the help."

"No worries," said Enid. "Don't lose heart, Pete. Bring your missus up here one day, get to meet them. They're a little odd, but they're good folk. And you never know what might happen."

She walked around the bar to the door, sliding the bolt free and opening it. Sunshine flooded the room, liquid and golden. Laughter, too, the sound of children playing nearby. Porter had to put a hand to his heart because of the sudden ache there, and he thought of Allie at home, thought of the same ache inside her, the same impossible dream.

Maybe not so impossible after all.

"Miracles are real," Enid said, gently ushering him out. "You'll see for yourself. Just believe."

He walked into the blinding light, into the shimmering heat of the car park, Enid's words chasing him all the way back to the car.

"Just believe."

CHAPTER TWENTY

KETT CLOSED THE DOOR OF PASTOR CAIRNS' INNER sanctum behind him, trying to make sense of everything he'd discovered. He could hear the old man weeping inside, although he wasn't sure if it was because his secrets had been exposed or because Kett was still holding the laptop with all his explicit chats.

He walked to the stairs, hearing Clare thumping around further down the corridor as he searched the other rooms. Cairns had claimed he'd left the cane right here, which means that anyone could have taken it. But why? What had brought them to the Manor's upper level in the first place?

Clare appeared, redder than ever in the stuffy heat of the landing. He rammed his hands in his pockets and jiggled his hips, trying to stretch his trousers. He looked like a madman trying to escape a straitjacket.

"Anything?" Kett asked, making him jump.

"Didn't see you there, Kett," he said, pulling his hands free. "Nothing. Except dust."

Kett waited for the Superintendent to catch up and they traipsed down the wide stairs together.

"You think he did it?" Clare asked when they reached the bottom. "Maybe our dead couple caught him in the act of self-worship and he went after them."

Kett spluttered out a breath. It was a possibility. Caitlyn or Liam could have ventured up here before dawn on Friday morning, looking for guidance but instead finding Cairns hard at it with Busty Bronwyn. How far would he have gone to protect his perversion?

But that didn't make sense because they died in their room. And Kett still couldn't see Cairns murdering two fit, healthy adults. Even if he'd managed to stab Liam as he slept, he still would have had to grab the cane and attack Caitlyn too. It was a big ask for such an infirm man.

"He's very weak," he said. "But it's more than that. He seemed ready to confess about the websites, the chat-rooms. Despite the tears, he seemed almost grateful. I can't see him murdering two people just because they found out about his obsession with tits and vegetables. And even then, what would he have done with the baby?"

They reached the door that led into the servant's quarters and Kett opened it, letting Clare through first. The first room they reached was Caitlyn and Liam's and he stared into it, trying to picture what had happened.

"If Caitlyn was killed with the cane, the killer would have had to walk past this room and up the stairs to get it. But they already had the knife, because it came from the kitchen they'd presumably just walked through. Why did they look for another weapon?"

"Unless one of the Browns went upstairs and took the cane first," Clare replied. "They brought it to their room, and it was sitting there ready for the killer to pick up and use."

"Maybe," said Kett, shaking his head. "But *why* would they take the cane?"

He didn't wait to see if Clare had an answer. He ducked into the room, the smell of blood punching him right in the back of the throat. The dead rabbit still lay in the crib, those dark eyes seeming to watch Kett over the ruin of its body. It was crawling with flies now, almost lost beneath them. They pushed themselves away from its bloated body and batted against Kett's face, his eyes, his lips. He thought of the baby that had lain there, the one that had been taken.

Little Adam.

If Porter was right and the killer hadn't driven away from Whytetail then there was every chance they were still here. But a crying baby would be audible for miles and nobody had heard a thing.

Dead, then?

Kett wouldn't let himself believe it.

"Where are you, Adam?"

He turned to the chest of drawers and the framed photograph that sat on it. Caitlyn and Liam lying in a hospital bed, her eyes full moons of panic and wonder, him wearing an idiot's grin. Adam lay between them, caked in blood, his mouth twisted open in a cry that felt almost physical.

"Did we speak with the hospital?" he asked Clare.

"I thought Savage was going to do it but she's tossed off somewhere."

"I asked her to take the kids home, sorry."

"You couldn't have called a taxi?"

Clare stomped off, muttering to himself. Kett pulled out his phone with his free hand, Googling the Norfolk and Norwich University Hospital's maternity department. The signal wasn't great and his battery was in the red so he followed the echo of Clare's brogues back through the kitchen and out into the courtyard. Mark, the man with the haystack hair, was standing by the door, one finger rooting around right at the back of his nose.

"Any chance of a cuppa?" Kett called to him.

"We don't have caffeine here," he replied, making no effort to remove the finger. "No tea, no coffee, no alcohol, no cigarettes."

"Well, that's just brilliant," Kett said with a little more sarcasm than he'd intended. "No tea."

"No tea?" said a voice on the phone. "Sounds like a disaster."

"It is," said Kett, walking across the cobbles. "Sorry. My name's DCI Kett."

He was surprised at how easily it still slipped off the tongue, even after all this time.

"Norfolk Constabulary. I was hoping to check some information."

"What do you need?"

"A young couple came in two weeks ago. She'd just given birth to a little boy, Adam Brown."

"Here?" asked the woman.

"No, it was a home birth. Or a community birth. I don't know what you'd call it."

"Oh, you mean the Whytetail baby?"

"Yeah," said Kett. "You remember it?"

"We've had a few of those. And I think there's another on the way soon. It's a religious community and they prefer to handle the births there. But they always let us know if a baby's coming so we have an ambulance on standby."

"You ever needed it?"

"No, there are a few midwives down there. They know what they're doing. And they often bring the mother and child to hospital to be checked. Seems a little daft to me, going through all that stress if you end up driving here anyway. But hey, what are you gonna do?"

"And they were okay? Caitlyn and Adam?"

"Right as rain," said the woman. "But I wasn't there. I think it was Mo."

He heard her talking to somebody else, a brief conversation.

"Argh, we've got a baby on the way. All hands on deck, I'm afraid."

"Can you ask Mo to call me, when she gets a chance?"

"She's right here, hang on."

A clunk, like she'd dropped the phone. Then another voice, older.

"You're police?" she asked.

"I am. DCI Kett. You're Mo?"

"Ramona, yeah."

"You helped with the Whytetail baby?"

"Nothing to do. Mother and child both healthy and happy. A lot of blood. I thought we might have to hook mum up to an IV, but she refused. Not unusual for religious folks. Plenty of toast and tea did the job and after a couple of days we sent them home. A little tearing, if that's not too much information. No stitches, though. Can't remember how much the kid weighed but he was healthy. Eight pounds something, maybe. I could check, but not now."

"I'll call back later," Kett said. "You think I could get Caitlyn's maternity records too?"

"For that, you'll need to head up here yourself," she said. "And you'll need to bring mum and dad with you. Gotta run."

Mo hung up and Kett slid the phone back into his pocket, grateful that he didn't have to explain why bringing mum and dad to the hospital would be impossible. He made his way out of the Manor grounds, texting Porter as he went.

Get tea!

He was walking beneath the brick archway back into the meadow when he heard the sound of shouting from up the hill. He upped his pace, out of breath by the time he'd reached the totem. Several members of the community were gathered around the steps of the wooden church, Paul Palmer standing at the top like a preacher and doing most of the talking. The big man's face was damp with sweat and he paced anxiously from side to side, like a caged bear. Facing off to him was the bald man, Tom Faulkner.

"Nothing," Palmer grunted. "Nothing else. Just a computer."

"Who cares?" said Faulkner, his accent more Yorkshire than ever. "None of your business anyway, Paul. Pastor's entitled to a bit of privacy."

"But if he's allowed a computer why aren't we?" said a woman. "A phone, the internet. Seems a little hypocritical if you ask me."

"Nobody's forcing you to stay here, Sandra," Faulkner said. "Pack your stuff, I can drive you to the village myself."

Sandra's mouth snapped shut and she stepped back into the arms of a tall young man who stood behind her, shaking her head.

"Everything okay?" said Kett when he reached the back of the group. The people parted for him and he saw that another party was approaching from the direction of the chalets. This one was led by Summer Cairns, and he saw his mother there as well. Neither of them looked happy.

"What did you see in there?" Palmer asked Kett, the sweat actually rolling off him now.

"That's not for me to say," Kett replied. "Nothing illegal, don't worry."

This, at least, seemed to placate the big man.

"See," said Faulkner. "Panties in a twist over nothing, as always."

"What's going on here?" asked Summer when she arrived. Her voice was as weak as the breeze, just a whisper. "Tom?"

Faulkner stood to attention at the sound of his name, running a handkerchief over the sheen of his scalp.

"Just keeping the peace, ma'am," he replied.

"And doing a poor job of it," Summer said. She came to a halt and studied the group with the stern expression of a boarding school governess. Her eyes landed on Kett and stayed there.

"I'm growing a little tired of the stress your visit is causing, Mr Kett," she said. "My husband asked you here to help us find a missing child. I didn't expect to see you interrogating our own people, and certainly not the leader of this community."

"All part of the j—"

"Carry on like this and I will ask you to leave," she said, riding over him. "And you can take your mother with you."

There was the anger again, burning bright inside him. Mary stood with her head hanging low, her eyes darting from Summer to the ground and back again. It reminded Kett of the way she'd been when his dad was alive, on those awful nights when he'd been drinking, and it hurt to see her this way—a physical pain right in the middle of his chest, worse even than the fragment of Keefe's bullet.

He took a step towards Summer but Faulkner moved to intercept him, positioning himself defensively in front of her. Two of the other men moved in too, flanking the big bald guy. Summer peered through the gap between them, her eyes sharp.

"Careful, Mr Kett," she said. "This is not your home."

He choked back the words he wanted to say, even though he could feel them right there on his tongue. People were moving slowly and quietly away from the group, as if they were afraid of drawing attention to themselves. His mum looked as if she wanted to go too but she stayed put by Summer's side. As if to make a point, the Pastor's wife threaded her sinewy arm through Mary's, leaning on her for support.

"We don't need you here," she said. "I didn't ask my husband to contact you. I didn't ask your mother. We are more than capable of finding our lost child."

"I don't doubt it," Kett said. "But the fact is we're dealing with two murders and a kidnapping. You send me away, the cavalry comes to take my place."

Summer didn't reply, and not once did she look away. It was Kett who blinked first, studying Faulkner and the other men before turning back to her.

"Do you mind if I ask you a quick question while we're here?" he said. "My colleagues told me that you brought the cane back to Cairns this morning. Where did you find it?"

"The cane?" she snapped back. "Over by the pigsty, when I was tending to the animals. He can't go five minutes without leaving something somewhere, those damned strokes. And he can barely walk without that thing so I don't even know how he manages to lose it so often."

Kett saw his mum glance at Summer again, a flicker of a frown.

"What kind of state was the cane in when you found it?" Kett asked.

"That's two questions," said Faulkner.

"It's okay," Summer said. "It was covered in pig dung, if that's what you're asking."

"No blood?"

"Why would there be blood?" she said, scowling. "Our pigs are perfectly healthy. I cleaned it for him and gave it back."

"Cleaned it with bleach," said Kett, and she nodded.

"Do you know anything else that can get rid of the smell of pig excrement?"

"Any idea how it got there? Cairns told me he left it at the top of the stairs in the Manor on Friday morning, early. When he came out of his room, it was gone."

"Well given what goes on in that room, I'm surprised he wasn't ramming it up his own arse," she shot back.

Kett flinched at the ferocity of the words, and so did his mum. Summer took a breath, and in the flexing of her jaw Kett understood that she'd known about the computer for a long time.

"He probably didn't even leave it there," she said, quieter now. "He doesn't remember things the way they actually happened. He probably won't even remember speaking to you just now."

"I don't think he's going to forget that conversation in a hurry," Kett said. "Look, Summer, if your husband doesn't remember things, if he has... I don't know what you call them, these breaks from reality, then is there a chance he might have hurt Caitlyn and Liam, maybe the baby too?"

He expected anger again, but she finally dropped her head, studying the grass beneath her feet.

"I don't think so," she said. "But the honest truth is, I don't know. He needs help. Serious help."

"Then we'll get it for him," Kett said.

He blew out a sigh, feeling the fabric of this community

tearing at the seams. Places like this were only as strong as their leader, and when Cairns was gone it would almost certainly fall apart. His mother knew it too because her face was a portrait of sheer misery, her eyes liquid.

"You mind if I take a look at the pigsty?" he said after a moment. "There might be something there that helps us find Adam."

Summer nodded. She tugged at his mum's elbow, like she was a mule pulling a cart, and together they started to walk.

"Take Tom, he'll show you where it is."

"I'd rather my mum did it, if it's okay with you," Kett said, and there was no question there.

Summer stopped, considered it, then nodded. She let go of Mary, one of the young men rushing over to take her arm. They hobbled away together, although Faulkner stayed behind, standing right behind Kett's mother. There was something of the gargoyle in his expression, and in the way he wouldn't take his eyes off Kett.

"Come on, Mum," Kett said, walking to her side and offering his arm. She didn't seem to want to take it, but after a second or two she did.

"Let me help," Faulkner said.

"We'll be fine," Kett replied.

He set off, surprised at how frail his mum felt, how much like a bird—as if she had grown hollow-boned. For a second he was convinced that it couldn't be the same woman, that somewhere between today and that last meeting outside the Cathedral in Norwich two decades ago she had gone, and something else had grown up in her image. Then her long dress brushed against his legs and he caught that same smell of vanilla that he remembered so well from being a child, and she was his mum again. It left him breathless and he squeezed her arm as hard as he dared so that she wouldn't blow away.

So that he wouldn't lose her again.

"I can't believe this is happening," she said. "I don't believe it."

Those words, too, seemed to break time, taking him back to those awful days before his dad's death, both of them powerless to stop the inevitable.

"It will be okay," he said, the words empty.

She didn't reply at first, she kept looking back to where Faulkner stood, watching them go. Only when they'd covered enough ground did she look up at him. There was something in her face, something urgent, and he was expecting it to be about him, or her, or dad.

"I don't believe it," she said again. "I don't believe *her*. She hates the pigs, she never goes to see the animals."

"Summer?" he asked, and she nodded.

"She's lying to you."

CHAPTER TWENTY-ONE

They walked in silence, weaving through the cluster of tombstone-like chalets. Mary didn't seem to know what to say and Kett didn't want to break this moment of contact between them. He clung to his mum and she clung back, both of them aware of the touch but neither wanting to draw attention to it. He hadn't walked with her like this for such a long time, arm in arm, and it wasn't until they broke back onto the meadowed hill and the sun struck his face that he remembered why.

The last time they'd walked like this was to go and watch his dad being buried.

The memory hit him like a sledgehammer, walking into Earlham Road Cemetery in the baking heat, holding each other up just as they were doing now. He'd been almost twenty back then, far taller than her, of course. But when he thought of that day he remembered looking *up* to his mum, he remembered the strength of her as they walked to the graveside to say goodbye to a man that neither of them had ever really known.

He wondered if she was thinking it too because she

heaved in a breath that seemed to rock her whole body, releasing it as a soft groan.

"I'm sorry I asked you here," she said. "I didn't know what else to do, and the Pastor was insistent that I send for you. I didn't want you to see me here, like this."

"Like what?" he asked.

"I thought this place would..." She faltered, struggling. "Reginald was always so good to me. He was always so kind. To everyone. But he's been so... so lost. What did you find in that room?"

"Nothing, Mum," he said, not wanting to upset her. "I think he was just lonely."

"That's no surprise. His wife is... She's..."

The words caught in her throat and she coughed hard.

"Yeah," said Kett. "She seems it. Do you think she had anything to do with the deaths?"

He glanced back as he spoke, and he wasn't surprised to see that they were being followed. Faulkner walked a respectable distance behind them, the sunlight gleaming off his head as he stumbled through the long grass.

"No," said Mary. "Oh gosh, no. She loved Caitlyn and she loved that baby. She can be cold. *Is* cold, often. But she dotes on the people in this community and she gives everything of herself to those children. Everything. She was a midwife for many years, she's so loving with them."

"But there's tension, right?" Kett said. "The men she hangs around with, Tom Faulkner and the one with the haystack for hair."

Mary smiled.

"Mark," she said. "He doesn't seem to be able to tame that hair for love or money."

"Yeah, Mark. They don't seem to like Cairns very much, or Palmer for that matter."

"Paul's harmless," she said. "A gentle giant with nothing but faith and devotion. He means well, and he'd do anything for Reg. The other men can be sullen, and Tom isn't a particularly nice man. They probably don't seem very friendly to you. But this place is sacred to them, and they are in danger of losing it if we can't find Adam. This tension isn't always here. Most of the time it's... it's like heaven, Robert. Your children loved it."

She broke into a smile, one that was almost a *grin,* and it seemed to make her twenty years younger.

"They're quite the characters, aren't they, your girls? Loopy as anything. You should have seen them in my home, singing about farting."

She snorted, gripping his arm even more tightly.

"Oh, I haven't laughed like that for so long. They're lovely girls. You should be proud of them."

"I am," he said, feeling that aching loss again, that so much time had passed. "They can be hard work. Alice especially, with her autism."

Mary flapped her free hand through the air to dismiss it.

"Your wife told me, but she'll grow out of it."

Kett bit back his response, even though it made his skin prickle.

"They're amazing," he said instead. "They've been through a lot this last year. Their mum too."

"She's a keeper," said Mary. "A beautiful woman, Robert, and kind. You're lucky."

"I am," he said, thinking about Billie and the girls, missing them as if it had been weeks since he'd last seen them, not hours. "I am very lucky. It's a miracle, really, that we're all here. That we're all okay."

"I said it to you before. This is a good place for miracles."

They walked through the grass, kicking through dandelion clocks and filling the air with fluff.

"They've missed you," he said after a moment. "They've missed having you, I mean. Their grandmother. It's good for them to know you."

The smile slid from Mary's face and he felt her contract, pulling away. He wasn't sure what he'd said, and before he had the chance to ask her he heard a booming voice call his name. He squinted up the hill to see Porter bouldering down it in his microscopic T-shirt, holding a carrier bag. About fifty yards behind him, shadowed by the enormous hedge, was a young man.

"Pete," said Kett with a nod of welcome. "How's it going?"

"Okay," the DI said, his eyes even redder and wetter than they'd been when he'd left. "But I didn't think they were going to let me back in."

He threw a thumb over his shoulder like a hitchhiker.

"Got this arsehole stuck to me like a rash."

"Yeah, we've got one too," Kett said, nodding up the hill to where Faulkner had come to a stop, still watching. "He's about as good at discreetly tailing a suspect as you were when we first made detective."

Porter laughed, sneezed violently, then frowned.

"Wait, what's that supposed to mean?"

"Nothing," Kett said. "You got tea?"

"I did," he said, fishing a box out of the carrier bag. Kett felt his heart sink.

"What the hell is that, Pete? Why would you buy decaffeinated tea? What's wrong with you?"

Porter frowned at the box.

"How do you know it's decaffeinated?"

"Decaf," Kett said, pointing at the enormous word on the box.

"I didn't know that's what it meant."

"What *else* could it mean?"

"I thought it was just regular tea from a café. *De. Caf.* Like, I'm going to get a cup of tea from *de caf.*"

Kett stared at him for a moment, open-mouthed.

"It's the pollen!" wailed Porter. "I can't think straight!"

"Right. Good to know. Anything new from the pub?"

"No, just the same things we've heard here," Porter said as he slid the box back into the bag. "Great place to make a baby. Something in the water, apparently."

"The Well of Our Lady," said Mary. "I showed your family earlier, and your female friend too."

"Female friend," said Porter with a wry smile. "Bet Savage'll love that. Enid at the pub told me Summer was the one who ran things around here."

"Yeah, I picked up on that too," said Kett.

"They charge for it. If you want to have a Whytetail baby, you have to pay."

"That true, Mum?"

"It's an honorarium," Mary said. "A tithe, to show that you're serious about adopting the rights and practices of our community."

"How much?"

"Whatever you can afford," she said. "But there is no price too high, I feel, for something like this."

Kett made sure Faulkner and the other man were out of earshot, speaking quietly.

"I'm more convinced than ever that the cane is our murder weapon. Summer says she found it by the pigs but Mum doesn't think she's telling the truth."

"She's never there," said Mary. "She hates the smell.

She spends her time on the other side of the river, mainly, the gardens and the old village proper. She doesn't like people crossing the water, not even us."

"Old village?" asked Kett.

"The original Whytetail was left to rot," she said. "There are dozens of houses in the woods over the river, all ruins."

"You think she found the cane somewhere down there?" Porter asked her.

"Found it, or *left* it after she'd used it on the Browns," Kett said.

"I... I don't know," Mary said. "I shouldn't be saying this, I'm sorry."

"Worth a try, though," said Kett.

"If they'll let us," Porter added, waving to the men who were watching. "It's starting to feel more like they're trying to keep us away."

"Yeah," said Kett. "It is."

He looked at his mum.

"You fancy providing a distraction?"

"What do you mean?" she asked.

"Like, it's a hot day and there's a lot going on. You're feeling faint. You could do with some help. There's three of us, two of them, they can't follow us all."

"No," she said. "I can't, it's..."

She met his eye and frowned, as if it was the first time she'd noticed who she was talking to. Her mouth opened and closed, the words not coming. Then her hand was there, cupping Kett's cheek, her thumb scratching his beard. He'd seen her look that way at the girls earlier, full of wonder, full of disbelief.

"You... you look so old, Robert," she said, her eyes filling.

"You look like your father, before he... before life gave up on him. Before he gave up on life. You look *so* much like him."

And he might have burst into tears right there if Porter hadn't been standing beside him. He placed his hand over hers.

"I must look old to you," she said. "It's been so long."

"You don't," he said. "You look fine, Mum."

She smiled, then to his surprise she winked.

"You know, I do feel a little faint. Don't let me fall."

She went limp and Kett caught her easily. There was nothing to her, just a bag of bones and old cloth, but she was still smiling when he lowered her to the grass.

"Thank you," he said quietly.

"Find that baby," she whispered back.

"Help!" Porter yelled. "We need help!"

Faulkner had broken into a shambling run but the other man was quicker, sprinting down the hill towards them.

"I've got this," Porter said.

Kett nodded, walking away at a pace and ignoring the shouts that followed him. He glanced back once to see the young man by his mum's side, his expression of panic almost funny. Porter was walking off the other way, his phone to his ear. Faulkner looked back and forth between them, stewing, then he bounded off after Porter.

It wasn't far to the treeline and a minute or so later Kett jogged into the shade, pausing to catch his breath. He could hear shouts from up the hill. It wouldn't be long before he had company. He wasn't even sure why he was being so clandestine about the whole thing, because it wasn't like anyone had explicitly banned him from crossing the river. The community had asked him here to investigate, and they wouldn't have done that if they truly had something to hide.

Except Summer Cairns *hadn't* invited him. Her husband had.

He followed a dusty track through the trees, the pollen from the cow parsley almost thick enough to taste. Dandelion seeds explored the shifting shafts of sunshine and the river gurgled contentedly. It was so much like something out of a dream, he thought again, and he felt tired enough to lie down and let it consume him.

The river saw him first, reflected sun like a searchlight as he left the woods. He had to throw his hands up against it because it was so bright, and in doing so he almost walked right into a shallow lake that sat beside the river. He reeled, his head full of light, and for a second he thought he saw a woman beneath the rippling surface—a girl, really, there for a heartbeat and then gone.

He blinked, searching the wide, flat expanse of water. There *were* things there, he saw, the gnarled trunks of long-drowned trees and happy clusters of tadpoles sunning themselves in the shallows. Rocks, too, patterned like faces. Enormous banks of reeds separated the lake from the river it had once, presumably, been a part of, and a weeping willow watched over it all, casting shadow puppets on the water.

What had his mum called it? The Well of Our Lady? It wasn't a well, that was for sure. It wasn't a spring, either, like the legend said. A lake, if you were feeling generous, a pond if you weren't. But if this was where the magic of Whytetail rested it was clear to see why people believed it. It was almost supernaturally beautiful, and the vision of the woman shaped from water and light still flashed across his retinas every time he blinked.

Pull yourself together, Robbie.

He skirted around the edge of the lake, pushing through the rushes and seeing the river. It was wide and flat, the water moving gently. It was hard to see over the high bank on the far side so he unlaced his boots and slipped them off, stuffing his socks inside and rolling up the legs of his jeans. The water was cool but not cold, the riverbed made from soft sand and flat, slippery rocks. Halfway across, the water was up to his knees, wetting the cuffs of his trousers, but it shallowed out again almost immediately and he scrambled up the steep slope, using the bulrushes to help him.

Ahead was an almost perfect mirror image of the other side of the river, except here there was no lake, just a garden of impossibly bright flowers. Fifteen rectangular beds had been dug in a rough semicircle, and in most grew rosebushes of differing sizes and colours. It was a work in progress because somebody had started digging another two beds. The closer he got, the more he understood that these weren't just flowerbeds. Little copper plaques had been laid into the grass beside each one, some new and others green with verdigris and lichen.

He walked to the nearest, seeing the words *Cressida King, Beloved Matron*. The others bore names and dates too and it took him a moment to find the earliest resident of this bizarre graveyard.

"*Gretchen Abigail Bird*," Kett read.

He made his way back to the two new graves, seeing a spade propped up inside the deeper of the two. Were these for Caitlyn and Liam, he wondered. And he was relieved he didn't see a third grave here, much smaller than the others.

There was no way of telling who they were for and he didn't want to hang around to ask whoever was shouting for him on the other side of the river. His feet had dried a little so he put his socks and boots back on and set off up the hill. The ground here was rougher and rockier, far fewer wild-flowers in the grass. Grasshoppers protested, hundreds of them leaping for safety as he traipsed and slipped into the front line of trees.

They seemed sicker here, the limbs crooked and more leaves on the ground than in the branches. The smell of this place wasn't blossom, it was rot, and his feet ground deep prints into the wet, pungent soil. After a few minutes it began to flatten out, and after a few more he arrived at a line of buildings standing on the top of the hill. They were short and long, made from the same dark stone and white render as the Manor and topped with black tiles, most of which had opened up to form gaping mouths in the roofs. Ivy clung to them with hidden claws, bringing them down like a lion with a gazelle—only over centuries instead of seconds.

He paused, listening for movement, voices. The trees whispered as they watched him but there was no other sound. Even the birds on this side of the river were muted. The shouts from behind him had stopped, too. Maybe they'd given up.

Was this where Summer had found the cane? There was no way of knowing. Kett made a break for it, running across the patch of soft grass that led to the nearest building. There were no windows on this side so he peeked around the corner to find a village there. Five or six stone houses led down the slope, more clustered at the bottom. A road had joined the houses once but the gravel was almost lost beneath an ocean of brambles and cow parsley.

Still, there was a car parked at the bottom. An old school green Defender with the driver's door open.

Kett paused again, his head cocked, his breath locked in his lungs.

And he heard it, a mobile phone ringing from inside one of the houses to his right. It grew louder and a man appeared in the doorway. He was dressed in jeans and a white shirt, and as he spoke he looked up the hill to the trees, his eyes passing over the place where Kett was hiding. He said something that Kett didn't catch, nodded, then slid the phone into his pocket.

When he spoke again, his words were all too clear.

"You out here, Mr Kett?"

And his intentions were pretty obvious, too, because the next thing he did was reach back into the dark house and pull out a crossbow.

CHAPTER TWENTY-TWO

SAVAGE WAS LOST.

It was easily done out here because the roads were laid out like an urban planner had dropped a pan of spaghetti onto the map and traced over the mess. What made it worse was that Kett hadn't updated his TomTom in what must have been decades, so every time she thought she was driving the Volvo the right way she found herself looping back onto the main road or rattling halfway up a farmer's track that ended in a cattle grid and a five-bar gate—all while the robot voice yelled at her to turn around.

"You bloody turn around," Savage said. "And jump out the bloody window while you're at it."

It didn't reply, and when she pulled over by the side of the road to check her phone she saw that she still didn't have a signal. She kept going, ignoring the sign for Whytetail that she'd followed ten minutes ago which had led her into the new village. The roads weaved left and right, narrowing so much that finger-like branches dragged along both sides of the car. The Volvo was a nightmare to drive, like trying to pilot a wardrobe on wheels, and twice she thumped into the verge as she took a corner too fast. She didn't see a single other car on the entire journey until she plunged into the shade of some overhanging trees and, in the sudden dark, almost hit a Rover parked halfway across the road.

"Come on!" she shouted, leaning on the horn.

A hand emerged from the Rover's window, waving her past, but she wasn't sure there was enough room. She blared the horn again and tried anyway, glaring at the driver as their wing mirrors clipped. She had stepped on the accelerator and driven another twenty yards before she realised that she knew him.

She reversed the Volvo so fast that she almost didn't hit the brakes in time. Then she was out, walking to the boat-like Rover. The man inside squeaked when he saw her, ducking into the passenger footwell. But it was Norman Balls, clear as day. How could she forget him, when he'd almost knocked her out on their last case fleeing the house of a murder victim?

The odd little internet conspiracy theorist, owner of the Balls Knows It Alls website, made no attempt to sit back up.

"I can see you there, Balls," she said, leaning through the window.

Balls rose slowly, pushing his glasses back onto his face. He was wearing white shorts and a cream polo shirt that was way too tight for his bulbous frame, and there seemed to be more sweat on him than was humanly possible, like a melting candle. He cleared his throat, regaining some composure.

"DC Savage," he said. "I didn't see you there. I was looking for something on the floor."

"Course you were," she said, studying his outfit. "Your tennis racquet, maybe? What are you doing here, Norman?"

"Just out for a drive."

"Near Whytetail. Funny coincidence, that."

"So you *are* in Whytetail," he said, grinning. "I knew it."

Savage mentally kicked herself.

"This is an active case, Balls. You can't be here."

"Ah!" He lifted a finger like a lawyer in court. "Only it's not, is it? Because there's nothing official. You're down here for something else, you and Kett and the rest of them. And I want to know what it is."

"How do you know that?"

"I have my sources," he said, tapping his nose. "And you're wearing gym clothes. Not exactly a brass approved detective suit, is it?"

"It still doesn't explain why you're here."

"Because somebody needs to keep the people informed!" he said. "Somebody needs to hold the authorities to account. Balls Knows It Alls, my website, is the font of all truths in a sea of ignorance."

"Go home, Balls," Savage said. "Or I'll call somebody to come and pick you up."

He swallowed, like he was wondering whether to call her bluff.

"You're lost, aren't you?" he said. "You're looking for the church, the commune. I can do one better."

He wiped a hand over his face, flicking beads of sweat onto the dashboard.

"I can show you the old village."

"Already seen it," she said.

"Not this one you haven't. The road's not there anymore. It was dug up when the village moved, the whole thing, substrate and everything. They planted blackthorn to hide it, and dumb cane to lock the evil inside. Nobody knows it's there, now, because the only way to get to it is through the commune and over the river."

Savage frowned and Balls beamed.

"Unless you're me, of course."

"This isn't some legend, Balls. This is a serious case, and I can't have you down here."

"Missing baby, right?" he said, and Savage shook her head.

"*How?*"

He answered by waving her back so that he could open his door. He was out before she could stop him, jiggling with excitement.

"You know the legends? Whytetail? The Cliffords and their baby?"

"Balls," she said, but he was off, walking into the trees that barred the side of the road. He waved her on.

"They couldn't conceive so they prayed to the heavens for help."

"Balls, get back here."

He kept moving, vanishing into the woods. Savage swore beneath her breath and went after him, clutching her whistle to her chest as she leaped over the ditch, and grabbing the rough bark of a tree to steady herself. Balls was still talking, his words almost lost beneath the sound of him stumbling through the thick undergrowth.

"But God didn't answer their prayers," he said. "He turned a deaf ear, no surprise there. And what did they do? They looked for help elsewhere."

Savage ducked under a branch, her hair getting tangled. She pulled herself free, chasing Balls deeper into the trees. The woods had closed up around her with frightening speed and she couldn't see the road or the cars from here. Balls was a spectre of white and cream bobbing up and down behind a bush.

"They asked the devil for help," he said, his words

floating back. "And it was the devil who gave them a child. Ah-ha!"

Savage rounded the same bush to see Balls right in front of her. He gestured with a flourish.

"Welcome to Whytetail."

Behind him was a scene that might have come from a horror movie, a street of forgotten houses lost to the wild. Stone cottages stood like gravestones, stained green by algae and lichen. Roof beams sat exposed, skeletal ribcages wrapped tight in ivy and bramble. The deeper Savage looked the more of the little buildings she saw, stretching up a slope. The forest had claimed them as its own, so much so that they were almost invisible.

"How did you know about this?" she said.

"Balls Knows It Alls," he replied, stepping tentatively over a patch of nettles. His stubby legs were cut to pieces but he didn't seem to mind. "Shortly after the Cliffords had their devil child, everything went wrong. The mother went down with Tuberculosis, died when her child was a few weeks old. The father met the same fate about a year later. People refused to work the land, they moved away, claiming that they saw the devil roaming the estate at night, checking on his baby. After a few years, the entire village and the estate were left to ruin."

"But those are just stories," Savage said, following him.

"Every story holds an element of truth. A seed. Even these ones. Our job is to work out what really happened. Our job is to peel away the mythology and solve the mystery."

Her granddad had always said the same thing, but it was still annoying hearing it come out of Balls' mouth.

"You do realise you're not actually a copper?" she said.

Balls pouted but carried on walking. The cottages

watched them go with glassless windows that looked like eye sockets. There were things moving in there, Savage saw, pigeons exploding out as they passed, clapping their way into the trees overhead. And crows, too, who stood firm, refusing to be bullied. The darkness was their domain, and it *was* dark here. The entire village was hidden beneath the heavy canopy, as if she'd stumbled upon a cave in the woods, or a cathedral. There were rabbits here, hundreds of them. When they moved she caught glimpses of their cotton-white tails, like sunlight on the tips of the waves.

Balls led her slowly up the hill, struggling in a monstrous carpet of vegetation that seemed designed to slow them down.

"So what do *you* think happened to the Cliffords?" Savage said.

"I'm glad you asked," Balls answered, swatting at a fly. "They were one of the richest families in the county, in a time when money could buy you anything. *Anything.*"

They were closing in on the top of the hill now. Savage thought she could hear the sound of the river and she wondered how close they were to the spot where Mary Kett had taken them a little while ago, the Well of Our Lady. Balls was oblivious.

"Like most rich folk, I'm not sure they so much did a deal with the devil as they *were* the devil."

"Shut up," Savage said. Balls actually gasped.

"I don't think you have any right to talk to me like that, DC Savage. I—"

"No," she said. "Shut up and listen."

She stopped walking, angling her head into the silence of the woods.

"I can't hear anything."

"Because you're still talking," she replied. "Shut it."

He did, although his wheezing breaths were just as loud. It came again, the sound of a voice raised in anger. It was coming from her left, past the nearest row of ruined houses.

"Wait here," Savage said, moving quietly in the direction of the sound.

"Like hell I will," Balls replied, matching her step for step and jutting his elbows out so that she couldn't overtake him. "This is my case."

She gave up, reaching the nearest cottage and peering into its gutted interior. Through the window on the other side she saw a car, an old Defender. A man stood next to it in a white polo shirt, and she had to shuffle along a little more before she realised it was Kett. He looked worried.

"That's—"

She slapped a hand over Balls' sweaty face to silence him.

"Just be quiet," she said, and she felt him nod.

She moved along the back of the cottage then down the side, aware of every twig that cracked beneath her feet. Somebody was still talking but it definitely wasn't Kett. Whoever it was, they were hidden from her behind the Land Rover. She couldn't make out a single word of what they were saying.

She jogged to the low wall at the end of what had once been the front garden, ducking down for a moment and motioning for Balls to stay where he was. He was already on the move, everything wobbling as he ran red-faced down the path. She half expected him to try a combat roll but he dropped onto his haunches beside her, sweat rolling off him and hitting the ground like rain.

"I wouldn't do that if I were you," Kett said, talking to the man.

Savage peeked over the wall. Kett still looked miserable but now his hands were held out by his sides, palms up—never a good sign.

She jabbed a finger at Balls' face, giving him the sternest look she could muster, the message clear.

Stay. Here.

Then she climbed over the wall and moved quietly towards the Defender. The windows were tinted but she could see the outline of the other man. He was waving something big as he spoke.

"Can't just have you pissing around, though, can we?"

His voice was rough, definitely local.

Savage reached the car, resting her fingertips on the metal to ground herself. She eased herself up as carefully as she could, seeing Kett over the high bonnet. She wasn't sure if he'd noticed her or not, his eyes locked on whatever the man was holding.

She ducked again, making her way around the back of the car in slow, sloth-like movements.

"Now I don't know what to do," the other man said.

"Just stay calm," Kett replied. "Don't do anything stupid."

Savage peeked around the filthy rear bumper, finally laying eyes on the other man—the back of him, at least. He was dressed in black jeans and a white shirt, his greying hair putting him somewhere in his fifties.

But it was the crossbow that made her heart suddenly shift gears.

It was a new model, sleek and black with a scope that belonged on a sniper rifle. It was pointing towards Kett, although she couldn't see from here if it was loaded. The man was agitated, his old boots scuffing the soil, his head twitching.

Savage didn't really have a choice.

As slowly as she dared, she stood. Kett glanced at her but he didn't give her away. He nodded softly, a bead of sweat rolling from his brow into his eye, making him wink.

She lifted her arms and took a step, ready to take the man down.

Only for Balls to start screaming.

The little man came bounding out from behind the garden wall, gargling a wet war cry as he went. He obviously hadn't noticed the crossbow, though, because as soon as he cleared the front of the Defender and saw the other man his roar became a squeak, and then a squeal. He turned in an impossibly tight circle and started to run the other way, making it all of three feet before tripping and falling. He landed on his face, his legs jerking up almost vertically before crunching down again.

The man swung his crossbow towards Balls and Savage didn't hesitate, grabbing the weapon and planting her foot in the back of his leg. He dropped to one knee, crying out in pain. His hand tightened and the crossbow fired but Savage was holding it upright and the bolt snapped into the branches overhead. Kett moved in, grabbing the weapon and hurling it into the bushes before pushing the man all the way down. Savage pinned him with a knee, bending his arm back until he cried out into the dry soil.

"Where on earth did you come from?" Kett said. "And was that...?"

"Balls," Savage said, nodding. "You okay, Norman?"

He pinged back into sight over the bonnet of the Land Rover, his face streaked with sweat and dirt.

"I would have had him," he said. "If you hadn't barged in. I would have had him."

"Sure you would," Savage said. "Who is he?"

The man answered with another shout into the dirt.

"Wouldn't say," Kett said. "But he's part of the commune and he's got a phone. Knew I was coming."

"Was he going to shoot you?"

"Let's find out," Kett said.

Savage took her knee from the man's back and he lifted his face from the ground, puffing big breaths to try to get the dust out of his nose. He wasn't as old as he'd looked from behind, mid-forties maybe, his cheeks mottled with veins and his nose swollen from years of drinking. Savage was about to ask him a question when Balls crouched beside her.

"What's your name?" he said.

"Norman, we've got this," said Savage.

"What are you doing here?" he persisted.

"Balls," Kett growled. "Bugger off."

Balls pouted again, then stood up and dusted down his tennis shirt.

"I shall wait for you over yonder," he said.

"Want to tell me your name?" Savage asked the man. "And what you're doing out here with a crossbow?"

"Nothing," he said. "Got every right to be here. It's you two who are trespassing."

"Name," Kett said.

"Glenn. And I were 'unting rabbits. Nothing illegal about that. Saw you here and thought you were poaching."

"I don't think so," Kett said. "I heard you on the phone. You knew I was coming. Where were you yesterday morning, Glenn? Friday, between two and eight? Did you have anything to do with the deaths of Caitlyn and Liam Brown?"

The man shook his head, squirming in the dirt.

"Just 'unting rabbits, is all."

"He's lying," said Balls, reappearing. He was holding a

bag in one hand, and he reached in with the other and pulled out a sleek black shaft tipped with an evil looking broadhead bolt.

"Bit much for a rabbit, isn't it?" Kett said.

"Was just 'unting," the man answered.

"Yeah, I believe you," said Kett. "Not about the rabbits, though."

He stared into the woods, into the dark spaces between the trees.

"I think you were hunting something else."

CHAPTER TWENTY-THREE

IT DIDN'T TAKE LONG FOR THE CAVALRY TO ARRIVE.

Kett saw Faulkner first, the big bald arsehole crashing through the bushes at the top of the hill five minutes or so after Savage had taken down the man with the crossbow. It took him a moment to see them all in the shadow of the Defender, and when he did, his face creased with rage.

"Oi!" he yelled, breaking into a run. "What the hell do you think you're doing? Get off him."

More men followed, first the guy that had been tailing Porter, then haystack hair, Mark. Their trousers were wet from where they'd waded through the river. Kett heard more shouts and was surprised to see another couple of men approach from deeper in the woods. Paul Palmer was the last to appear, lumbering down the hill like a dinosaur, every step slipping and sliding. They converged on the Land Rover at the same time, all talking at once. But Faulkner's voice was the loudest.

"I said get off him."

Kett wasn't exactly sitting on Glenn but he backed off anyway. Savage stood up, moving to Kett's side. Balls was hovering by the front of the Defender, looking a lot like he'd wished he'd stayed at home.

"Glenn?" said Faulkner, squatting beside the man. "What they do to you?"

"Ambushed me," Glenn said, letting Faulkner help him up.

"It was hardly an ambush," said Savage. "He was threatening us."

"Hunting rabbits," Glenn said, giving Savage a filthy look.

"Which is illegal, if you're hunting with a crossbow," Savage went on. Kett reached out and touched her arm, gently. Whatever else she'd been about to say became a frustrated breath.

"We might have had crossed wires," Kett said. "Glenn was on the phone when I came down the hill. I think I startled him. My friend arrived before we could sort the situation out."

"*Friends*," said Balls from behind Savage's shoulder. Everyone looked at him. "I'm his friend too."

"I don't think you're being honest," Palmer said. "Glenn doesn't have a phone. None of us do. The Pastor doesn't allow them."

"Stay out of it, Paul," Faulkner said, making Palmer shrink back. "I don't know what the hell is going on here but this side of the river is off limits."

"Says who?" Kett asked. Faulkner stepped forward, as broad as a bouncer.

"Says me."

"Last I heard, the baby is still missing," said Kett. There was something about the bald man that made him angry, something he couldn't quite put his finger on—other than that he had the air of a short-tempered security guard or prison officer. "And *you* are the ones who asked us to find him."

Faulkner scratched his cheek, looking like a lizard with his bald head and his wattle and his dark eyes.

"We've got this side of the river covered," he said after a moment. He nodded at the men who had emerged from the woods. "We've been searching the old village for two days, near enough, and there's no sign of the baby, or the man who took him. You hear that?"

Kett listened, hearing nothing and realising that was his point.

"You hear a baby crying?" Faulkner went on. "Me neither. This is our land. Private land."

"Sacred land," said Palmer, earning a withering look from the other man.

"So piss off back over the river. There's nothing here. Maybe piss right off out of Whytetail while you're at it."

Kett looked between the men. Other than Palmer, whose entire body rocked with uncertainty and doubt, they were all tense. Mark had one hand behind his back, resting on something in his waistband. One of the guys who'd stepped out of the woods had a satchel over his shoulder and his fingers clasped at it reflexively. There was an air of violence here, the feeling of something about to boil over.

Kett held up his hands.

"My mistake," he said. "I didn't understand the boundaries. We'll go."

Savage shot him a look but Faulkner stood down, visibly relieved.

"Summer's waiting for you by the river," he said.

"Then we'd better get to it."

He walked past Faulkner, Savage by his side.

"Wait for me," Balls squeaked, running after them. Kett smiled at Palmer as he reached him.

"You mind showing us the way? I'm not sure I'll remember it."

Palmer nodded. Kett followed him in silence until he was far enough away for his voice not to carry.

"You and Faulkner don't get on, do you?"

Palmer snorted a laugh.

"Tom? He's an arsehole. A bully. Thinks he runs the place but he's only the second in charge."

"I thought you were the second in charge."

"I am," Palmer replied, flustered. "I mean, I'm Cairns' right-hand man for sure. Tom works for Summer, not Reg."

"But Cairns doesn't run this place, does he?"

They were at the top of the hill now, the sound of the river greeting them on the other side. The trees thinned out down the slope, sunlight piercing through in glorious golden shafts. The sun was lower than he would have expected it to be, as if they'd lost hours in the woods, but even so, Kett couldn't remember a time he'd been happier to see it.

"He does," Palmer said, frowning. "He's the one we all turn to for advice. He's the one who keeps our faith alive. But..." He huffed at the sky like a child, biting his broken lips. "But Mrs Cairns is the bossy one. She's always telling him what to do. She's not kind to me. And the men she hangs around with, Tom Faulkner and the others, they're not kind either."

"How many men does she hang around with?" asked Savage.

"There are seven of 'em," said Palmer, counting them on his fat fingers. "Including Tom."

"Paul," said Kett, making sure they were definitely alone. "Do you think Summer might have hurt Caitlyn and

Liam? Do you think she might have taken Adam? Or asked somebody to do it for her?"

"No," was his immediate response. "No, Summer wouldn't hurt anyone."

He looked over his shoulder, not at Kett but down the hill.

"But Tom, he's different. He's mean. *He* could have hurt them."

"Why didn't you mention this before?" asked Savage.

The answer was clear in the way Palmer flinched, in the way he glanced down the hill again with wide, wet eyes. For all his size, he startled as easily as a deer.

"What are they doing down there?" Kett asked. Palmer shrugged.

"Just looking for rabbits," he said. "And looking for the baby, I guess."

They broke out of the trees into the rose garden, enveloped by the smell of them. Kett heard Savage gasp as they walked through the beds.

"They *are* graves," she said. "I thought that when I saw them."

"Not graves," Palmer said. "At least not the newer ones. Cremated, their ashes used to feed the roses. It keeps them with us. You can cross easier downstream. This way."

He led them along the river to a spot where the rushes thinned. Somebody had laid flagstones in the calm water and Palmer stepped purposefully across them, his tongue jutting out from his pursed lips.

"Water's shallow enough here," he said from the far side. "But it gets deeper further down where it joins the Little Ouse. Treacherous."

Kett paused to take off his boots and his socks again, following Savage and Balls after they'd done the same. He tried to look further along the river but the reeds grew even thicker downstream, towering over the sandy banks.

When they cleared the rushes on the other side Kett saw Summer Cairns waiting for them by the little pond, in the shadow of the weeping willow. Clare was with her.

"Kett," barked the Super, his voice startling the birds into silence. "Tossing hell, what happened to you?"

Kett didn't know what he was talking about until he looked down and saw that his clothes were almost completely green, covered with leaves and burrs.

"You look like a tossing yeti. And who... *Balls*?"

Norman Balls studied the Superintendent, tight trousers and all.

"Balls," said Balls, aghast.

"What?" said Clare.

"*What?*"

"I think we made it very clear," Summer said, the tremble in her voice less to do with her age than her anger. "We do not like visitors to cross the river."

"Why?" Kett replied. "You think whoever took the baby wouldn't cross over? There's a whole village over there they could be hiding in."

"With a screaming child?" said Clare. "Would never happen. We'd hear them for miles."

"I think..." said Summer, chewing on something then nodding decisively. "I think that perhaps we no longer need your assistance. You've done nothing but upset the balance here. Nothing but ruin my poor husband. If I'd known the harm you were about to cause I never would have listened to Reginald."

"Look," Kett started, but Clare silenced him with a raised hand.

"We've done what we can," the Super said. He checked

his watch and Kett did the same, surprised at how late it was. "We've searched the community, we've spoken to your people, we've studied the evidence, and we're no closer to finding our baby."

Summer gave Clare a look of gratitude, but it didn't last.

"We're running out of time and chasing rainbows. Note or no note, threat or no threat, I'm making this one official."

"What?" Summer said. "No, that's not what I meant. We can't have the police here if it puts Adam's life in danger."

"She's right," Kett said.

"It's out of my hands," Clare replied. "And it's what we should have done in the first place. Porter's SIO, wherever he is. Savage, back him up."

"And me, sir?" asked Kett.

Clare shrugged.

"You're not police, Kett. This is your mother's home. I can't tell you to leave or to stay."

"I'll stay," said Balls. "I can provide—"

"Balls off!" Clare yelled.

The Superintendent turned his back on them, walking up the hill towards the trees. Kett jogged after him.

"Sir, this is a mistake. I think the child is here, some-where. I don't know for sure, but I think they know who's taken him. A bunch of uniformed police is the last thing we need, it will drive the kidnapper deeper into hiding, or force his hand."

"You've got proof?" Clare asked.

"Just an instinct. The jigsaw pieces are there but they're not coming together yet."

"I'm going to need a little more than jigsaw pieces," Clare said. He reached the treeline and stopped, panting from the effort. He tugged at his belt, grunting in pain. "I'm leaving. If I don't get these trousers off in the next few minutes then I'm going to end up accidentally castrating myself. But it will take me some time to organise a Task Force."

He checked his watch again.

"Which gives you until the end of the day to find the child."

CHAPTER TWENTY-FOUR

THE END OF THE DAY.

It wasn't far off. The sun was falling fast but the earth was refusing to let go of the heat, holding it in as if the community was a tin can over a hot stove. Kett watched Clare vanish into the trees, and when he turned to head back down to the river he saw Summer and her entourage approaching.

The Pastor's wife looked exhausted, so pale that she might have been transparent—a ghost, with the Well of Our Lady behind her. It reminded Kett of the vision he'd seen in the water before he'd crossed the river, the spectral girl, and for a moment he wondered if this place truly was haunted.

Or cursed.

"What happens now?" Summer asked when she was close enough. She was holding onto Faulkner's arm, the bald man glaring at Kett like he thought *he* might be responsible for taking the child.

"In a few hours this place will be swarming," Kett said. "A full Task Force, in uniform."

"But the letter," she said. "He will kill the child."

"We're getting nowhere, Mrs Cairns. And you haven't exactly been forthcoming. Somebody here is hiding something. I think *you're* hiding something. If you want to find this baby, you have to be honest with me."

She opened her mouth but Faulkner tightened his grip on her, making her wince.

"Shall we speak alone?" Kett asked her, and she shook her head.

"I don't wish to speak with you at all. It was my husband's idea to bring you here, and your mother's. My job is to keep this community safe from further harm. I shall await the Task Force and we shall pray that my people find Adam before they arrive."

"Let me—"

"*My* people, Mr Kett," she said. "We will handle this, like we always have and like we always *should* have. I would appreciate it if you left us. I have no power over the police, but *you* are no longer welcome here."

It seemed futile to argue, so Kett let them pass. The only one to look back was Faulkner, his face full of fury.

"What was all that about?" asked Savage as she climbed the hill, Balls trotting to keep up with her.

"She wants me out," Kett said. "Because we're getting too close to the truth."

"Whatever the truth is," Savage said.

"The truth is always stranger than fiction," said Balls, sagely. "If you like, I can start making a list of—"

"We'll be fine, Norman," Kett said. "You should go home."

Balls jutted his bottom lip out, planting his hands on his sizable hips.

"I'll call you if I need you," said Kett.

"Promise?"

"Hand on my heart. But you can't be here. It's too dangerous."

"Danger is my middle name," he protested.

"Danger Balls?" said Kett, raising an eyebrow.

"Well, no, not my actual..." He spluttered out a breath. "Okay. I shall return to my chariot and await your call."

He waddled into the woods, stopping after a few seconds to stare back down the hill. The lake shimmered in the dying light, the swaying bulrushes whispering.

"Before I go, do you know why it's called the Well of Our Lady?"

"A reference to the Virgin Mary," said Savage. "Right? Mother of Jesus. Like the totem pole up the hill."

"The woman who gave birth free of sin," Balls said, nodding. "Apt, isn't it? In a place like this, where babies spring from nowhere."

His words turned a key in Kett's head but the door didn't open. He reached for whatever it was he thought he'd seen, only for Balls to knock it away with a dramatic flourish.

"Farewell, fellow detectives!"

"You're not a detective," Savage shouted after him, but Balls was gone.

Kett turned to the lake, thinking of the ghost of the woman he'd seen there.

Our Lady.

He pulled at the threads of his thoughts but whatever was there remained hidden.

"Find Porter, will you?" he said. "We need to regroup. I'll meet you up the hill."

"Sure," Savage said, walking away. "I can't call him. No signal. I'll look for him on the way. I need to collect our stuff from the church anyway, if they'll let me."

"Good luck."

Kett waited a moment then set off, using the trees to haul himself up the steep slope.

Caitlyn and Liam. A regular couple who'd struggled to get pregnant. Neither of them religious and yet somehow they'd ended up here, in Whytetail. Home to the Well of Our Lady, the silver spring which Lord and Lady Clifford had dug over a century ago when they, too, couldn't conceive. *A holy place*, Pastor Cairns had called it. But faith couldn't give you a child, could it?

What, then?

He reached the path that led up through the meadow, gravel crunching beneath his boots. The birds sang their evening chorus, hundreds of them, as if they meant to drown out his thoughts, scream the truth into oblivion. They wanted to keep the secrets of Whytetail hidden too.

And what had happened to the baby? Was that why Caitlyn and Liam had been killed? Had somebody here been jealous of their child? Somebody who couldn't have one of their own? Reginald Cairns had claimed that nobody had ever failed to conceive a child here, but he could have been lying.

Or it could have been somebody from outside the village.

He pulled out his phone and called DS Alison Spalding. It took three attempts before she finally answered.

"What do you want, *former* DCI Kett?"

"Hey, Spalding. Can you do me a favour?"

"No," she said.

"See if you can get some information from fertility clinics in the region. Support groups. Somebody who's been trying to have a child for a while, and somebody who might have been desperate to steal one."

"Um, I'm pretty sure I said no."

"It'll be hard," he said. "It'll be confidential. But see what you can dig up."

"No."

"Thanks," he said, hanging up. He climbed the hill towards the wooden church, the sun nestling in the tops of the chalets and making their shadows stretch towards him like a giant's fingers. It was as if the community meant to pick him up and crush him. This place was getting beneath his skin and he didn't know why.

Or maybe he did. Somewhere out there a baby was screaming for his parents, and they were fast running out of time to save him.

If they weren't already too late, that was.

Two people stepped out from the darkness between the chalets and at first Kett thought it was Porter and Savage. He almost waved until he realised it wasn't them at all. It was Faulkner, and he was standing over Kett's mum just like he had been before, like a security guard. Mary's mouth was downturned, her eyes puffy, and it wasn't hard to see why.

There was a suitcase at her feet.

"What's going on?" Kett shouted, upping his pace. "Mum?"

She replied, but he was too far away to hear what she was saying. He broke into a jog, the pain worrying its way back into his chest.

"Mum?" he said again as he closed in.

"They want me to leave," she said, smudging her hand over her eyes. "They want me to go with you, Robert. I... I don't know what I did."

Faulkner put a hand on Mary's shoulder and Kett pointed a finger at him.

"Let go of her or I'll fucking end you," he said.

Faulkner was a big man but he must have seen the truth in Kett's threat because his hand dropped to his side. Mary staggered away from him, tripping on her own feet, and Kett caught her. Impossibly, she seemed to weigh less now than she had just an hour ago, as if she was wasting away, as if she was being devoured.

"You're better off well away from here, Mum," he said, picking up her suitcase with his free hand. "Come on."

They walked towards the towering hedge, people watching them go from the windows of their chalets.

"I don't know what I did," Mary said again.

"Nothing, Mum. They're using you to make sure I leave. You didn't do anything."

"But I don't have anywhere else to go."

Kett stopped walking, looking down at his mum. How had she got so small, when once she'd been as big as the world? When she wouldn't look at him he put his fingers beneath her chin, gently lifting her head until she met his eyes—the same way he did with his girls when they were sad, he realised.

"You *do* have somewhere to go," he said. "Always."

Mary sniffed, nodded. She took his hand and held it in both of hers, just for a second, then she let go. They walked the rest of the way in silence, pushing through the gap in the hedge into the graveyard of the old stone church. Kett was surprised to see a group of men there, haystack hair and a couple of others he didn't recognise. Further down towards the road stood Porter.

"Got turfed out," Porter said when Kett reached him. "Same as you."

"They can't do that," Kett said. "You're police."

"They're saying we need a warrant, and I wasn't about

to test them. I'm pretty sure they've got knives in their belts. You okay, Mrs Kett?"

Mary nodded, although she looked anything but okay.

"Savage is picking up some files from the church, she won't be long," said Kett.

"I don't like her being in there on her own," Porter replied, glaring at the hedge and the people who guarded it.

"She can handle herself. Where's the car?"

"On the road."

They walked past the church. The sun was on the other side of it now, turning the old stone to fire. The whole world felt like it was burning. The Whytetail men followed them through the cemetery, their faces full of promised violence. There was no mistaking what would happen if Kett tried to go back.

They reached the road, the Volvo angled so high on the bank that it looked like it might topple over.

"Nice parking, Pete," Kett said. "Go on, you're driving."

Kett opened the passenger door for his mum, helping her in. He threw her suitcase into the boot, waiting for Porter to close the driver's door and then climbing in the back. Porter turned the key and the car wheezed, the engine stuttering. It caught and Porter bumped them down onto the road, waiting there. From the growing dark, the men watched them go.

"We're really leaving," said Porter, disappointed. "What about the baby?"

"He's here, I'm sure of it," Kett said. "Either they know where he is and they don't want us to find him, or they know who did it and don't want us involved."

He stared out the window, the commune lost behind the hedge, behind the trees, doing its best to keep its secrets to itself.

"Porter, I need you to drive Mum to my place. Can you do that?"

"Sure," he said.

"Then come back."

"What are you doing?" the DI asked, glancing at Kett in the mirror. "You're not leaving?"

"No," said Kett. "I'm not going anywhere."

CHAPTER TWENTY-FIVE

THE COMMUNITY OF WHYTETAIL WAS GROWING MORE unfriendly by the second, and Savage's heart was thumping in the back of her throat as she approached the wooden church. She wondered if the residents had been ordered back into their chalets because the only people she saw—other than the man who tailed her twenty yards back—were the ones who stared at her through windows that were full of the sinking sun.

"Be quick now," shouted the man.

She hadn't seen this guy before, she would have recognised the ugly beard that hung all the way to his chest. But the same could be said for a few of the people who had crawled from the woodwork in the last hour or so. Like Faulkner and Palmer, this man was broad and tall. Not exactly athletic but farm fit, as her granddad would have said. She didn't doubt that he was stronger than he looked, which isn't something she would have worried about except he hadn't stopped glaring at her. She could feel the cold heat of it singeing the back of her neck. There was anger there, and every single muscle in her body had grown tense in anticipation.

She patted her pocket, wishing for Old Betsy, the baton she'd carried as a PC. Then she pulled the whistle free from her T-shirt and clasped it tight.

She passed the last line of chalets, crossing the path to the steps of the church. The circle of mown grass around the totem was deserted, the tables cleared away. The distant Manor stared at her from behind its shroud of trees, still in mourning.

"Hurry up," said the bearded man.

"I'm going," she replied, wondering how wise it was to be alone with him. She wasn't sure what had happened to the others but there was no sign of them.

She jogged up the church steps and opened the door, quickly realising that she wouldn't be alone at all. Reginald Cairns sat in the front row of pews, hunched over and trembling. She approached down the centre aisle, hearing the bearded man enter behind her, the clomp of his heavy boots on the floor. Glancing back, she saw him close the door and plant himself in front of it like a bouncer.

The folder with Caitlyn and Liam's passports was on the low stage at the front, although it hardly seemed worth the effort to collect it. She picked it up then turned to the old man who sat there. He didn't look well.

"Pastor Cairns," she said. "Are you okay?"

He blinked his way out of whatever trance he'd been in, finding her.

"No, child," he said. "My sins have caught up to me."

"Hey, we're all human. Don't punish yourself."

"Don't talk to him," the bearded man shouted from the back of the church.

"And come on," Savage said, ignoring the threat. "It's

not really a sin, is it, in the grand scheme of things? It's not a sin to be lonely."

He looked at her with such a profound expression of sadness that it threw her. He held out a trembling hand and she took it, his skin paper-dry and cool.

"Hey!" said the bearded man. "I said don't talk to him."

He was walking towards them, his footsteps so loud they made the floor sound hollow, like the skin of a drum.

"I didn't mean for it to end here, young lady," Cairns said, quietly. "I didn't mean for it to end like this. I genuinely wanted the best for people when I took on my role of Pastor. I wanted to help. I don't know how it got so out of hand. All this time I was looking up, looking for *Him*. But I think we looked down instead."

"Stop!" said the man, speeding up.

"I think you should look down too," Cairns said, urgently.

His grip on her tightened and his eyes began to roll back. He slumped into the pew and she had to grab both of his hands as he slid right off onto the floor. The quakes had grown more severe, foam bubbling from his mouth.

"Mr Cairns?" she said. "Help him!"

The other man faltered, unsure. Savage wrenched her phone from her pocket, still no signal. She hurled it onto the bench.

"An ambulance," she said to the bearded man. "*Now*."

He looked at her, wide-eyed, before turning and bolting for the door. Cairns was properly fitting now and Savage dropped to her knees beside him, searching her pockets for a pen to stop him from biting off his own tongue. Then the door of the church slammed shut and just like that, Cairns fell still.

"Don't judge me," he said. "Don't judge us."

He lifted a crooked finger and pointed to the door at the side of the stage.

"Please," he said.

Savage pushed herself up and ran for the door, her feet pounding out a hollow rhythm. It was open, and through it was a small corridor leading past a toilet into a kitchen. It was tiny, no bigger than the one in her own flat. What had Cairns been pointing to? Did he just want water?

She doubled back into the corridor, opening the toilet door. A small room with a sink and past that a solitary cubical that reeked of bleach. A couple of coats, a janitor's closet, some buckets. Nothing.

Out into the corridor again. The walls here were vertical hardwood logs, the same as the rest of the church. What was she missing? She ran her hands along them, pushing, pushing, pushing, then feeling the slightest of gives.

There was a door here.

She pushed again then shoved it with her shoulder, feeling a latch pop free. The door opened into darkness but there was enough light in the corridor to see the stairs. She reached for her phone, remembering she didn't have it, hesitating for all of a second before walking onto the top step.

I think you should look down too.

It creaked out a warning that could have been heard from the other side of the commune. She took another step, something rushing out of the darkness and landing on her face. The scream was halfway up her throat before she clamped her mouth around it, feeling a cord there, the tassel batting her forehead. She pulled it and the bulb in the ceiling blinked on.

The stairs led down to another door and she clattered her way towards it. It opened into a space that was dark and bitterly cold, a draught playing with her hair and planting unwelcome kisses on her skin. She shivered, her fingers fumbling down the wall, finding the switch.

The room was smaller than it had seemed in the dark, the walls and floor made of concrete. It was bare except for a large, bare wooden bed that sat against the far wall, a brass crucifix mounted above it. The only other thing here was a door to her left which seemed to chatter excitedly in its frame.

She was halfway to it when she heard the shouts. She hesitated, unsure what to do. But the door was close enough to run to and she did, grabbing the handle and ripping it open.

There was a tunnel, the walls dirty white—chalk, she thought—and the far end a gaping maw of pure darkness. A gust of wind grabbed her as if it meant to pull her in and she shut the door before it could.

More shouts, the sound of feet on the steps of the church. Savage retreated, switching the light off and closing the door before tripping her way up the steps. The church was filling up, the sound of shoes like thunder. She made it into the corridor, gently pushing the door until the hidden latch caught. She bolted into the kitchen, finding a glass on the drainer and filling it from the tap.

She was walking back into the corridor when the bearded guy burst through the door. Even though she'd been expecting it she still jumped, the water sloshing over her hand.

"What are you doing back here?" he said.

Another man appeared, Mark, just as angry. Savage saw his eyes drift to the hidden door then back to her.

"I was getting the Pastor some water," she said, her heart

drumming its frantic beat into every word. "Did you call an ambulance?"

"No need," said Mark, one hand in his unruly hair. "He'll be fine. We need you to leave."

She wasn't about to argue. She handed the glass to the first man, who placed it on the floor so he could take her arm. He wasn't gentle, yanking her through the door into the church. Cairns was back on his pew, his face so drawn it might have been about to slide right off his skull. He met her eye, asking something wordlessly, and she nodded. He nodded back and something seemed to lift from him.

"Come on," said Haystack, manhandling her down the side aisle. Beneath her feet, the floor groaned and creaked like it was trying to scream something at her, like it was trying to call her back to that hidden room.

A third man was waiting by the door holding the folder and her phone. He passed them to Savage as she walked by, the bearded man giving her a shove that almost sent her flying down the steps onto the grass. It was only luck that kept her standing, and she turned around and gave them a look she hoped would knock them onto their backsides.

They stared back, and there wasn't just anger in their expressions now, there wasn't just violence.

There seemed to be a streak of madness there too.

"Go," said Mark, pointing up the hill towards the hedge. "This is your last warning."

"Sure," Savage replied, doing everything she could to keep her cool, to show them she wasn't afraid. It was better to obey the command than fight it. This place was a powder keg.

She turned slowly, the adrenaline burn-off making her legs feel like lead weights.

What the hell is going on here? she thought as she went, thinking about the room, about the tunnel. *What are you hiding?*

"And don't come back," came another shout.

But that was an order she wasn't about to follow.

CHAPTER TWENTY-SIX

Kett was on the verge of leaving the car to go and find Savage when she finally pushed free of the hedge. She looked back over her shoulder, leaves caught in her hair and her face lined with panic, before turning and seeing the Volvo. She practically ran across the last half of the overgrown cemetery, past the men who stood there like sentries. Wrenching open the door, she clambered in next to Kett, perched on Evie's car seat, and blew out a long, juddering breath.

"You okay?" Porter asked from the front.

"Just get us out of here," she replied. "I honestly thought they were going to start coming after me with pitchforks."

She wasn't laughing, and neither was Kett. It was rare that he saw Savage this rattled.

"What happened?" he asked as Porter accelerated.

"Went to get our stuff and Cairns was there. He pointed me to a room beneath the church. The wooden church, that is. Hidden door and everything."

"Pastor Cairns showed you that?" said Mary, looking at them from the front seat.

"You've been down there?" Savage said, and Mary shook her head.

"It's a sacred space, the most sacred space. We're not allowed."

"Yeah, neither was I," said Savage. "Nobody saw me, and I get the feeling that if they had I wouldn't have got out so easily. There was another door there that led to a tunnel. I couldn't see where it went."

Mary frowned, uncertain.

"Might be one of the mines," said Porter.

"Seems weird to build a church over a mine," said Kett. "What else was down there."

"Just a bed," said Savage. "That was it."

A bed. Something crawled its way across Kett's skin, leaving a trail of goosebumps.

"I don't think it's anything bad," said Mary. "The church is a holy place. A safe space."

"Yeah, Mum," Kett said. "But different people interpret holy in different ways. You ask me, a bed in a secret underground dungeon doesn't seem like good news."

"It's hardly a dungeon, Robert," she said, although that frown was back, bigger than ever.

"Does it have anything to do with the couples?" Savage asked. "The ones who come to Whytetail to have a baby."

Mary turned to her window, drowning in worry, her hands making invisible shapes in front of her as Porter did his best to steer the big car around the tight, darkening bends.

"Those are miracles," she said eventually, although there was none of the conviction she'd held before. "Pastor Cairns is a good man. A man of God."

"It's not him I'm worried about," said Kett.

"Cairns seemed relieved that I'd found the room," Savage said. "He *wanted* me to find it."

"I get the feeling he's a man who wants to unburden himself of all his sins," said Kett. "Big and small."

The car turned a corner and plunged into the shade of some overhanging trees. Kett couldn't be sure but he thought they might be the same ones they'd passed that morning. It felt like a million years ago, as if Whytetail was a place where time moved differently. He wondered whether they'd get back to Norwich and find that years had passed, that the rest of the world had aged beyond recognition, and he had to shake the notion from his head.

"What now?" said Porter, rubbing his bloodshot eyes. "We need to get the Task Force here ASAP, right? There's definitely some weird shit going on there."

"No," said Kett. "If Clare wanted a Task Force here now, it would be here now. He's giving us more time."

"Why would he say it, then?" asked Porter.

"To gauge their reaction. He was baiting them. And it worked. They're closing ranks, pushing us out. And I think he's worried that the initial threat still stands. So am I. Whoever took that child, I think he's close and I get the feeling he'd hurt it to keep himself safe."

But that didn't feel right, did it? The piece of the puzzle looked okay, but it wasn't fitting with everything else he'd learned. He reached for it, searching, almost seeing what he wanted to see before Porter scuffed the curb and chased the thoughts right out of his skull.

"I think the community knows who took the child," he went on.

"They're hunting him," Savage added. "The man with the crossbow. Those were broadhead bolts, you don't need one of them to take down a rabbit. But if you're hunting a person, they're perfect. Are you sure you don't have any idea who it might be, Mrs Kett?"

"I don't," she said, her face open and honest. "Nobody was missing at lunch today. Everyone was there, other than the dead. They're not killers, they're kind people."

"Even men like Tom Faulkner?" Kett asked her.

"Tom was clergy once too," she said. "Up near Hebden Bridge. He's a little rough in his manner but he's never hurt anyone. And some of those other men may have had to swim through troubled water to find us, but there has never been aggression in Whytetail, there has never been violence."

"What kind of troubled water?" Savage asked.

"Drugs, prison, the usual things that lead to redemption. I sat in on some of their sessions when they arrived here and all they want is peace and a good life. All they're looking for is forgiveness, and God grants it to them."

"He might," said Kett. "I'm not sure I would."

"So where does that leave us?" Porter said. "Clare's right. If the Task Force gets here now, we risk somebody killing the child. But if we leave, then our window for getting Adam back closes, possibly forever. What do we do?"

Porter met Kett's eye in the mirror and shook his head.

"I don't really need to ask, do I?" the DI said.

"You're off the hook on this one, Porter," Kett said. "You too, Savage. You're police, and Clare will have your heads."

"Like he'd ever be able to catch us in those trousers," Savage said.

Porter barked out a laugh that almost made Mary hit the ceiling.

"He's driving home in his pants and socks right now, guaranteed."

"Nice image," said Kett, wincing. "Pull over here, will you, Pete?"

Porter stopped the car by the side of the road, keeping the engine running. He slung his arm over Mary's seat as he turned around.

"Can you take Mum home?" Kett asked. "She's going to be staying with us for a while."

A smile landed on Mary's lips and she trapped it beneath her trembling fingers.

"Drop Savage home too. I've got this."

Savage shook her head, opening her door and leaping out.

"Whoops," she said, stretching. "I seem to have fallen out of the car, sir. I'm not sure I'll be able to get back in."

"Don't do anything without me," Porter said. "I'm coming right back."

"Couple of bloody idiots," said Kett, but he was smiling.

He manoeuvred himself over Evie's chair, Savage offering him a hand which he shot down with a glare.

"I'm not that old, Savage," he said, groaning as he dropped to the verge. He turned back, seeing his mum lost in the gloom of the Volvo.

"Be careful, Robert," she said. "Please. Cairns is a good man, they're all good people, but... But even good people can do terrible things, can't they? If they believe they're doing it for the right reason."

Another flash of something in Kett's head, like sunlight flickering through the sweeping branches of a tree. It blew into nothing, caught by the breeze.

But he was getting closer to the truth.

"I'll be careful, Mum. And I'll see you soon."

"Find the boy," Mary said. "And God bless you, Robert."

I doubt it, he thought, offering her a smile and a wave.

"And I mean it, don't do anything until I'm back," said Porter, jabbing a finger at Kett.

"Hand on heart," Kett said. "Drive safe. But drive fast."

He slapped the car twice and Porter pulled away, gunning it up the road. Savage was already walking into the trees that rose beside them like prison bars.

"The old village is this way," she said. "I think that's our best bet."

Kett nodded, setting off after her.

"That was nice of you," she said. "Letting her stay."

"She's my mum," said Kett. "What else could I do?"

"Does Billie know?"

"Oh, shit. I should probably tell her."

"That's a good idea."

Kett pulled his phone from his pocket, seeing that the battery was a thin slice of red. He called Billie and it went straight to her voicemail, so he called the house number instead. It rang a handful of times before somebody picked up. He heard breathing, a sniff.

"Hello?" he said.

"eh-lo," came the reply.

"Moira? It's daddy. Is mummy there?"

He heard Evie in the background, whispering conspiratorially. Moira laughed so loud he had to pull the phone away from his ear.

"Utt cheese," she said, giggling. "Farty utt cheese."

"Moira, please," Kett said. "I don't have much battery left."

"She's saying farty butt cheese!" screeched Evie,

breaking into howls of laughter. Then there was a bleep and the line went dead.

"We need a better receptionist," he muttered, and he'd only just slid the phone back into his pocket when it started to ring—the *Mexican Hat Dance* seeming to scatter every single bird from its roost.

"Billie?" he said.

"Sorry," she replied. "They beat me to the phone."

"What on earth is farty butt cheese anyway?" he asked, grimacing. He didn't wait for an answer. "Look, my phone might die, but I just wanted to warn you that Mum's coming to stay for a bit. Is that okay? They basically kicked her out because of me. I didn't—"

"It's fine," Billie said. "Robbie, it's fine. She's your mum. I think it will be good for her, and you, and the girls love her."

"You're sure?" he said. "I know it's a big ask."

"I'm sure. You coming home with her?"

"No, not yet. There's something I've got to finish here."

"Be careful," she said, reading the hesitation in his voice. "I got a bad feeling from that place. I don't think there's much they wouldn't do to protect what they've got. They're religious zealots, Robbie, and those are the worst kind of people to deal with because they will never accept that they're doing anything wrong."

"Yeah, Mum said the same, give or take. I'll be careful."

Savage threw a look over her shoulder—*yeah, right*—and he lifted his middle finger in her direction.

"Hang on, Robbie," said Billie. "Alice wants a word."

"I really should—"

"Dad!" screeched Alice, loud enough to make his ear whine. "Is she really coming to live here? Can she share my room? Can I feed her?"

"She's not a pet, Alice," said Kett. "I think she can feed herself."

"Is she really coming, though?"

"She is. Just for a little while."

"And she's really our gran? Like, our proper gran?"

"She is," Kett said. "It'll take some getting used to, but—"

"She's gone," said Billie. "I don't think she really believes you're related."

"Why?" Kett said.

"Alice says she has a grumpy face, and you've got a fluffy face."

"A fluffy face?" said Kett.

"Friendly."

"I don't have a friendly face!" he shot back. "Why do people... It's mean and ferocious."

"Very mean. It's why I love you. But anyway, it's Alice that needs convincing. She insists she's not your real mum."

Kett stopped walking, feeling that key turning again inside the chamber of his skull, feeling the door of his thoughts finally open.

"Oh shit," he said, cutting off whatever Billie was saying. "I've got to go. I love you, Billie. Thank you."

He hung up, looking at Savage. She'd stopped too, waiting.

"That's it," he said. "I'm such an idiot, I never even considered it."

"What?" said Savage.

She insists she's not your real mum.

"Caitlyn and Liam, I don't think they're Adam's parents. I don't think he's their son."

"What?" she said again. "But they were at the hospital,

right? There was a photo in their room. And you called the maternity ward and they confirmed it."

"Yeah, they were in hospital after giving birth *here*. Shit, Kate, they *all* give birth here, every single Whytetail baby. I don't think..." He put his hands in his hair, his head reeling. "Did you see any pregnant women? I didn't, not even in the Manor. The maternity ward said they were expecting another Whytetail baby soon and I didn't see a single woman who looked ready to give birth. All those couples that couldn't have babies, travelling to Whytetail for a miracle. What if they weren't miracles at all?"

"You think they stole the babies?" Savage said, frowning.

"No, I think they *made* them."

Savage shook her head, not understanding. Then her mouth fell open.

"No," she said.

"You saw a bed, a tunnel. The whole Virgin Mary thing, immaculate conception. It fits."

Savage was still shaking her head, but she knew. Every line harrowed into her face told Kett she knew.

"That's why everyone was present at lunch, why nobody was missing," she said. "That's why the room is hidden beneath the church. There's somebody else here, somebody they haven't told us about. Somebody that most of the people here don't even know about."

"My mum didn't know what happened in that room. Maybe none of them do, the regular folk in Whytetail."

"A surrogate," said Savage.

"It makes sense, Kate," he said. "Christ, it makes an awful kind of sense. What if the person who killed Caitlyn and Liam, the person who took the baby—what if it's Adam's *real* mother?"

"They got her pregnant? Then they took her baby?"

Even good people can do terrible things, can't they?
Mary had said. *If they believe they're doing it for the right
reason.*

"And she took it back," said Kett. "She killed Caitlyn
and Liam and she took it back."

CHAPTER TWENTY-SEVEN

Kett pulled his phone out again, calling Clare. It was his wife Fiona who answered, and she sounded out of breath.

"He's unavailable," she said. "We're having a bit of a trouser emergency."

"I... Wait, *what?*"

"They won't come off!" Clare roared from nearby. "Just get the scissors and cut the tossing things!"

"I can't, Colin, they're hired!"

"Look," Kett said. "Can you tell him that we think we know who killed the couple out in Whytetail? We think it's the child's birth mother, that she was somehow paid or coerced into giving up her baby. She... *hello?*"

He looked at the phone, seeing that it had died.

"Fuck! Savage, can you call him?"

She produced her own phone, studying it for a moment before shrugging.

"I would, sir, but there's no service out here."

"Seriously? We're not in the bloody rainforest."

"You think the boss got any of that?"

"I don't know."

He looked back to the road, cursing Alice for playing *Roblox* on the journey down. He couldn't even charge it in the car because Porter had taken it. After a second or two he began walking again, using the low branches to help him navigate the uneven ground. Something was nagging at him.

"The photo," he said. "The hospital. I spoke to the maternity department and they said they'd checked Caitlyn when she came in. If she wasn't the mother, they would have seen it. They would have known."

"Maybe these things can be faked?" said Savage as they went. "Covered up?"

He didn't know. That didn't sit right.

"Or somebody at the hospital is in on it," she added.

That felt more like it.

"There's nothing illegal about surrogacy," Savage went on. "But you're right, I didn't see any pregnant women, so if they're using surrogates then they're keeping them hidden."

"Of course they are. Because that's their secret. If it gets out that Whytetail isn't home to miracles, that it's just some kind of baby farm, then nobody's going to go there anymore. It's so obvious, that's why they charge so much. Nobody pays that kind of money for fresh air and farm food."

"Secret, then?" Savage said, tripping over a tree root as big as a crocodile. "Or forced?"

"I guess we're about to find out."

And just the thought of it made his body sag with exhaustion, his own batteries drained.

"It's why Summer was so pissed that we turned up," Savage went on. "Right? It's why she was so angry at the Pastor and your mum. They didn't want anyone here because the truth would have destroyed everything they'd built."

"But Cairns didn't care," said Kett, nodding. "He wanted us to find out. He wanted it all to end. He's dying. Those TIAs. He wanted to be free of it all before he went."

"'*There are no secrets in the eyes of God*.'" Savage quoted. "I'm sure that's what he said to us inside the church when we first got here. He was confessing, cleaning his conscience. He might not have even been a willing participant. Everybody told us that Summer was the one who ran the place."

"Her and Faulkner." Kett nodded. "And the rest of the men who chased us out. But maybe nobody else knows. Not Mum, not Paul Palmer. They're happy to believe in miracles."

"Who isn't, sir?" said Savage.

They pushed deeper into the woods, into the stagnant smell, into the clouds of flies that choked the hot air.

"That's why the mother wrote the note, though," Savage said. "That's why she threatened to kill the baby if anyone came after her, if *we* came after her. Because she'd rather kill her son than lose him again."

Kett grew cold at the thought, but he could understand it. If they were right, then the mother had been made to carry a child to term only to have it taken away. Even if she'd agreed to it, what would that do to somebody, especially after the trauma of birth? Would you kill to get your child back?

He would, he thought.

He *had*.

"There," said Savage, crouching and pointing into the trees.

Kett squinted, seeing nothing. Then he spotted the grass-green roof of a cottage between two withered trees, perfectly camouflaged.

"You think she's here somewhere?" Kett said.

"I think that's who they were hunting," Savage replied. "Whytetail was a big place before they abandoned it. There are mines here too, remember? Tunnels. Maybe miles of them."

Kett blew out a breath.

"That's why we never heard a baby," he said, suddenly realising. "That's why we never heard Adam crying."

"Because he's with his mum," Savage said. "They knew that too, they even mentioned it. What did Faulkner say to you? '*I can't hear a baby.*' They knew."

"Fuckers," said Kett.

He set off again, the coils of bramble making it impossible to be stealthy. Twice he tripped, landing hard on his hands and then his elbow. It was like wading through an ocean, like he could drown, and he felt the panic radiate from his injured chest.

"She could be anywhere," Savage said as they reached the first cottage. It seemed as if it had been grown here, not built, its ancient stone the same colour as the mossy ground. Only three of its walls were intact, the fourth reduced to rubble. Trees grew up inside it, their branches holding the roof in place. "We don't even know where to start looking."

"We don't even know if we're right," said Kett. "If you were her, where would you go?"

"Far, far away from here," she said. "But we know she didn't because there was no sign of her on the camera that Porter found."

"Unless she got out through the woods. Hiked it, or hitchhiked."

"Covered in blood and carrying an infant child?" Savage shook her head. "We'd have heard."

They skirted the cottage, seeing another one almost

directly behind it. It was in better shape, ripped lace curtains hanging from the glassless upstairs windows and the remains of a lean-to clinging to the back wall.

"No, something is keeping her here," Savage said. "She's too scared to go far. Maybe Whytetail is all she knows."

"She's young?"

"Young or... I don't know, maybe she's never lived anywhere else."

"Maybe she grew up here?" he asked, answering his own question before Savage had a chance to. "But nobody was missing, everyone was accounted for. If the community knew who she was, somebody would have mentioned her."

Kett was liking the sound of this less and less.

"I think you're right," Savage said, her face a mask of misery. "Nobody knew, other than Summer and her men. She's been here all this time and nobody knew about her."

It was still speculation, of course, but it was becoming harder and harder to dismiss.

"What if they brainwashed her?" he asked. "All the legends, the religious talk. What if that's why she can't leave, because they've messed with her head?"

"Makes sense," said Savage. "My Mum's religious, like yours. I told you that, right? She's got the mind of a doctor but she won't do anything without a prayer, and she won't go anywhere without her crucifix."

They made their way past the second cottage, the woodland thinning. There had been a road here once, Kett thought, seeing the fractured paving beneath an impenetrable net of undergrowth. The trees stretched their long arms overhead as if they were praying, their fingers interlocked. As quiet as it was, it didn't feel calm, it didn't feel peaceful. This wasn't a restful place.

It wasn't a safe place, either.

Savage heard them first, crouching quietly and waving for Kett to do the same. He ducked down, both of his knees releasing a gunshot crack.

Voices. Two men, maybe more. They were speaking quietly, which meant they had to be close. He could hear the snap of branches underfoot, one of the men sniffing repeatedly. Their words drifted through the hot air, through the droning swarms of flies.

"... knows what was going on up there, him and that computer. Must have been in there every night wanking one off, the old pervert."

The other man laughed, but there was anger in it.

"Wouldn't let us do the same, though. No phones, no computers. Hypocrite."

"Yeah," said the first guy. "You wanna check that one?"

"We've done it already. Haven't we? They all fucking look the same."

The sound of their footsteps drew closer and Kett braced himself, his fist bunched. Then they quietened, their voices fading as they headed deeper into the trees. Kett stretched, risking a look. It was dark enough in the woods now that he couldn't identify them, but there was no mistaking the crossbow that one of the men held and the loops of rope that hung off the other man's shoulder. They were heading for a third cottage but Kett was pretty sure they'd be back.

What to do?

He felt something on his hand, prickling his skin, and when he looked down he saw a stag beetle crawling over his knuckles. His first instinct was to shake it off but he resisted. It was only a little one, and after a second or two it left him, scuttling over the dirt, looking for somewhere to hide. He thought of the one that Alice had held in her hand just a day ago, long dead.

He didn't believe in omens, of course, but as he watched the beetle escape into the tangled roots he couldn't help but think that this was one.

He just didn't know if it was good or bad.

"Come on," he said.

They set off like Commandos, keeping low. The ground was dipping, heading into the valley where they'd seen the Defender earlier that day. He thought he could hear more voices from that direction as the men searched the woods. He had no doubt in his mind now that they were after the mother, but these were people who knew the old village, who knew the woods above and the tunnels below. If they couldn't find her here, what chance did Kett have?

Unless she *wasn't* here.

He came to a halt, rubbing his temples as if to squeeze out the thoughts that hid there. Savage had disappeared into a monstrous swathe of cow parsley and he heard her whisper his name before reappearing. Her face was damp with sweat and marked with dozens of little scratches.

"What is it, sir?"

"Let's just say we're right. A young woman who's lived here for a while, who's been fed a cocktail of dogma and lies. She's obviously a believer, think about the note. *You knit me together in my mother's womb.* Whatever she's done, I think she believes in this place."

Savage waited, batting at the flies.

"If I was going to hide from Summer and her men, I'd come here," he went on. "Because you could lose yourself in these old buildings, in the trees, the tunnels."

"Right," said Savage.

"But she's not us. She's not thinking like us. She won't

hide here because she knows the village won't protect her. She thinks something else is protecting her."

"God?" asked Savage.

"Close."

"Mary," Savage said.

Kett thought about when he'd stumbled onto the lake, the Well of Our Lady, and seen the vision of the girl in the water, there for an instant and then gone again.

Not a vision.

A *reflection*.

"Shit," he said, looking up the hill. "I know where she is."

CHAPTER TWENTY-EIGHT

KNOWING WHERE SHE WAS HIDING WAS ONE THING.

Getting there would be harder.

Kett took the lead as he cut back up the hill, heading for the river. The forest did everything it could to stop them, the trees like soldiers on a battlefield, jabbing their bayonet branches, going for their eyes, their throats, while the birds screamed from their roosts. *They're here! They're here!*

Thick coils of brambles conspired with the roots to trip them, and Kett tumbled onto his hands and knees half a dozen times. Savage only fell once but it was a bad one and her cry echoed off the low canopy, the loudest thing in the woods.

"You okay?" Kett whispered.

He offered his hand and she took it, holding her other arm to her chest as she struggled up. He thought it might have been broken but she shook it a couple of times and offered a grimaced nod. Her granddad's whistle had fallen out of her T-shirt and it swung there on its chain—like his mum's crucifix, like Cairns' key.

Everybody worships something, he thought as she tucked it back in.

The slope grew steeper, and through the gaps between the trunks Kett saw the old village spilling away to their left. Two dozen cottages clung to the hill but he couldn't work out if they were the same ones he'd seen before. In the muggy heat of the evening, he wondered whether they'd all risen on little legs and beetled to new positions just to confuse him.

The air was poisonous; the stifling, suffocating, dizzying atmosphere of a mythical kingdom lost to dark magic. Even though they were taking it slow he had to pause every few steps and suck in as much oxygen as he could, his heart hammering against his ribs surely hard enough to punch that little shard of bullet right out of him.

It seemed like hours had passed here, but when Kett checked his watch he saw it had only been thirty minutes. It took another five to hit the top of the hill and by that time he heard the growl of an engine from down below. He braced himself on a tree trunk, angling his body until he found a line of sight through the tangled weeds.

The Defender was back, crawling down the remains of the old road. After a few seconds it stopped and all four doors opened, five men climbing out. He was too far away to see who they were, but the gleam of a bald head told him the driver had probably been Faulkner.

They fanned out, Faulkner scanning the woods, seeming to stop when his eyes fell on the place where Kett was hiding. He pulled something from his belt—a knife, Kett thought—then pointed to his left, barking out an order that was swallowed by the thick forest. The men followed it, fanning out.

"This is bad," Savage said, looking past his shoulder. "I

don't get the feeling they're going to let this woman go if they find her."

Kett didn't either. There wasn't just violence in these men. There was murder. He thought of the graves he'd seen, wondering who they'd find there if they dug them up.

The anger drove him on and he pushed through the shell of another little cottage, cresting the hill and finally seeing the river below. It was after nine and they were losing the day fast, but the river still held a little light, reflecting the inferno of the setting sun. He could see the lake from here, wrapped in bulrushes and shielded by the weeping willow.

"Come on," he said.

They descended as gracefully as they could but they were a long way from the path here and gravity wasn't doing them any favours. Halfway down they had to duck as more voices floated above them, but after a couple of minutes they faded, joining the distant calls from below.

"Wolves," said Savage as they started moving again.

"Huh?"

"That's what they remind me of. A pack of wolves."

They slipped and slid their way down the last of the hill, hitting the open meadow below. Even from here, fifty yards away, Kett could smell Summer's roses.

"Where now?" Savage asked.

Kett looked upriver, seeing it curl back through the trees towards the Manor. There had been plenty of people there earlier, too many eyes for somebody who wanted to remain secret, so he turned the other way instead. The river gurgled its way past the flower garden, then the lake, vanishing into its castle of bulrushes. It would be a good place to hide.

"That way," he said, breaking into a jog as they covered the open ground. "When I was here earlier I thought I saw a woman in the water. Just a flash. I figured it was a trick of the light, one of the logs beneath the surface or something, but what if it was her?"

"She'd have to come out from hiding sometimes," Savage said. "If only for something to eat and drink."

They sprinted through the garden, between the beds of roses, slowing down only when they reached the river's edge. Here the rushes and the cow parsley provided a blanket of cover. Kett pushed into it, the heads soft against his face, the air cooler thanks to the rushing water. Compared to the woods, this place was heaven.

The skirts of the willow didn't quite hit the ground, and even from this side of the river Kett could see there was nobody there. He followed the water into the growing dark. The birds sang the final verses of their evening chorus, the river singing with them. Every now and again the rushes would break and Kett saw the Well of Our Lady, the surface dancing in the breeze.

"We're going to have to cross," he said.

Savage skipped ahead, finding a gap in the rushes.

"Pretty shallow here," she said.

She started to unlace her shoes but Kett put a hand on her shoulder to stop her. It was growing quite hard to see but the river seemed to lean abruptly to the right a little way downstream. At the turn, on this side, was a high, sandy bank punctured by hanging tree roots. Kett approached it slowly, hearing the hushed whisper of the river ebbing and flowing.

A whisper that seemed *far* too human.

He glanced back at Savage and saw by her expression that she heard it too. He put a finger to his lips, creeping towards the bank as quietly as he could. The trees along the river arced their arms overhead protectively, the ground rising. Kett dropped from the grass to the wide, sandy bank, his boots crunching the wet gravel.

And the whisper suddenly stopped.

He walked as quietly as he could, hearing a gurgle, a panicked *shhh* of breath. There was a hollow in the high bank, a narrow split barely wide enough for a person. The last of the sun's rays still reached this place and Kett saw her there, a young woman folded around the child she held tight against her chest.

She stared at him with eyes that were liquid with fear, with madness, her mouth falling open into an awful, silent scream. She was wearing a white dress that was now filthy with blood and dirt, her red hair hanging in knotted clumps. Her bare feet were covered in sand and she dug them into the silt, pushing herself back even though there was nowhere to go. The baby was a bundle of rags with dark eyes, surely too small to be real.

"Hey," Kett said quietly, holding out both of his hands. "Hey, it's okay, it's okay."

The baby must have sensed his mother's fear because he started to cry, the loudest sound in the night. She shushed him, trying to push him onto her breast, his chubby fingers grabbing at her through the blankets he was wrapped in.

"It's okay," Kett said again.

He'd taken a step towards her before he realised what she was holding in her other hand. It was too dark to see whether it was a knife or a stick but there was no denying it was sharp. She thrust it towards him, sobbing through bared teeth, her eyes wild.

"We're not with them," he heard Savage say. "We're friends. We won't hurt you."

"We won't hurt you," Kett echoed. "We want to get you out of here. You and Adam."

At the sound of her child's name, the girl groaned, still trying to push herself deeper into the hollow. The baby's cries were getting louder, his body flexing as he fought to get air into his lungs.

"We don't have much time," Kett said.

The girl held her weapon out for another second or two.

Then she drew it close and pushed the tip against the baby's throat.

"No," she said, her voice thick with an accent. "I do it. I do it."

Kett retreated, his arms still held out in front of him. His heel hit a stone and he tripped, landing hard on his backside in the wet silt.

"Don't," he said. "You don't have to hurt him. We're not here to take him away."

She didn't comprehend what he was saying. Or she didn't believe him. She pushed her weapon with more force, talking to the baby in a language that Kett didn't know but with an urgency he understood all too well.

She was going to kill him.

He didn't know what to do, so he did the only thing he could think of. He dug his hand into his pocket and pulled out his wallet, ripping it open.

"Wait," he said. "Just wait."

There were photos of all three of his girls in there and he pulled them out. Two fell to the riverbank but he lifted the third. He knew which one it was, Alice and Evie and Moira on one of those bucket swings in the little park around the corner from their old house in Stepney Green. Alice was in the middle, caught mid-howl of delight, Evie to her left with a wild grin. You couldn't see Moira's face because on the upward swing her legs had gone over her head and she'd almost rolled right out of the bloody thing. But he could still hear her laughter.

Back before Billie had been taken. Back before the Pig Man and the newspaper girls and Hollenbeck and the horror of Whytetail.

"My girls," he said, holding the photo up. "My children. Alice, Evie, Moira. I know what it's like, I know how much you love him. I don't want to take him away."

The woman studied the photograph with eyes as big as moons. The baby still screamed, loud enough to shatter the whole world in two.

"Your child," he said, nodding to the baby. "Your baby. Your son. Nobody else's, okay? Yours."

"Mine," she said. "My son. Not Adam. Luca."

"Luca," said Kett, nodding.

She relaxed, but the weapon didn't drop far from the baby's throat and she clung to it so hard her knuckles burned white. Kett slid the photograph back into his wallet, picking up the others from where they had fallen. The woman was trying to get her baby to feed but he was still screaming. She looked past Kett, past Savage, the tears leaving tracks in her dirty cheeks.

"Help," she said. "Help us, please."

"We will," said Savage. She walked past Kett, offering the woman her hand. "Trust us. What's your name?"

"Mihaela," she said.

"Mihaela, I'm Kate."

There was still doubt in the woman's face, but she must have known she didn't have a choice. She let go of the stick and took Savage's hand, clutching the baby to her chest as she stood on legs that seemed too weak to hold her. Kett could see how exhausted she was in every movement, and it was only Savage's strength that stopped her from dropping again. When she was ready, she let go, using both of her hands to hold Luca. Now that they were upright the child had settled a little, and she shushed him through her own sobs.

But it was too late.

A shout from upriver, echoed by another in the woods. A beam of light broke free of the trees, penetrating the darkness, searching.

"Shit," said Kett. "They found us."

Another shout, closer this time.

He looked at Savage, seeing the fear there, feeling it himself.

"Run."

CHAPTER TWENTY-NINE

KETT KNEW BETTER THAN TO ASK TO CARRY THE BABY. He offered Mihaela his arm instead but she shook her head, clutching Adam tight as she ran down the riverbank. The air behind them was full of shouts now, the men sounding more like a wolf pack than ever as they hunted. The torch they were using was a good one because it lit up the tops of the trees, exploding in the canopies like fireworks.

"Where are we going?" Savage asked, jogging beside Kett.

He didn't know, so he didn't answer. Mihaela was tired but she was quick, and she knew how to move quietly. She scrabbled up the bank onto the grass, vanishing into the cow parsley.

"Wait," said Kett, one foot slipping on the loose earth and depositing him onto his chin hard enough to make his teeth clack and his ears ring. "Fuck!"

Savage bounded up beside him, chasing the girl into the foliage. Kett got to his feet, spitting dirt as he lumbered after them. To his relief, they were both waiting when he pushed through the branches. Mihaela had managed to get Luca to latch on and even though the baby didn't seem happy he was no longer crying. The blankets were coming loose and his hands grabbed her dress, squeezing.

"How do we get out?" Savage said.

"Not out," Mihaela replied. "Cannot leave. Mother here, she keep us safe, I cannot leave her."

"Mother?" Savage asked, and Mihaela nodded. "As in Our Lady?"

Savage and Kett shared a look but Mihaela didn't reply. Kett turned back, peeking through the foliage to see the light bouncing down the river as the men ran this way. They were maybe a hundred metres away, close enough for him to make out their words.

They weren't good.

He ducked back into cover, looking up the slope. The woods had fallen further into darkness and it wouldn't be long before they were pitch black. That way lay the old village, its crumbling cottages and its impenetrable carpet of thorns. If they ended up there in the dark then they'd be snared like rabbits.

"We need to cross the river," he said.

"But that'll take us back to the commune," said Savage.

"They're not all part of this. I'm sure of it. If we can reach the Manor then somebody will help us. And there's a phone in the old church."

"That's a big gamble," said Savage.

"Not as big as staying here."

He took a breath, trying to steady his pulse, then stepped out of the bushes. The torch beam swung over his head but whoever was holding it was still a little way down the river, hidden by the rushes. Everything else had been swallowed by the night—so much so that Kett didn't see the shadow until it was almost too late. There was a man a dozen yards away and sprinting hard, just a silhouette against the glow of the river.

Kett stepped back, the bushes rustling, and the man skidded to a halt. He was panting, his head swinging left and right. It was hard to see him but even in his white polo shirt Kett was almost invisible too, just so long as he didn't move, just so long as he stayed quiet.

Behind him, Luca gurgled.

"Hey!" the man shouted. "Hey, they're here!"

Fuck.

Kett pushed himself out of hiding, breaking into a run, building up speed.

"Hey," said the man. He was fumbling for something in his pocket. "Hey, they're—"

Kett thumped into him, knocking the words clean out of his throat. The man hit the ground hard, Kett landing on top —a knee in his crotch and an elbow in the soft cavity of his solar plexus. Momentum carried him over and he rolled away.

He struggled back to his feet but the man beat him to it. He was trying to call out but he couldn't get the air in. He lunged towards Kett, something flashing in his hand, then another shadow rushed up behind him. There was the sound of a stick cracking against bone and the man dropped hard.

"Kett?" Savage hissed, dropping the branch.

"Down here," he said. "Come on!"

The men were almost on top of them, the bulrushes glowing with torchlight. Savage looked back just as Mihaela appeared.

"Not river," the girl said. "This way."

She bolted. Kett swore again, accepting Savage's hand and letting her haul him up. His chest burned with cold pain, as if a knife was worrying its way between his ribs. Mihaela was following the river, looking more like a ghost than ever in her white dress. As soon as the men rounded the corner they'd be able to see her, but when Kett called out quietly she ignored him.

"Quick," Savage said, chasing her.

Kett glanced back, blinded by the torchlight, and when he looked forward again the young woman and her baby had vanished.

"Mihaela?" Savage hissed, slowing to a jog. She looked at Kett. "Where'd she go?"

"Here," came the reply.

A face in the trees, a beckoning hand. Kett ran towards her, the torchlight breaking over the meadow a second later, snapping at his heels. Mihaela was right there and behind her, set into the slope of the hillside, was an iron door. It was open, and the darkness that sat on the other side of it was absolute.

"This way," she said, swaddling the baby against her.

They didn't have a choice. The shouts had turned from urgent to angry as they found the man that Savage had taken down.

"They cross the river?" yelled one—Faulkner, Kett thought, based on his accent. "You see them over there?"

Splashing, but footsteps were coming this way too.

"Please hurry," said Mihaela.

She ducked through the door, disappearing instantly as if the darkness had simply swallowed her. Savage looked at Kett, and even in the night he could read her expression— *please don't make me go in there*. He was wearing it too. He took her hand and squeezed it, before letting go and following Mihaela inside.

It wasn't just dark, it was bitterly cold. A current of stale air touched his face as if trying to work out who he was and it took every ounce of willpower he had not to scream. Phantom shapes formed from the shadows, leering eyes and monstrous grins. He put his hands out in front of him, feeling nothing but that breeze, as if he was standing on the edge of a cliff.

"Mihaela?" he said.

She didn't answer but he could hear Luca whimpering.

"Hang on," said Savage.

There was a rustling, then she appeared in the gloom, her phone's torch muted by her glowing fingers. She lifted the light and Kett saw a round room with a brick pillar in the middle, supporting the low ceiling. Mihaela was walking away, heading into another shaft of darkness—one the size and shape of an upright coffin.

"Oh, fuck this," Kett muttered.

He moved after her, one hand on the wall to steady himself. Whatever this place was, it was doing a good job of muting the shouts from outside. It might have been another world in here, another universe. But the men weren't stupid. It wouldn't take them long to find the door.

He needed to turn sideways as he entered the tunnel and even then it seemed to push on his chest and his back, threatening to crush the air from him. Savage was right behind him, one hand holding the torch, the other holding Kett's polo shirt. Ahead, Mihaela was a phantom of shadow, breathing hard and doing her best to hush the child. She must have reached a junction because she vanished to the left.

"Wait," said Kett.

It wasn't a junction so much as a bend, and he angled left as he followed it. The breeze still blew but the air was ancient, stagnant, full of dust. *Dead* air, and even as he hauled in breath after breath he felt like he was drowning. He looked back, blinded by the torch, Savage right there, and the panic screamed inside his head.

Was it getting narrower in here? The walls seemed to be closing in, the ceiling dropping. He had to duck to stop it from scraping the top of his head, then he had to duck some more, contorting his body to fit.

"Hey," he said. "Mihaela, wait!"

What would it take for the tunnel to collapse? For the hillside to bury him here? They'd never find him, he thought. They'd never know what happened. He tried to lift a hand to wipe the sweat from his eyes but the rock wouldn't let him.

Then the tunnel began to widen. He could straighten up, stand tall. He almost wept with the relief of it as he stumbled into another room. Savage held up the torch to reveal a long, wide chamber carved into the chalk of the hillside. Kett put a hand to the wall and just breathed, hearing nothing but the wet roar of his pulse in his ears. If the men had chased them in here, they were doing so silently.

"Where are we?" he asked, his voice muted.

"Tunnel," said Mihaela, somewhat unnecessarily. She had Luca over her shoulder now, jiggling him. "I hide here. Tunnel everywhere."

"Chalk mines," said Savage, scraping a nail down the wall and then studying it. She held up the torch but the end of the chamber was lost in darkness. "Do you know where it goes?"

"Out to old town," she said.

"That's no good to us," Kett replied, scrubbing the sweat from his face. "We need a way *out* of Whytetail."

"Not without Mother."

"Mother?" asked Savage again. "Who do you mean? Mother as in the Virgin Mary, as in the Well of Our Lady?"

Mihaela frowned, shaking her head.

"Mother, she look after me. And the others. I won't leave without her."

"The others?" said Kett. "Other women like you?"

Mihaela nodded.

"How many?"

"They come and they go," she said. "There are four of us right now, all with child."

"They use you to give them children?" Savage said. "Is that what happens?"

"Make babies," Mihaela said, nodding. "I came here for job, but they not let me go. They make me..."

She groaned, the sound coming from deep inside her.

"They make me sleep with the father until it happens. Father and other men."

"The room beneath the church," said Savage, and Mihaela nodded.

"What happens to you afterwards?" she said. "When you've had the baby?"

Mihaela shook her head, still making that awful sound in her throat.

"I don't know. We never see them. They take baby and we never see them again, never see the mother again. They made me make baby, but he's *my* baby. I won't let them take him."

Her entire body seemed to be trembling, something about to break inside her. Something was breaking inside Kett, too. He held out his hands again.

"Let us help," he said. "Let me carry him for a little while."

She shook her head, her arms like steel wires as she pulled Luca closer.

"You not take him."

"Not take him," Kett said. "Just carry him. Just for a little while."

She studied his face, everything shaking. She held his eye. How long had it been? Nearly two days now since she'd entered Caitlyn and Liam's room and taken back her child. Two days of terror, hiding in the wet, in the cold, feeding Luca to keep him quiet, to keep him alive. She looked like she might snap clean in two if she tried to take another step, but Kett saw the endless strength in her, an unimaginable courage.

"Just for a little while," he said again.

Finally, she nodded, and he stepped gently towards her. She lifted the baby from her shoulder and handed him to Kett, but even when he took Luca she didn't let go. He held the baby to his chest with one arm and placed his other hand on top of hers. For a moment they stood there, not talking, barely even breathing. The baby whined in protest, his little fingers exploring Kett's beard, his nose, studying his face with those beautiful, dark eyes.

"Hey Luca," Kett said to him in as gentle a voice as he could muster. "My name's Robbie. It's good to meet you."

The baby cooed like a pigeon, and whatever he'd said his mother must have understood it. She let go, stepping back, her arms wrapped around herself.

"*Multumesc*," she said, or something like it.

Kett turned to Savage, pulling the blanket close around the child's head. It had been so long since he'd held a baby and he couldn't stop himself picturing one of his girls shivering in his arms—so lost, so small, so fragile.

"We can't stay here," he said. "We should follow the

tunnel, see if we can get out through the old village. Porter will be on his way back by now, he might even be there. And Clare's Task Force should be on its way."

Savage nodded but she seemed unsure. She looked past Kett to the young woman.

"Mihaela, do you know where your friends are being held?" she asked.

Mihaela nodded.

"There's a... a *moară*, a... *mill* down the river, they keep us there."

"We can come back for them," said Kett. "The priority has to be getting the baby to safety. If those arseholes find us they'll take us out, all of us, if it means protecting what they have."

"That's the problem," Savage said. "If they think we've escaped then they'll move the women. They'll take them someplace else. We'll never find them."

She was right, they'd end up disappeared.

Or dead.

"I know," he said, half words, half sigh.

"You help them?" said Mihaela.

"They'll be under guard," said Kett. "These people won't give them up easily."

"Please?" the young woman said.

"And it's just us. We're not an army."

Mihaela looked at him, desperate now. He glanced at Savage.

"Your call, sir," she said. "But I think I need to let you know that I'm going after them whatever you say."

Kett breathed a laugh through his nose—a nose that currently had at least three baby fingers wedged up it. It didn't last long because he knew there was a chance he might not laugh again. He thought about his own girls, about that night inside Bingo's house, all the fire and fury of hell and the pig-headed devil who stood over them.

He thought about the devil who had come to rescue them, too.

Four women, all of them pregnant, all of them prisoners. He had a feeling it would take the same devil to set them free.

And that's what scared him.

"Okay," he said, holding the baby close. "Tell me where they are."

CHAPTER THIRTY

MIHAELA CUT THE MAP INTO THE SOFT WALL WITH A piece of flint, gouging the lines of the river, the Manor, the old church and the new one. She hammered out the little collection of ruined cottages like she was trying to chisel her way to freedom, and when she reached the mill she attacked the wall with such fury that the flint cut through the skin of her hand.

She gasped, dropping it and putting the wound to her mouth.

"You okay?" Kett asked, jiggling the baby. She nodded, using her other hand to point to the outline of the mill. There was blood on her teeth.

"Here," she said. "Hard to see from the village. They keep us hidden. You cannot get there along the river, it too, uh, grown up?"

She ran her finger down through the line of cottages, then back around.

"Have to go this way. Not easy."

"That's how you escaped?" Kett asked.

"Da," she said. She held up her hands and in the light

from Savage's torch Kett saw the welts around her wrists. "Tied. I bit them. Took me many days. We kept in cages, but not always. Not when men…" She made a noise that was almost a snarl. "Room upstairs. I climb through window at night, while the others sleep."

"To get Luca back," Savage asked, shuddering in the cold.

"I know they keep the men and women in the Manor, the men and women who pay for the baby."

"You've been there?" Kett asked.

"Tunnel goes from Manor to church, they bring us along in a… how you say it?"

"A ceremony," said Savage.

"So I go to Manor but I do not know what to do. I do not know how to get Luca back. I…"

Her face fell, her eyes scrolling the wall as if remembering for the first time what she had done to reclaim her baby.

"I find room, I see him. I want to ask them if I can have Luca but I know they only send me back to mill. Then I hear people and I run up the stairs to hide and I see the stick."

"Pastor Cairns' cane?" Kett said. She nodded.

"I do not know where he is but I think he left this for me, to do what I needed to do."

"Wait, you think he left it there *deliberately*?" Kett said.

"Why else? He was always kind to me. Kinder than *her*."

"Summer?"

"Mrs Cairns," she said, almost a hiss. "Never Summer to us. She says she does God's work but she is a Devil. She tells the men what to do. I take stick back down stairs and I look through the door and… And I see her with Luca. I…"

Michael scrubbed her hand over her face, leaving a streak of blood from her nose up to her forehead.

"I wonder if he would be happy with them, you know? I wonder if he have a good life with them. But she calls him Adam, she calls him Adam and I... He is not Adam, he is Luca. And I *lose* it."

"It's okay," Kett said, jiggling the baby to keep him quiet. "We don't have to do this here."

Mihaela studied her hands, stained beetroot-red with old, dried blood, and loosed another almost subsonic groan. She scrubbed them on her dress, shaking her head.

"I was going to wait. I was going to wait until they were asleep. I thought I could take him and run but Luca was crying so much, I could not bear it. He cry and cry. For *me*. And she woke up and saw me. I had no choice. I... hit her... and I drop the stick but he was waking too and I... I saw the knife."

"It was already in the room?" Savage asked.

"By bed. I took it and..."

"It's okay," Kett said again. "None of this is your fault."

She didn't hear him, or she didn't believe him. She stared into her memory with eyes that drowned in horror and madness.

"I did not want to kill them. I... I did not want them to think it was me, so I write note like one of them, a note full of their religion. I put rabbit in crib to confuse them, to make them fight each other. But it did not work. They knew I did it. I did it. I did it."

Something in her head was breaking, her fingers gouging at her face, her eyes.

"How many people guard the mill?" said Savage, trying to bring her back.

Mihaela froze, blinking at Savage.

"The mill, Mihaela. How many men?"

"I do not know," she said after a small eternity, calmer now. "There is sometimes one, sometimes many more. They all look the same. They come and they go to bring us food and water and to... They say they are *priming* us but they are not. They are evil. One always watch the door."

"Is there another way in?" Kett said, his stomach rolling in great, nauseating waves as he took in what she was saying. "The window you escaped through?"

"Very high," she said. "Over river. Deep water, not like here. Everything else closed with nails."

"We might get lucky," Kett said to Savage. "Most of the men will be in the woods looking for the baby."

"Yeah, but they'll come running as soon as they hear us," she replied.

"Unless there's a distraction."

"You're going to use me as bait, sir?"

"Well, I was thinking that *I* could be the bait, and *you* could break into the mill and get the girls?"

Savage almost smiled.

"You know, bait sounds fine."

"Mihaela, can you wait here for us?" said Kett.

"No. They find me here eventually, they crawl every-where, like insect. I know how to hide."

She did. She'd managed to evade a search party for thirty-six hours. She held out her hands and Kett passed her the baby, but not before giving him a gentle cuddle, breathing him in—still that unmistakable smell of baby even though he was filthy, even though he'd been living in the woods and the wet and the weeds for all this time.

You're going to be okay, Luca, he told him, silently. *You and your mum. I promise. You'll be okay. You'll be safe. I'll bring you home.*

"How will we find you?" he said when she had pulled Luca to her chest.

"I will be close. I will see you. Tell the girls that Mihaela sent you, or they will not trust you. Tell them I have Luca."

Kett nodded.

"Which way?"

Mihaela stared down the length of the chamber into the ink-thick dark, then pointed to the cottages on her map.

"Right tunnel will bring you out on edge of village."

"Right," said Kett. "Be safe, Mihaela."

"You too," she said. "They are bad men. Evil men. They will kill you if they find you. They will kill me too. Promise me, if I die, don't let them take Luca. I have family in Ramnicu Valcea. Nicolescu. Take him home."

There was such sadness in her face, such desperation, that all Kett could do was nod.

He made his way down the chamber, trailing his hand along the greasy stone. Savage walked behind him, her light turning his shadow into something inhuman and unrecognisable. Each step felt like it might carry him over the edge into some terrible, bottomless darkness, but he took one after the other until the ground started to slope upwards. The breeze was stronger here, carrying with it the heat of the dying day. It was impossible to see for sure but Kett could tell by the shifting sound of his footsteps that the tunnel opened up ahead.

"Kill the light," he said, and Savage did. It was as if he'd been blinded, but after a few blinks he saw the dull outline of the end of the tunnel, the grey night waiting for him.

He kept low, moving slowly. He couldn't hear anything except the last of the birds. There was a brick archway here but no door, and he put a hand to it and leaned out. They were deep in the woods, somewhere to the east of the valley where they'd seen the Defender. Kett tried to picture the map that Mihaela had drawn them, the swathe of cottages clustered to the slope like decaying fungus and the old mill downriver.

"This way," he said. "I think."

"It is," said Savage. "You want me to take the lead?"

"Probably for the best."

He felt her push past, seeing her silhouette pull ahead and spirit between the trees. He did his best to keep up with her, his feet catching on the tangled undergrowth, the brambles gouging their claws down his arms, his face. He could still hear the men who chased them but their cries were distant. There was room to breathe here and he did, deeply, to counter the growing panic.

What the hell are we doing?

He thought about Mihaela, about Luca, about the other women. And like so many other times in his life he said to himself, *the right thing.*

It has to be.

Savage was moving up the hill, framed against the burgeoning stars as they pushed their way through the dark sky. She stopped when she got to the top, waiting for Kett to catch up. From here they could see all the way down the slope to where the river waited for them.

"There," Savage whispered, and he followed the point of her finger.

A building sat by the water's edge, a square of shadow that was caged by the crooked trees. No lights burned there, and when Kett's heart had stopped thrashing from the climb he couldn't hear a single thing.

The group of men had been moving in that direction, but Mihaela had said there was no access to the mill along the river because of the woods. If they wanted to get there, they'd have to follow the same tunnel, or head down into the valley, through the old village, and back over the hill.

Right?

He wasn't sure.

Savage was a streak of darkness moving like a ninja. Kett tried to follow in her footsteps but he was nowhere near as graceful. Twice he tripped, scraping his arm down the bark of a tree then jarring his knee on a root. At this rate, the woods were going to kill him long before Summer Cairns and her men.

But he kept going, dropping steadily down the hill. More of the mill came into sight, a slim, tall chimney and a peaked roof. Its wheel was a fractured spine arching from the wall, frozen by time. It looked utterly abandoned, even by the river, which was clogged by the same enormous banks of reeds that grew further up.

Savage stopped again by the last line of trees, pulling twigs and leaves from her hair. The mill was maybe fifty yards away, utterly still and unnervingly silent.

"Maybe they've already moved the women," she said, so quietly that he had to lean close to hear her. He scanned the walls, squinting when he saw a tiny, flickering light. It flared up and died away.

A cigarette.

"Somebody's there," he whispered, smelling smoke on the breeze.

"You still want that distraction?"

He nodded, then realised she wouldn't see him.

"Yeah," he said quietly. "Head for the river. Can you make a sound like a sad baby?"

"How hard can it be?" she said. "Two minutes?"

Kett checked his watch, the digits glowing.

"Two minutes," he said. "If it goes to shit, get the hell out of here, okay? Don't wait for me."

She said something that he didn't catch as she shuffled away. In a second or two she was gone, as if she'd never been there at all. He couldn't even hear her as she ran.

The light flared again and a man coughed, then spat. He sounded closer than he looked, the night playing tricks. Kett was grateful for the dark, though. It made him invisible as he cut across the meadow, even in his white polo shirt, and the short grass muted his footsteps. He checked his watch as he went, seeing that a minute had passed.

The closer he got to the mill the more he could see— details picked out in starlight. The smoking man stood on what looked like a wooden veranda. He must have been pacing, because the boards creaked softly with every step. He took another drag of his cigarette, coughing again.

Ninety seconds.

He flicked the butt and it landed half a dozen yards from where Kett was standing. The veranda groaned. He was going back in.

Come on.

From somewhere to his right came a feeble cry. It sounded less like a baby than a dying pigeon, and it was so quiet that the man didn't hear it. He was still coughing, hawking up a throatful of snot and launching it into the night.

Savage cried again, louder this time.

Kett swore beneath his breath as he heard the sound of a door. They were going to miss their opportunity. He opened his mouth to get the man's attention but Savage beat him to it, another whimpering sob that echoed off the side of the mill.

The man stopped. Kett could see his outline, frozen like

a piece of video footage had been paused. The cry came again, a weak gurgle.

"Fuck," the guy said.

He made his way back, the veranda a concertina beneath his heavy feet. There was a thump as he dropped to the grass, moving towards where Savage was hiding.

"Who's there?" he asked, his voice hoarse. "Mihaela?"

"Waaa," said Savage, followed by what sounded more like a bark than a cry.

It was the least convincing baby noise in the world but it was working, the man down by the river's edge now.

"That you?" he asked. "You've come home? Good girl."

Kett upped his speed. He couldn't see much but he could see enough, the man a blob of stationary shadow against the shifting reeds.

"Come out now," the man said. "We can get you cleaned up, settle you in again. I'll make it easy for you."

Sure you will, Kett thought.

He put in a final burst of speed, everything in his body aching. He was ten yards away by the time the man heard him, the shadow spinning.

"Who—"

He didn't have time to finish before Kett charged into him, a rugby tackle that lifted the other man from the ground and punched him into the reeds. They landed in the muck, stagnant water exploding in Kett's face. The man struggled beneath him, grunting, his hands grasping at Kett's face.

"Stay down," Kett growled.

But he wasn't listening, fingernails raking down Kett's cheeks. Kett slapped his hands away only to feel the man's teeth bite into the flesh of his chest. It took everything he had not to scream and he threw a punch instead. It missed, his fist sinking into the mud.

"Get off, you fuck!" the man said, breathless. "Get off me. Help!"

The man's hand was thumping into Kett's side but he couldn't get any strength behind the punches. Kett pulled his arm free, his fist full of mud. He slammed it down onto the man's mouth, turning his cries for help into desperate, gulping chokes.

"Stay down," he said again. "And shut the fuck up."

Savage skidded down beside them, her hands on Kett, working their way down to the man. She grabbed hold of his arm, clamping it to her chest. The man was still fighting with everything he had, his body bucking like a mule. Kett fought to stay on top, grabbing another fistful of mud and pushing it into his mouth, clamping it there until his breaths became screams.

"You done?" Kett said and the man nodded, his eyes wide and wild.

Kett took his hand away and the man twisted his head to the side and vomited, the stink of it filling the night. Kett braced both hands on his head and pinned him there, leaning in.

"How many of you are in the mill?"

"Fuck you," the man said, retching.

"You want to eat shit again?" Kett said. "How many?"

"Just me," he said.

Kett leaned a little harder, the man's head sinking into the mud.

"The truth."

"It's just me," he squealed. "They're all looking for her."

His eyes scrolled the dark and Kett realised he must have mistaken Savage for Mihaela.

"You're dead, bitch," he said. "You don't know what the fuck you've—"

Kett pushed hard, half of the man's head sinking beneath the surface.

"I'll bury you here," he said. "I swear to God. How many men out there? How many are looking for her?"

"Six," he said. "Six and me. But you're too late, you're too fucking late you piece of shit."

"Why?" said Kett. "You've moved the girls?"

He could feel the man shake his head.

"We've got people coming to get them. To tidy up this mess. You're fucked, mate."

"Who?"

"You'll see," he said, the words bubbling as his mouth sank beneath the mud. "They're bringing an army. You're—"

Kett hit him on the side of the head and the words died in his throat.

"Fucked," Kett said. "Yeah, I get it."

He grabbed the man by the collar of his jacket and dragged him onto solid ground, giving him a couple of slaps to make sure he was unconscious. Then he rooted in the man's pockets, pulling out a set of keys.

"Bullseye," he said as he stood.

Savage pulled out her phone and fired up the torch, shining it on the man at their feet. It was Mark, although it was hard to tell because his haystack hair was caked in so much mud.

"What was that?" Kett asked, bracing his hands on his hips and doing his best to catch his breath.

"What?"

"The noise you were making? It sounded like a dog stuck in a washing machine."

"It was a baby, sir," she said. "Wasn't it?"

Incredibly, he laughed.

"You haven't met many babies, have you, Kate?"

"I..." she started, then she gasped. "Oh, shit, I've got a signal."

She ran her finger over the screen, lifting it to her ear, then to the sky.

"Come on," she said. "Come on, come on, come on."

It rang, the sound of it almost bringing Kett to tears. After a second or two, Clare answered.

"Sir, it's Savage," she said, cutting him off. "I don't know how long I've got. Whytetail is trafficking girls. We've found one, and the baby. We're going after the others. There's a mill downriver, that's where they're holding them. There's a lot of heat here, and more on the way. We need backup and we need it right now."

There was a moment of stunned silence, then Clare's voice.

"Toss me off. I'm on it. Hang tight, Savage, don't Kett this up."

"I'm right here, sir," said Kett.

"I mean it. Do not move. I'll call you back."

The line went dead and Savage lowered the phone.

"It's going to take them a while to get here," she said.

"So let's go," Kett replied. "We're running out of time."

CHAPTER THIRTY-ONE

"Fuck the fucking countryside all the way to fuck."

Porter slammed a fist on the wheel of Kett's Volvo, craning towards the windscreen to try to make sense of the winding roads that peeled themselves from the night. The satnav had given up a few miles back, the robotic woman sounding like she was having an aneurism as she demanded that he turn around and go the other way. But he was certain he'd driven back the exact same route he'd taken after dropping Mary Kett home, and unless the streets had simply picked themselves up and tied each other in knots there was no way he could be lost.

He drove on, keeping his speed low so as not to mount the steep banks. He'd only spotted a couple of cars since leaving the A11, and nothing in the last twenty minutes.

"Because nobody else is stupid enough to be arse deep in the middle of cow shit central," he said, if only to hear the sound of his own voice. It was as creepy as hell out here, the headlights turning the trees into skeletal figures that reached out for him from a dark that seemed far too heavy.

"Pull yourself together, Pete," he said.

But what he wouldn't give to have Kett or Savage sitting next to him. He couldn't even remember where he'd said he'd meet them, and they weren't answering their phones.

"Bastards."

He turned a corner, relieved to see another vehicle up ahead—a brand new Ford Transit. It was parked on the side of the road, the glowing interior lights making it look like a submarine in the depths of the ocean. Porter slowed so he didn't collide with it, raising a hand to the woman and the teenage girl in the front seats. He passed them carefully, grinding the Volvo along the verge as he went, keeping his speed low as he drove around the next corner because he was convinced he recognised the van, and the people in it.

He pumped the brake, frowning as the car shuddered to a halt.

Enid. The woman from the pub. He was sure it had been her and her daughter.

He slung the Volvo into reverse and backed up as fast as he dared. If it had been her she would almost certainly know the way to Whytetail.

When he wobbled around the corner, though, the van had gone.

"Fuck," he said.

He kept reversing, because he couldn't understand how they'd moved out of sight so fast. Maybe they'd turned the headlights off, but he couldn't even see the outline of the Transit on the side of the road. He braked, leaning out and trying to spot the Ford's headlights. It was only when he turned and looked over the verge that he saw them, a light-show in the trees.

They'd driven into the woods.

"Fuck this place," he said, sitting back in his seat. He

didn't close the door, though. He tapped the wheel for a moment then climbed out into the mild evening, running to the place he'd seen the parked van. There was no road here, no track or path or gate. But he could see the van moving in the woods, its engine revving hard.

He pulled out his phone and beamed the torch into the bushes that guarded the side of the road. There was only one place where the verge dropped, but a thick hedge barred the way. Not even the heavy Transit could have pushed through it.

Unless...

He scrambled up the steep bank, then jumped down the other side. There was a dirt road here, winding into the trees. He turned to the hedge, the beam of the torch picking out the metal five-bar gate covered in plastic greenery.

What the hell?

The gate wasn't locked and when he tugged hard it swung open towards him, creaking like a banshee. He moved it as far as it would go then ran back to the Volvo, reversing it a little more before bumping onto the track.

He had no idea where he was going but Whytetail had to be around here somewhere, and he had more chance of finding it this way than by driving aimlessly around the countryside all night. He kept his speed up, the Transit's taillights appearing out of the gloom. When he flashed the headlights the world glowed red as Enid hit the brakes.

Porter put the car in park and cut the engine, opening his door at the same time Enid opened hers.

"Hey," he said, lifting a hand in welcome. He sniffed, grateful to the night for at least putting the pollen to bed.

"What...?" she started.

She glanced into the van and said something before leaning out again.

"We spoke earlier," Porter said, walking towards her. "At the pub?"

"So?"

There was none of the joviality he'd seen before. Her face was as hard as stone in the Volvo's headlights, lines chiselled into her forehead.

"I'm lost," he said.

"No shit," said Enid.

"Uh..." Porter's stomach was churning but he didn't know why. "I'm looking for Whytetail, the old one. The commune. Was hoping you could point me there."

"Told you before, if you want their help, there are channels," she said. "You don't just turn up."

There was a soft thump from inside the back of the Transit.

"Unless you're not telling me the truth," Enid said. "Unless you're not who you say you are?"

Another thump, and this time Porter thought he saw the van rock on its wheels.

"What you got in there?" he asked, trying a smile. "Horses?"

Enid didn't smile back. The girl in the front said something and Enid hushed her with a stern word.

"Off you trot," she said when she turned her attention to Porter again. "Head back a way, half a mile, and you'll see the road. Ignore the signs, they'll take you to the new village."

"Half a mile," said Porter. "Sure. Thanks. You need a hand with whatever it is you're doing? It's late, dark. I'm happy to help."

Before she could answer, Porter's phone started to buzz. He held up a hand in apology as he pulled it free, seeing Clare's number.

"Alright guv," he said. "What's up?"

"Where are you?" Clare demanded, so loud that Porter had to pull the phone away from his ear and fumble with the volume. He walked back towards the Volvo as he spoke.

"Heading back for the others. I'm lost."

"Well un-fucking lose yourself, Porter. They're in trouble. The whole place is a trafficking ring, they're using the girls to provide the babies, and for God knows what else. That tosspot Kett found the baby, they're going after the other women."

Porter swallowed, looking over his shoulder to see Enid staring at him.

"I've called for backup but so have they," Clare went on. "Savage says they're expecting more men, and I don't think they're fucking around."

The Transit wobbled again. Something was definitely moving in there.

"Get to Whytetail, find Kett and Savage," Clare went on. "There's a tactical team *en route*. You hear me? Thirty minutes. Get Kett and Savage the hell out of there and they'll handle the rest."

"Yes sir," said Porter.

"You're close?"

"Closer than you'd believe," he said.

He met Enid's eyes, seeing the exact moment she worked it out.

"Fuck," said Enid.

"Fuck," said Porter.

"Chris!" Enid yelled, thumping on the side of the van. "Now!"

"Porter?" said Clare.

"Ford Transit," Porter yelled back. "AT20 BB—"

And that's as far as he got before the back door of the van swung open and a shotgun ripped the night in two.

CHAPTER THIRTY-TWO

KETT HEARD THE GUN GO OFF AS HE WAS RUNNING towards the mill—a concussive thump from deeper in the woods that woke the birds as if dawn had broken.

There was no time to worry about it. The old building rose up before them, Savage's torch doing little to illuminate it. Kett reached the veranda first, grabbing hold of a post that felt powdery with rot. The whole thing seemed to creak and shift beneath him, like a boat on rough seas. He had to stop to catch his breath, everything aching from the fight. He felt as old and infirm as Pastor Cairns.

Savage hopped up beside him, shining the torch left and right. The windows here had been boarded, the plywood brand new, and when Kett made his way down the building's broad flank he saw that the door was sealed as well. He put an ear to it but the mill was as silent as a tomb.

He crept around the side to see another door there, almost hidden by the suffocating woodland. It was closed, but when Kett turned the handle the old wood shuddered open, almost bringing the frame with it. Beyond was a darkness so absolute it was like the world simply ended.

"Age before beauty," whispered Savage with a nervous laugh.

She aimed the torch inside, revealing a small room with shuttered wooden walls. Part of the ceiling had fallen to the floor and things scuttled into the debris, frightened by the light. The only other door was nailed shut but the wall next to it had been almost entirely destroyed. Savage's light chased the dark through the gap where it waited for them.

"You getting that?" Savage said.

Kett cocked his head, trying to hear past the rush of the river outside.

There, a woman singing. It was so gentle he wasn't sure if it was real.

He nodded, leading the way through the ruined wall into a much larger room. It felt empty here, and it was only when Savage lifted the phone that he realised it wasn't.

"Christ," he said.

There were two cages in the middle of the space, long and thin with wheels and a hitch. Kett thought they might be livestock trailers, the kind you saw on the back of tractors.

But these held women.

There were three here, two in one cage and one in the other. The two who shared a cell were as young as Mihaela, and both were very pregnant. They put their hands up to the light, cowering against the bars, speaking in a language that Kett didn't know but understood anyway because there was no denying the sheer terror in those words.

"Hey," he said. "Hey, calm down, it's okay."

The woman who sat on her own was older, although it was hard to tell exactly how old because the lines on her face had been etched in dirt, as thick and dark as tattoos.

She wore a loose dress like the others, one which had been mended countless times.

"We're friends," said Kett. "Police."

"Sir," said Savage.

She was aiming her phone at a switch on the wall, and when she shone it upwards he saw the bulbs hanging from the ceiling. He shook his head. If the lights went on, the mill would be visible for miles. It would bring the wolves right to the door.

Savage turned the torch to the floor and Kett picked his way through the detritus, making for the cages. The women were growing more agitated but he kept his hands high, his voice calm.

"Police," he said. "We're here to help you. We found Mihaela."

It wasn't working, the two younger women shaking their heads as they pushed themselves against the back of the cage. Only the older one seemed to pay any attention.

"You're Mother?" Kett said to her.

She didn't nod, but the way she tilted her head in surprise gave away the answer.

"Mihaela has Luca, her baby. She found him."

"Luca?" said Mother.

"Yeah, Luca," said Kett. "We're going to get her out of here. She wouldn't leave without you."

Mother lifted her head and spoke to the others in a series of hissed, urgent sentences.

"There is a man," she said when she turned back to Kett, her accent almost identical to Mihaela's. "He has keys."

"No he doesn't," said Savage, holding them up. The woman smiled, but only for a second.

"He is not alone. Another man."

"Here?" said Kett, and she nodded.

"Another woman too. Upstairs."

Savage lifted the torch and Kett saw the stairs at the back of the room, so rickety it was a wonder they were still standing. They led to a small landing and another door, the barest trickle of light leaking through the cracks.

"They're together?" Kett said.

"He take her, not so long ago."

Kett nodded, turning to Savage.

"Get them out, and get out of the building."

He paused, no idea where to go next.

Savage must have read his mind.

"We'll figure out the rest when we get there. Go find her."

She approached the cages, the keys flashing. Kett went the other way, stumbling towards the stairs. Without the light he couldn't see the floor and he slipped and tripped a dozen times before he reached them. When he stepped on the first one it sang out a tune that sounded deafening in the silence.

He waited, his heart roaring. Then he took the next step only for it to squeal twice as loud.

He looked back to see that Savage already had the first cage open. The light from her phone jiggled as she helped the two younger women down from the trailer, both of them cradling their swollen bellies.

Upstairs, something moved.

Kett took the third step, this one quieter. But the next one seemed to make the entire building groan, dust raining down from the shadowed ceiling.

Fuck it.

He moved fast, ignoring the symphony from the old wood, making it to the landing. The door was open a crack and he shouldered it the rest of the way to see a long, narrow corridor lit by a bare bulb, one door to the right and another at the far end. He reached the first door in two long strides, opening it to see another room, a flickering lamp on the floor beneath the boarded window.

The room was bare, except for the mattress that sat on the floor.

And empty, except for the woman who lay there.

She blinked at Kett, pulling a thin, filthy sheet up to her throat. She was just as dirty, her face streaked with tears, her hair matted. All she wore was a pink slip, and even from here, even beneath the sheet, Kett could see the bulge of her stomach.

"No," she said. "No, please, no."

"I'm police," he said, entering the room. "Police, I won't hurt you."

She didn't seem to understand, pushing herself further back against the wall.

"Don't," she said. "Don't."

"I'm not going to—" Kett started.

Then he realised she wasn't looking at him. She was looking *behind* him.

Kett turned, but not fast enough. Something hit him like a train, punching the air from his lungs and snapping his head back. He was off the ground, he realised, a pair of arms locked around his waist. The man was thundering towards the boarded window, grunting with the effort.

"Fu—"

Kett hit the window in an explosion of wood and glass, the night opening up its maw to swallow him. He reached out as he fell, grabbing hold of his attacker's hair with both hands. The man screamed, losing his balance. Then they were both falling—too far, too fast.

The river caught him, impossibly cold. The other man landed on top of him, pushing him down into the weeds, into the silt. Kett opened his mouth, desperate for air already, but the man was a shifting weight on top of him, his hands on Kett's face as he tried to shunt himself back to the surface, his foot crunching on his knee.

Then he was gone, but the river wasn't going to let Kett go so easily. Weeds tangled his legs, his hands, the current sucking him down. His chest was a clenched fist, every last scrap of oxygen gone. He swung his arms back, managing to twist his body around then giving himself a mighty push— kicking, kicking until finally, he managed to break free.

He opened his mouth, sucking half a lungful of air, only for the man to come at him again, pushing him back under. It wasn't deep here but the ground was mush and he sank into it, the man's hands on his face, his fingers in his eyes. Kett groped for him, finding his arm, then his throat, grabbing what he could and squeezing hard.

The man let go, kicking out as he tried to get away. Kett pushed himself to the surface, fireworks blasting in his vision. The man was half swimming and half lunging as he entered the reeds, hacking up big, wet coughs.

Kett moved after him, gulping as much water as air, every muscle already failing. He reached him just as he was hauling himself onto land, grabbing the back of his jacket and yanking him back into the water.

He struggled but Kett left him there, using him as ballast to kick himself through the leaves and onto the river-bank. He clawed his way through the mud, screaming each breath. When he was well clear of the water he rolled onto his back, his body too heavy to pick up, both of his calves on the verge of cramping.

The man was splashing, grunting, and a second or two later

he emerged from the reeds. It was too dark to see his face but there was no denying his intent as he lumbered towards Kett.

There was a dull crack and the man suddenly stopped. An object thumped into him, knocking him back. He growled, raising his arm as another missile flew his way.

Bricks, Kett saw when one thumped into the mud by his foot. A woman stood by the riverbank, picking bricks off the ground and hurling them with one hand while she clamped a baby to her chest with the other.

"Fuck off!" the man yelled.

One brick glanced off his head and he reeled like a drunk. Then he turned and bolted, his shoes squelching.

"Are you okay?"

Kett recognised Mihaela's voice and the whimpers of baby Luca. He pushed himself up, although it took a few attempts before he was standing. The world danced around him, as if he was still tumbling in wild circles in the river.

"Yeah," he said after a moment. "I'm alive. Thank you."

There was a drum of feet and Kett braced himself, but it was Savage who ran out of the mill's side door. All four women were with her. She blinded him with her torch before lowering it.

"Sir?"

"I am getting way too old for this shit," he said. "Anyone see where that arsehole went?"

"No," said Mother, moving to the front of the group. "But he'll be back."

From somewhere in the woods, the man shouted.

"And he won't be alone," she added. "Come on."

For a second, Kett wasn't sure if he could remember how to walk. His body felt too heavy, too weak. Then somebody was there by his side, one of the young women from the mill. Her left arm was wrapped protectively around her stomach, but she took his hand with the other and tugged him gently forwards. Mihaela took his other arm, and between them they got him moving.

"You know the way?" the first woman said, her head twisting left and right, her eyes like moons.

"Up the hill," Savage replied. "If we head that way it will take us around the edge of the old village and back onto the main road. That sound good to you, Mihaela?"

"Da," she said, shifting Luca to her other arm.

The man was still shouting, and his calls were being answered. When Kett looked back he saw torches further down the river, too close. He sucked in air, pushing on. The ground was growing steeper with every step and after a minute or so they were deep in the woods again. The women spoke in their language, guiding each other as they followed Savage's light.

The shouts were fading, the lights falling further back. By the time they'd crested the hill Kett couldn't even hear them anymore. Maybe the men had given up? Maybe they were going to cut their losses and get the hell out of Whytetail while they still could.

Please, thought Kett. *Just fuck off.*

Savage battled her way through the undergrowth, carving a path for them like an icebreaker. Kett followed as fast as he could in his wet clothes, his skin numb, his teeth chattering. There was no sign of the cottages here, they'd come too far south, but after another few minutes he stepped onto what felt like gravel. Sure enough, when Savage aimed the light to the left and then right he saw that they were on a dirt track.

"Which way?" she asked.

"Main road's got to be that way, right?" Kett said, pointing to his left.

"So is the village," said Mihaela.

"And the wolves," said Savage.

"So that way," Kett said, turning. "Gotta go somewhere, right?"

"Anywhere but here is good with me, sir," said Savage.

She started walking, the gravel crunching beneath her feet—almost loud enough to hide the sound of footsteps coming from the other direction.

"Savage, wait," Kett hissed.

But it was too late. A shaft of light burned its way down the road, bright enough to blow off the back of Kett's head. He buried his face in his hands, calling Savage's name, hearing the sound of boots running towards them and an all-too familiar Northern voice.

"Found you, you fucks."

CHAPTER THIRTY-THREE

PORTER HIT THE GROUND AS THE GUN WENT OFF, SHOT scattering into the trees and ricocheting off the Volvo. Something bit into the skin of his shoulder but he didn't stop, scampering on all fours and diving behind Kett's car. The shotgun went off again, kicking up dirt and leaving a crater in the space he'd just left.

Past the whine in his ear, the air was full of shouts, and he could hear the shotgun being reloaded. He looked under the car, through whorls of gunpowder smoke, to see a pair of boots drop down from the back of the Transit. Then another. Then another.

Fuck.

"Go round, Chris!" yelled Enid. "He's right there."

Porter glanced into the woods, knowing he wouldn't last five seconds if he bolted. The fucks would shoot him in the back. There was nowhere else to go.

He reached up, finding the Volvo's tailgate. He couldn't remember if he'd locked the car or not but when he tugged the handle the boot whined open. He climbed inside and pulled the door shut as the shotgun detonated again, the passenger side windows exploding in a hail of glass. He threw himself over the back seat just as the gun slid through the shattered window, the face behind it grinning.

"Got you," the man called Chris said.

Porter grabbed the barrels, jamming the gun against the ceiling as it went off. The sound of it was so loud that he thought he'd been shot, pain ripping through both ears into his skull, turning his brain to jelly.

Chris was trying to wrench the gun out of his hands, opening the door to get to him. Porter refused to let go, lying on the seat and kicking the door as hard as he could. It sprung open into the other man's face, knocking him back.

Before Porter could sit up, the door behind him opened, somebody grabbing his head and pulling him out. He slid to the ground, still holding the gun, twisting away to avoid a stamping boot. Another man was there, his face full of fury as he launched a kick. He had tattoos on his hands, a lion and a bear. Porter had seen him before.

He let go of the gun and grabbed the man's boot, yanking hard. The tattooed guy fell with a shout, then Porter was up, collecting the shotgun from the ground. He used it like a golf club, striking hard. The man's head snapped back and he lay still, other than the haggard rise and fall of his chest.

"Wanker," Porter said, the word muffled by the ringing in his skull. He braced a hand on the side of the car so that he could recover his breath.

The third man was approaching, and he was holding a carving knife. He was young, maybe in his twenties, and he looked scared. On the other side of the Volvo, Chris was recovering, both men circling the car to pincer him. Behind them, Enid watched. She was on the phone, Porter saw. Never a good sign.

The gun was empty, so he lifted it like a bat, testing its heft.

"Come on, you piece of shit," he said to the kid.

The kid glanced at Chris, still unsure.

"He's not gonna help you," Porter said. "I'm police, son. You go through with this, you're fucked."

"Don't listen to him," said Chris. Or at least that's what Porter *thought* he said, because he couldn't hear much of anything. Chris was older, bearded, and he was wearing a pair of cheap camouflaged overalls. He kept looking at the gun like he couldn't believe he'd lost it. "Just fucking get him."

The kid lunged, the knife flashing. Porter stepped back, pivoting on his heel as he swung the improvised bat. The heavy stock connected with the boy's hand, the knife flying free and vanishing beneath the car. He cried out in pain, falling onto his backside and cradling his injured wrist against his chest.

Porter heard running. He tried to turn but he wasn't fast enough, Chris rounding the Volvo and planting both hands on Porter's chest, shoving him backwards. Porter tripped over the injured kid and fell, just managing to hold onto the gun, his head ringing off the hard dirt. Chris was right there, pinning him down, a fist striking him just beneath his left eye.

Porter pushed his hips off the ground and rolled to the side, sending Chris flying. But the guy grabbed the gun as he went, pulling it free and taking it with him. He'd snapped it open in a heartbeat, jamming a cartridge into the barrel. Porter swore, pushing himself to his feet and vaulting the high bonnet of the Volvo just as the gun went off.

The car rocked, the windscreen exploding. Porter

landed hard, feeling his ankle give. He could hear the man reloading.

You fucking idiot, Pete, he thought. How had he lost the gun?

Chris would be on him in seconds, and Porter didn't think he'd miss again. The Volvo was a wreck, the woods were too far away.

There was only one place to go.

He ran for the Transit. The gun barked, the air seeming to shudder with the force of it. Something thumped into the back of his leg, making him miss his footing, but he didn't stop. Enid saw him coming, her face falling. She tried to get back into the driver's seat but she was too slow, her shoe slipping on the step.

Porter grabbed her by the scruff of her shirt and hurled her out of the way, sending her rolling into the weeds.

He climbed into the van, flinching when he saw Enid's daughter there. She curled her feet beneath her and lifted her hands in defence.

"Do not move," Porter told her as he slammed the door shut. The engine was still running and he slid the gearstick into first, his injured leg burning as he gunned the accelerator.

The gun detonated again, a fist of shot punching the side of the Transit and ripping the wing-mirror away. The van thumped and bumped its way down the rough track, turning a corner into silence.

Porter put a hand to his aching shoulder, feeling the blood pooling in his shoe. He turned to the young woman again.

"I'm police," he said. "Do I have to worry about you?"

"Police?" she echoed with a heavy accent. "*Politisti?*"

Not Enid's daughter, then, Porter thought.

"Yeah, police," he said, and the girl managed the smallest of smiles before burrowing her head between her knees and starting to sob.

"Let's get you home," he said to her.

He reached for his phone before realising he'd dropped it when the gun went off. It didn't matter, the road was going in the right direction.

"I've just got to make a quick stop first."

CHAPTER THIRTY-FOUR

THE WOLVES HAD FOUND THEM.

And they were hungry for blood.

Kett blinked the angry torchlight from his eyes, seeing Tom Faulkner standing in the middle of the gravel track wearing a fat, wet smile. There was no humour in his eyes, though. They were like gimlets, full of cold hatred.

In his hands he held a big, black crossbow, the broadhead bolt gleaming.

Flanking him were four men, one armed with another crossbow, the others holding knives.

"Where the fuck were you gonna go?" Faulkner asked, looking around him. "This place is vast, and we know all of it."

Baby Luca began to cry, as if he knew what was about to happen. Kett could hear Mihaela trying to calm him with sweet words but there was terror in her voice. Faulkner looked past Kett and his shit-eating grin grew wider.

"There's my lad," he said. "Little Adam. Why don't you bring him back, love?"

Mihaela spat a word in her own tongue and Faulkner laughed.

"Yeah, I love you too. Go get her."

Two of the men started walking but Kett moved himself between them and the child.

"Don't," he said.

"Or what?" Faulkner replied. He lifted the crossbow, aiming for the middle of Kett's chest. He was ten yards away. It would be almost impossible for him to miss. "You'll get blood on me?"

"Kill a copper and you're done," Kett said. "You're finished. They'll never stop hunting you."

"But you're not a copper, are you?" said Faulkner, taking a step towards him. "Your mum told us you'd left the Force. You're just a civilian. And her..."

Faulkner turned his attention to Savage.

"I don't think I'm going to kill her. I think we can use her. Looks like a good little breeding machine to me."

The anger was a living thing inside Kett, powerful enough to make his ears ring. Savage didn't reply but he saw the same fury there, silent and dangerous.

"Go get the child," Faulkner said again, gesturing with the crossbow.

"No," said Kett. "You so much as touch that baby and I'll fucking kill you."

He glared at the two men, and neither of them took another step.

"We've been here all day," he said to them, to *all* of them. "We know every one of you. They're coming for you right now. Even if you kill me, you'll never make it out of Whytetail. I swear to God, your lives will be a living hell."

"We'll get out," said Faulkner. "We've got roads you'll never find, and we've got another place all set up. You think you're smart, *Robert*, but you're as thick as pig shit. As thick as your mum was. She couldn't see what was happening in front of her eyes and neither could you, neither could any of the fuckers here. By the time your lot get to town we'll be gone, it'll just be Reg's shitbrained flock left to take the fall."

"And Summer?" said Kett.

"Aye, she'll be coming with us," Faulkner said. He looked back, talking to the man behind him. "You see her yet?"

"She's coming," said one of the men.

"You can't kill me until she gives you permission," said Kett. "Right? She's the boss. She's behind this whole thing."

"We're a team effort," said Faulkner. "She had this place, I had my connections. We made it work. We've made it work for years."

Luca was screaming now, and his mother was crying into him. Savage had moved to her side, holding her close, the rest of the women forming a protective circle between them and the men.

"Go on now," Faulkner said. "Get the fucking baby."

"You know, I've met a lot of men like you," Kett said to Faulkner. "You think you're something special, but you're not. You think you're clever, but you're not. You think you're above the law, but you're not."

Faulkner grinned, his hands flexing on the crossbow.

"You know what happens to men like you?" Kett went on. "You don't get away. You don't get to go and live your life."

"What then?" Faulkner said, heaving a dry, wheezing laugh. "You'll send me to prison?"

"No," said Kett. "Men like you, they don't go to prison either. They drown in their own shit. They die in the night with a hammer in their head."

Faulkner's smile took flight.

"Because for every man like you, there's somebody like me," Kett said. "And you have no fucking idea what we're capable of."

Faulkner didn't reply, because they all heard the sound of footsteps at the same time. Somebody was walking up the track, shrouded by night.

"Summer, that you?" Faulkner asked without looking. "Can I kill this deluded wank-stain already?"

It was Summer, but she didn't reply. She walked slowly up behind Faulkner, standing there in the dark. It was only when one of the men aimed his torch back that Kett saw the other person in the shadows behind her, towering over her head.

Paul Palmer.

One of the giant man's hands was clamped on Summer's bony shoulder, and the other held a knife to her throat. She closed her eyes and swallowed, her fear palpable.

"Palmer?" spluttered Faulkner. "What are you doing, you stupid fat fuck?"

"It's t-true, isn't it?" Palmer said, his voice broken. "It's all true."

"I've tried to explain it to you, Paul," said Summer. "It's not what it looks like. We're doing the Lord's work, but you just can't see it."

"She's lying," said Kett. "It's exactly what it looks like. They're trafficking girls, forcing them to have babies. There are no miracles in Whytetail. Just murder."

"Shut the fuck up," said Faulkner, slowly and deliberately. "Palmer, you prick, put down the fucking knife."

"Put it down, Paul," said Summer. "And we can talk.

Remember, God moves in mysterious ways. This is one of them. I can explain."

Palmer was crying, the tears rolling down his big cheeks, over his chapped lips. He looked past Kett and seemed to see the young women for the first time, shaking his head.

"You're m-monsters," he said. "I won't let you do it."

"Put down the fucking knife," said Faulkner. The crossbow was still aimed at Kett, but it was wavering. "I mean it. I'll give you three seconds. One."

"It's not too late for you to see the light," said Summer, everything trembling. "It's not too late for you to make this right in His eyes."

"Two."

"Kill her!" Mihaela shouted, her voice rising over Luca's screams. "Kill her!"

But Palmer was stepping back, his eyes almost popping out of his head as if he'd only just realised what he was doing. Faulkner saw his opportunity, swinging the crossbow around.

"Three."

Kett hurled himself onto Faulkner's back just as he pulled the trigger. He felt the snap of the crossbow through the man's arms, then they both hit the ground. Somebody screamed but Kett didn't have time to look. He dug his knee into Faulkner's kidneys, pinning him there.

"Robbie!" Savage screamed.

The second crossbow snapped but the bolt went wide, skittering down the track. The man swore, starting to reload. Faulkner was pushing himself up, freakishly strong, and Kett punched him in the side of the head. It was a bad hit, pain clawing its way down his wrist. He used an elbow instead, driving it into the bald man's neck and forcing him down.

Only then did he look up, seeing Palmer standing there with a hand to his stomach. Blood poured out of him, staining his white shirt and spattering on the track as heavily as summer rain.

Palmer roared like a bear, running past Summer hard enough to send her sprawling into the nettles at the side of the track, heading for the closest of the men. He grabbed his head with bloody hands, actually lifting him off the ground. The guy lashed out with his knife, slashing at Palmer's arms, but the big man was like a berserker, he didn't even seem to feel it.

A scream. Kett looked back to see another of the men trying to pull the baby from Mihaela's arms. Savage was there in an instant, kicking his legs out from under him. He went down like a sack of bricks, Mihaela stamping on his head, the other women fast joining her in a storm of violence.

"Go!" Savage yelled at them. "Run!"

The women scattered into the night, Luca still shrieking. One of the men started to chase them while another rounded on Savage. She lifted her fists, bouncing on the balls of her feet, ready to give as good as she got.

Faulkner bucked hard and Kett fell back onto the gravel. He rolled onto his knees but Faulkner was faster. The bald brute scrambled to his feet, sliding a combat knife from a sheath on his belt.

"You know what happens to men like me?" he said, that grin back on his face. "We fucking win."

Past the thunder of his panic Kett heard an engine. Faulkner heard it too, squinting down the road as a pair of headlights burned their way out of the night. It was a van, a big one, but any hope that it was the police died when Faulkner's grin grew even bigger.

"Cavalry's arrived," he said. "So just die like a good boy, will you?"

He pulled back his arm, the knife glinting in the van's headlights.

The engine roared, the van accelerating. The man who was attacking Savage leapt out of the way just in time, but Faulkner wasn't so lucky. The van thumped into him and he bounced off the bonnet like he was made of rubber, ragdolling down the track in a cloud of dust.

Kett pushed himself up as the van squealed and shuddered to a stop. The driver's window was down, the door pitted with buckshot, and Porter was there, his face knotted with pain and damp with sweat.

"Get in the fucking van!" he yelled.

Kett didn't have to be asked twice. He ran to the back, meeting Savage there. The doors were open, the van empty, and Savage leapt inside.

"Mihaela!" she yelled.

The young woman burst from the bushes, holding her baby. The other women were right behind her and Savage hauled them into the van one by one. Kett followed them in, pulling the doors shut just as one of the men appeared there, his crossbow rising.

"Go!" Kett yelled, slamming the flat of his hand on the wall.

The van lurched forward, everyone stumbling. It bumped over something on the track that may or may not have been Tom Faulkner, then they were free, picking up speed. Mihaela fell into Kett and he caught her, holding her tight, the baby sandwiched between them. Luca was quietening, mesmerised by the rocking motion of the van, his little breaths hitching.

"It's over," Kett told him. "It's over."

The van crunched into something, everyone bobbing like puppets.

"It's over," Kett muttered. "As long as Porter doesn't drive us into the bloody river."

"We are safe?" Mihaela asked him, her breath hot against his face.

He didn't dare answer her because the van was slowing down, wheezing to a halt. There was a shout, then another. Every single person held their breath as they heard the driver's door open. More shouts, voices raised in anger.

Footsteps walking down the side of the van. The sound of the handle turning.

Then the door opened, revealing a world that shimmered with blue light.

Porter stood there, and he was grinning. A second later an armed police officer appeared beside him, nodding up at Kett through his visor.

"Everyone okay?" he asked.

"We're good," Kett said. "Bad guys are back that way."

The tactical officer moved away and a line of armed police followed him. Porter breathed out a long sigh as he watched them go. He was bleeding, Kett saw, the back of his yellow football shirt was slick with blood and two trails of it ran from his ears. When he tried to move he winced, and he had to lean against the van.

"You okay?" Kett asked him.

"What?" he said, wiggling a finger in his ear. "Deaf as a post."

"Are you okay?" Kett yelled.

"Just a scrape," he replied, looking at Kett's wet clothes. "You?"

"Fell in the river," said Kett.

Savage stepped past Kett and hopped down to the road.

"Good to see you, sir," she said to Porter. She smiled, but there was a deep vein of sadness in her voice. "One hell of a day, eh?"

Kett nodded, gently lowering himself onto the tailgate before dropping the rest of the way. He peeked around the Transit to see three police IRVs and a van blocking the road, an ambulance behind them, their lights beating back the night. More police were gathered there, and he could hear Clare barking orders from somewhere in the middle of them.

He looked back into the van to where Mihaela and the other women stood in a tight circle around the mewling baby. Something about them reminded him of lions.

"You're safe," he said. "You're free."

He stood to one side as the paramedics appeared, watching them clamber into the back of the van. Then he joined Savage and Porter by the steep verge. They both looked shattered. Hollowed out. Savage smiled sadly at him.

"A little piece of you dies so that they can live, right?"

Kett nodded.

And sooner or later, there will be nothing left to give.

"What?" said Porter. The big DI had tears in his eyes and he smudged them away with the back of his hand.

"Nothing," Savage said. "You crying, sir?"

"Huh?"

"Crying?" she said, rubbing her eyes with her fists to demonstrate.

"No," he said, sniffing. "Pollen, *innit?*"

But he was, and he pulled Savage close, holding her tight. She rested her head on his chest and held him back, her own tears coming quietly.

"I don't blame you," said Kett.

He collapsed into the long grass of the verge, closing his

eyes, the day replaying itself over and over and over. He could feel the tears burning his own eyes, the painful lump in his throat, the anger and the fear and the relief almost too much to bear.

"I don't blame you at all."

He thought of Mihaela. He remembered the weight of her son when he'd held him, those fingers exploring his face. He thought of all those women, and all those children. And the sobs wrenched their way out of him, rising into the night.

CHAPTER THIRTY-FIVE

Tuesday

KETT PULLED BACK HIS ARM AND LET THE STONE FLY. Every single muscle in his body responded with a cry of pain but he growled through gritted teeth, trying not to feel it. He'd done this job for long enough now to know how to tune out the pain.

The pain in his body.

The pain in his mind, too.

The stone hit the sea and bounced once before gravity pulled it beneath the surface.

That was the trouble, wasn't it? Gravity always won. No matter how hard he threw them, the stones always sank.

It was like his mood. Even though the late afternoon sun had thrown a blanket of warmth and light over the wide Yarmouth beach, even though his girls ran up and down the sand, laughing their way between their mother and grandmother, he couldn't shake the horror of the last few days. Every time he closed his eyes he was right back there in the river at Whytetail, drowning in the dark.

He wasn't sure if he'd ever feel warm again.

He ducked down, rooting in a galaxy of wet stones until he found another flat one. He worked it around in his palm as he stood up, gauging its weight and waiting for a quiet wave to meander onto the shore. Before he could throw it, Alice came galumphing over and grabbed his arm, turning his hand up to investigate what sat there.

"What's that, Dad?"

"Just a stone," he said, shaking her loose. "I'm skimming them. Want to see?"

She nodded and he waved her back a few steps. He put the stone in the curl of his forefinger, lined up the shot, then let go. The stone flew, but it only bounced off the tame sea twice before vanishing.

"Can I do it?" Alice said.

"Sure," he replied as she searched for a stone. "But it takes a bit of practice. The trick is to…"

Alice hurled the stone sideways and Kett watched open-mouthed as it skimmed off the water six times. He turned to congratulate her but she wasn't even watching, she was sprinting down the beach, kicking up fountains of sand as she made her way towards a lone figure approaching from the south.

Kett raised a hand against the sun to see DC Savage walking over the dunes, her hair dancing in the breeze, one hand trailing in the long seagrass. Behind her, the beach stretched on forever, the tuneless soundtrack of the arcades audible even this far north. She smiled, lifting a hand in welcome.

"Kate!" shouted Alice, thumping into Savage so hard

that Kett heard the *oof* over the rush of the waves. Savage hugged her, laughing.

"You tackle like your dad," she said when Alice had let go.

Evie was running over too, struggling on the sand, her cheeks blazing beneath Alice's enormous hat. She stopped after a moment, breathless, and Billie picked her up, holding her tight.

"Hey, Kate," Billie said. "How're you doing?"

"Good," Savage said, but Kett could see the lie there, in the tightness of her smile, in the way she wrapped her arms around herself straitjacket tight. She met his eyes for a fraction of a second before smiling at Evie. "Hot enough for you?"

"Too hot," Evie wailed. "I want ice cream."

"Pete's getting some," said Savage. "Clare's parking the car."

"Clare's here too?" asked Kett. "Why?"

"Said it was too hot to be stuck in the office," she said. "He's wearing medically prescribed shorts, Robbie, just to warn you. Hey, Moira. Mary. How's tricks?"

Kett glanced down the beach to see his mum carrying his youngest daughter. Even though it had been a few days since Whytetail it still gave his heart a mighty kick to see her, as if by thinking about it too hard he would somehow stop it from being real.

Mary Kett didn't look like the same woman he'd seen standing in the shadow of the old church. She stood taller, just like she did in his memories, and the smile was on her face more often than not. She was dressed in a flowing skirt and a white blouse, her feet bare. The crucifix still hung around her neck.

She still carried those old memories with her, of course.

Memories of the bad days, of his dad. She always would, he knew. But here on the beach with the blue skies overhead, Kett understood that it didn't matter. All that was important was that she'd soon be carrying *new* memories too.

Good ones. And lots of them.

She caught him looking and smiled, almost stumbling. Moira laughed, thinking that it was a game, and his mum started laughing too, bobbling her up and down in her skinny arms. Kett realised he was holding his breath, although he wasn't sure why. He unlocked his lungs, breathing hard, white flashes exploding against the horizon. He turned to Savage, the sun suddenly too bright, just like it had been in Whytetail.

Not warm, though. He was still shivering.

"Any news?" he asked. "How's Mihaela?"

"Who's Mihaela?" asked Alice, bending down to scoop up a handful of sand. She hurled it into the air, oblivious to where it might go.

"Don't throw sand, Alice," Kett said.

She looked like she was about to argue then she jumped up and started waving. Porter was struggling over the dunes in his designer suit, using both hands to hold the biggest ice cream Kett had ever seen. There had to have been five scoops of various flavours nesting in a waffle cone that could have doubled as a vase.

"Pete!" Alice yelled.

"Ice cream!" shouted Evie.

"Yo," said Porter. He licked the drips from his fingers. "Christ, it's hot."

"Nice of you to get them ice cream," said Kett. Porter frowned at him.

"What?"

"Ice cream," Kett said. "For the girls, right?"

Porter shook his head, pulling the cone to his chest.

"It's my ice cream," he said, followed by what almost sounded like a growl.

"Yeah, good luck with that," said Billie.

Alice was already on him, giggling as she lunged for the cone. Porter screamed, retreating, but Evie had torn herself loose from her mother and was joining the fight. It was over in seconds, before Moira even had a chance to help her sisters. The three girls ran off behind a dune to share the spoils of their victory.

"I was really looking forward to that," Porter muttered. "How's it going? How's your mum?"

Kett looked at his kids, at his wife, at his mum, hearing the laughter, seeing the smiles. But he felt cut off from it all, oddly distant.

"Good," he said. "It's all good. Mum seems okay. What are you doing all the way out here?"

"Got an update," Porter said, sniffing.

"And you couldn't use the phone?"

"On a day like this? Nope. Beach all the way."

"We can leave you to it," Billie said. "The girls want to head into the town anyway."

"Thanks," Kett replied. "It won't take long. I'll meet you there."

Billie kissed him on the cheek, squeezing his arm. She walked over to where their daughters sat, all three of them plastered in ice cream.

"Let's go to the arcades," she said to a round of cheers.

Mary hovered, unsure of what to do with herself.

"Would you like me to stay?" she said. "I'm happy to, if you need me?"

"No," Kett said, too abruptly. "We don't."

She nodded sadly as she turned to go, walking bent-backed over the sand in pursuit of her granddaughters. Kett sighed. It was true, wasn't it? He hadn't needed her for so long, because she hadn't been there.

But maybe every son needed their mother, whether she was there or not.

And his was right in front of him.

"Wait, Mum," Kett said. He chased after her, catching her in the hollow between the dunes. She turned to look at him and he saw himself in her face, in the lines around her eyes. It took his breath away, and for a second or two he couldn't speak.

"I'm sorry," she said.

"For what?"

"For calling after all this time. I didn't want to. I didn't think you'd even be able to help, because I thought you were still a policeman. It's just that Reginald asked me, and I couldn't say no to him. I never could. I didn't mean for you to get caught up in all this... all this *madness*."

He started to answer but she held up her hand.

"I didn't want to because I didn't think you'd want to see me. I thought you would be doing better without me. I didn't want all those bad feelings to come back."

A couple of gulls screamed their way overhead, fighting over scraps.

"What bad feelings, Mum?" he asked.

"About your dad," she said.

Kett closed his eyes, seeing his father the way he'd found him all those years ago when he'd finally given up on life, given up on his family.

"I thought you blamed me," Mary said.

He opened his eyes, the sun still too bright.

"I thought you blamed *me*," he echoed.

Mary shook her head, putting a cool hand to his cheek.

"Never, Robert," she said. "Never. Not once. What your father did was on him, nobody else. It was his choice to make. I never blamed you for it and..." She sobbed, putting the same hand to her mouth. "I'm so sorry, Robert, I didn't think... I never once imagined that you blamed yourself. I thought you hated *me*."

His tears broke like waves, threatening to drown him. He couldn't speak, and instead he opened his arms and his mum fell into him. For what felt like forever they held onto each other, and he was a child again. It didn't quite make up for twenty years of absence. But it was a good start.

And just like that, Kett felt the warmth of the sun.

It was Mary who pulled away first, using the hem of her long skirt to wipe her eyes then clean her glasses. She cupped Kett's face again, just for a second.

"I'd better go after those girls," she said, her voice trembling. "I've got a bag of pennies for the machines."

"Nobody uses pennies anymore, Mum," Kett said, scrubbing the heel of his hand over his own eyes, feeling the scratch of the sand against his skin.

She started to walk away, then hesitated. The serious look on her face made Kett feel as if she was about to say something else about his dad, and he braced himself.

"Robert, one thing," she said. "What is a farty butt cheese?"

He snorted a laugh, the relief washing through him.

"If you ever find out, let me know," he said.

She walked away, following the laughter of his daughters. She passed Clare as she went, the Superintendent wading through the sand as bow-legged as a cowboy. He was wearing his shirt and suit jacket but his long, bony legs poked out of the bottom of a giant pair of baggy black shorts. He looked like a badly dressed scarecrow.

"You okay, Robbie?" Savage asked, and he nodded.

"Just been an emotional week," he said. "How's Mihaela doing?"

"About as well as you'd expect. But she's safe. She's been doing a lot of sleeping. She was exhausted, dehydrated and had severe hypothermia, but she's strong. She'll pull through. They're letting Luca stay with her, for now. They figured it was best for the baby. Not sure how long it will last, because they'll charge her with murder."

"Any luck getting hold of her family in Romania?" Kett asked.

"They're flying over tomorrow," Porter said. "They've been looking for Mihaela for two years."

"*Years*?" Kett said. "She's been at Whytetail all that time?"

"Since she was seventeen," Porter said. "She was down in London, went for a holiday job and was never seen again. Enid's part of a massive ring of traffickers, we've discovered. Most of the girls went to brothels but some found their way to Whytetail. There have been dozens of babies born there over the years, we're still looking into where they came from."

"It's a massive operation," said Clare, huffing and puffing his way into the conversation. "Families are going to be torn apart. Many of them are still living in Whytetail. Those kids we saw, the ones running around..." He took a shuddering breath. "It's a right tossing mess. Breaks my heart. The other three women we found in the mill are all in advanced stages of pregnancy. They're being supported. There were more, though. Dozens, over the years. We're exhuming the graves beneath Summer Cairns' flowerbeds. We think they may have buried some of the women there, when they weren't useful anymore."

"Fuckers," said Kett.

"I don't think there will be many, though," Clare went on. "Testimony from Ioana Sandu, the woman they knew as Mother, makes it clear that most of the women were trafficked to other destinations after Whytetail. Enid transported them, along with her husband Chris. The woman you found in the van, Porter—Sylvie Rigo—was on her way to the mill to join the others."

"It was a lucky escape," said Savage.

"Enid has given us a lot of names and a lot of addresses. There was a woman at the hospital, too. She was in on it. I think you spoke to her."

"Ramona?" said Kett. "I knew it. That was the thing that didn't make any sense. The hospital should have known that Caitlyn wasn't the mother. They *would* have known. But they had an inside man."

"Woman," said Savage. "And because they always knew when one of their babies was going to be 'born' they could always make sure she'd be on duty. She made it look legitimate, let them get their hospital photos, their discharge records."

"It was a sophisticated system," said Clare. "They knew what they were doing."

"And we're going to get them back," said Savage. "All those kids."

"As many as we can," Clare said. "They've already started the raids. These arseholes are finished."

Kett exhaled a breath he'd been holding for far too long.

"What about Summer Cairns, sir? Tom Faulkner?"

"Faulkner is still in critical care," Clare said, giving Porter a look. "He won't wake up, I'm sure of it. Some of the details about how he sustained his injuries are still a mystery, right Porter?"

"Yes, isn't that right, Porter?" said Kett. "Some of the injuries to my car, as well."

The Volvo had been a write-off, too much damage from the shotgun. It was a sad end to their reliable old workhorse, but better the car than Porter.

"Officially, I'm not sure we'll ever work out exactly what happened to him," Clare said. "The other men who worked for Summer are all in custody and looking at a long time behind bars. There were eight of them in all, including Faulkner."

"And Paul Palmer?"

"He had no idea. Not a clue. It broke him. I'm not sure if you know, he didn't make it."

Kett felt an unexpected current of sadness at the thought of the big man's passing.

Anger, too.

"Tell me you've got Summer, though."

"She's been charged already. And so has her husband."

"He was in on it?"

"At the start, yes. He and Summer came up with the idea themselves. He believed he was doing the work of God. It's what the Cliffords did, you know? A century ago. Spalding's been doing some research. They couldn't conceive a child so they used one of their servants, got her pregnant, took the baby, murdered her and buried her body by the river. Forensics found bones beneath the lake, in the roots of that old weeping willow, unidentified. All still speculation, of course. But it makes sense."

"Lord Clifford wasn't digging a well," said Kett. "He was digging a grave."

"But the legends were true, in a way," said Savage. "Caitlyn and Liam made a deal with the Devil. Summer Cairns."

"Summer will spend the rest of her life in prison," Clare said. "I'm not sure Reginald will survive the next few days. Fiona's working on Mihaela's case. She thinks she can mitigate her sentence, if it goes to trial. The poor lass is going to get every bit of help she needs to get through this, and to keep her child. But the truth is, I don't know what will happen to her."

"It's something out of your worst nightmares," said Savage.

"What about Caitlyn and Liam?" Kett asked. "Did they know what they were signing up for?"

"That is something we are still trying to figure out," said Clare. "But yes, I think they did. Their medical records show they tried IVF numerous times, adoption too, although his mental health problems made that impossible. Witnesses say both of them were present in the room beneath the church when Luca was conceived, although nobody knows who the father is. There were..." Clare swallowed, wiping the sweat from his brow. "There were too many men involved. We'll need a DNA test. We're rounding up the other couples who had their babies at Whytetail, too, to see how many of them knew the truth."

"But nobody else in Whytetail had a clue what was going on," said Porter. "Can you believe that? Not one person knew what was happening right beneath their noses."

"They didn't know, or they didn't care," said Savage. "You have to be pretty deluded to believe in those kinds of miracles."

"We're interviewing everyone," Clare said. "We'll find out the truth. Either way, Whytetail is finished. Thanks to you lot."

The gulls were back, wheeling through the cloudless

sky. Kett watched them go, feeling the sun on his face, the breeze in his hair.

"You came all the way out here to thank us?" he asked.

"Yes and no," said Clare. "I'm still trying to avoid long periods of sitting. Doctor's orders. My crotchal area took quite a beating from those trousers. I still have so much tossing pain in my ba—"

"I don't need the details," Kett said, holding up a hand. "Please, sir. If I go my whole life without hearing the word 'crotchal' again, I'll die a happy man."

Clare cleared his throat, adjusting his shorts.

"I've come here to ask you a question, Kett," he said after a moment. "And I need you to think very carefully before you answer it."

Kett frowned, the cold clawing its way back into his bones. Porter and Savage were watching him and he realised they knew exactly what Clare was about to ask.

"What?"

"Things are getting worse out there," Clare said. "You've said it yourself. Something's going on. The crimes we're seeing, they're different somehow. Figg and Stillwater, your Pig Man, all of that Hollenbeck stuff, even those kids up by the coast. Now this; a trafficking ring working right under our noses. Those women, those poor children."

The Superintendent shook his head, staring out across the murmuring sea.

"There are monsters out there," he said. "And even with every resource at our disposal, it's getting harder and harder to stop them."

Kett could see where this was going, and he wasn't sure if the churning in his gut was from fear or excitement.

"Sir," he started, but Clare waved him down.

"We need you, Kett," the Super said. "We need your

instincts. But it's more than that. Because sometimes, I think, we need people to do the *wrong* thing. Sometimes, to stop a monster, you have to..."

He stopped, his brow buckling into a deep frown as if he wasn't sure whether to continue.

"You have to send a monster," Kett finished for him.

"Yes," Clare said. "I'm setting up a new Task Force. I want you to lead it. Officially."

"But sir," Kett said, only for Clare to override him again.

"I've spoken to the Chief Constable, and I've spoken to Larry Ling down at the Met. It wasn't easy, and there are more hoops we'll need to jump through if you say yes, but we've cleared a path for you, if you want to come back."

"Sir..." Kett started for a third time, but even though nobody else spoke he couldn't find the words to finish. He looked past the Super to see his family, almost off the beach now. Their laughter drifted back, louder than the gulls.

He'd made a promise to Billie. He'd promised her a fresh start.

But he'd made a promise to Mihaela, too. He'd made a promise to her child.

You'll be okay. You'll be safe.

And it wasn't just to them, was it? It was to every victim out there. To every mother's son, and every mother's daughter.

I'll bring you home.

"I get to pick my team," he said.

"Obviously," Clare replied. "Although, I've already allocated these two tosspots."

Porter and Savage grinned.

"And I'm going after Hollenbeck," Kett said.

"I'd expect nothing less. I want to find those arseholes as much as you do."

Kett looked at his family again, just specks, now, against the line of arcades along the seafront. He had his mum back, and the kids had their grandmother. He didn't think that was going to change. They had an extra pair of hands. It could work.

I'll bring you home.

"Okay," he said. "Okay. I'm in."

Clare's face morphed into something that might have been a smile and he thrust out one giant hand. Kett shook it.

"Tossing hell," the Super said. "I know for a fact that in about four months I'm going to regret this, but for now, I'm happy to have you on the team. Welcome back, DCI Kett."

DCI. It sounded strange. It sounded unfamiliar.

But it sounded *right*.

"Thank you, sir," Kett said.

"Don't Kett it up," Clare said as he turned and stumbled away over the sand.

"Good news, right?" Porter said.

"You're back," added Savage with a smile.

Kett nodded, and for a second the beach fell dark as a solitary cloud passed over the sun. He shivered, looking for his girls again and not finding them.

"I'm back."

Then the cloud moved and the heat rolled back in.

"Come on," said Porter. "Let's get ice cream to celebrate."

"All I need is tea," said Kett. "Let's see if we can get a cup."

He clapped the big DI on the shoulder.

"From *de caf*."

And Kett was laughing as he made his way back to the road.

BINGE THE SERIES NOW

www.ballsknowsitalls.net

LIFE IS NO FAIRY TALE

SWEET BRIAR ROSE

A DCI ROBERT KETT NOVEL

ALEX SMITH

THE INTERNATIONALLY BESTSELLING SERIES

SWEET BRIAR ROSE
THE EIGHTH DCI ROBERT KETT NOVEL

DCI Kett is back, heading Norfolk Constabulary's brand-new Extreme Crime Task Force.

And it's just in time, as the body of a woman bound in thorns is discovered in Norwich's historic Cow Tower. In her mouth is a severed finger wrapped in a scrap of red cloth, and the first few lines of a fairy tale.

"Once upon a time, a young maiden waited to be saved from a hideous monster."

The finger belongs to another missing girl, and if Kett, Porter and Savage want to find her alive they must follow a chain of blood-drenched riddles, each victim leading to the next and each crime more horrific than the last.

Because this killer is telling a story, and he'll do anything to stop it from having a happy ending.

Join DCI Kett, DI Porter and DC Savage on their most dangerous and disturbing case yet, in the internationally bestselling series that Thrilling Fiction calls "the most addictive and action-packed crime saga you'll ever read."

ABOUT THE AUTHOR

Alex Smith wrote his first book when he was six. It wasn't particularly good, but it did have some supernatural monsters in it. His latest books, the DCI Robert Kett thrillers, have monsters in them too, although these monsters are very human, and all the more terrifying for it. In between, he has published twelve novels for children and teenagers under his full name, Alexander Gordon Smith—including the number one bestselling series Escape From Furnace, which is loved by millions of readers worldwide and which is soon to become a motion picture. He lives in Norwich with his wife and three young daughters.

Find out more at alexsmithbooks.com

Made in the USA
Coppell, TX
03 August 2021